The Classics of the Eighties

Every year since 1971, *New Dimensions* has collected the best science fiction stories from the very best writers in the field. Many of the now-classic stories of the seventies were introduced in these pages, including stories by Harlan Ellison, Ursula Le Guin, James Tiptree, Jr. and Gardner Duzois.

Now, distinguished editors Robert Silverberg and Marta Randall, themselves among the most imaginative and versatile writers ever to be associated with science fiction, have assembled the first collection of the new decade. Here are the stories that will be regarded as the masterpieces of the eighties.

NEW DIMENSIONS 11

Edited by Robert Silverberg and Marta Randall

PUBLISHED BY POCKET BOOKS NEW YORK

Another *Original* publication of POCKET BOOKS

PS
648
S3NH8
VOL 11

POCKET BOOKS, a Simon & Schuster division of
GULF & WESTERN CORPORATION
1230 Avenue of the Americas, New York, N.Y. 10020

ISBN: 0-671-83085-6

First Pocket Books printing July, 1980

10 9 8 7 6 5 4 3 2 1

POCKET and colophon are trademarks of Simon & Schuster.

Printed in the U.S.A.

CONTENTS

NEW
DIMENSIONS 11

FOREWORD

≋≋≋≋≋≋≋≋≋≋≋≋≋≋≋≋≋≋≋≋≋≋≋

A TIME OF CHANGES

I FIRST SUGGESTED THE IDEA OF *New Dimensions* to a publisher in the summer of 1968, began buying stories for the initial issue the following year, and for the next decade was its sole editorial force. During that time I published some noteworthy science fiction stories—see the recently published anthology *The Best of New Dimensions* for those—and established what I think is a valuable standard of performance. The prototypical *New Dimensions* short story was addressed to an alert, sophisticated, intelligent reader, not necessarily a long-time science-fiction reader, and eschewed both the formulas of pulp-magazine fiction on the one hand and the vapors of obscurantist avant-grade fiction on the other.

But ten years is a long time to be editing a science-fiction publication. A certain weariness seems to set in after that; one tires of finding manuscripts in the mail, one loses patience with novice writers, one starts to concoct one's own formulas and conventions and become predictable and self-repeating. John W. Campbell, who took over *Astounding Science Fiction* in 1937 and used it to transform the field, had accomplished all his greatest glories by 1948. Horace Gold's tenure at *Galaxy* ran from 1950 to 1961. Anthony Boucher guided the *Magazine of Fantasy & Science Fiction* from 1949 to 1958. I would not presume to compare my achievements as an editor with the legendary work of those great men; but their example lies before me, and it tells me that ten years is enough. Effective with this issue, I have withdrawn from active control of *New Dimensions*, and, though my name

9

remains on the title page in an *ex officio* capacity, the book you now hold is largely the work of Marta Randall. I have served mainly in an advisory way; she has done most of the hard work of assembling the stories, and it is to her that praise and blame must be directed.

Marta Randall does not come to *New Dimensions* as a stranger. Her own stories have been an ornament to the collection since its fifth issue; and, as my friend and neighbor in California, she has frequently played a consultant role when I felt doubtful of my own judgment of some manuscript. Her own tastes in science fiction are, necessarily, not identical to mine, but they are not that far removed in matters of basic canons, and I think there will be a few radical changes in *New Dimensions* under its new editor. There will be changes, yes; and I would be greatly surprised if I approved of all of them. But the dedication to excellence in literary craftsmanship will remain, and I think the infusion of new energy that Marta Randall will provide can have only the most positive of effects.

ROBERT SILVERBERG
Oakland, California
May 1979

UNICORN TAPESTRY

by Suzy McKee Charnas

Suzy McKee Charnas entered science fiction in 1974 with the publication of her novel *Walk to the End of the World,* a gripping and imaginative work which led to her nomination for the John W. Campbell Award for best new science fiction writer of 1974. Since then she has published *Motherlines,* a sequel to the first book, and a third novel in the series is in the works. The novella which follows is part of a larger work, *The Vampire Tapestry,* to be published by Simon & Schuster/Pocket Books in the summer of 1980.

Born in New York, Charnas received her B.A. from Barnard College and subsequently taught in places as diverse as Ogbomosho, Nigeria, the University of Ife in Ibadan, and New Lincoln School in New York City before becoming a full-time writer, a loss to the teaching profession which is a boundless gain for science fiction. The following story is, we think, the best work that Charnas has done; it may keep you awake nights—for a surprising number of reasons.

"HOLD ON," FLORIA SAID. "I KNOW WHAT you're going to say: I agreed not to take any new clients for a while. But wait till I tell you—you're not going to believe this—first phone call, setting up an initial appointment, he comes out with what his problem is: 'I seem to have fallen victim to a delusion of being a vampire.' "

"Christ H. God!" cried Lucille delightedly. "Just like that, over the phone?"

"When I recovered my aplomb, so to speak, I told him that I prefer to wait with the details until our first meeting. I was a little late though."

They were sitting on the tiny terrace outside the staff room of the clinic, a converted town house on the Upper West Side. Floria spent three days a week here and the remaining two in her office on Central Park South seeing private clients like this new one. Lucille, always gratifyingly responsive, was Floria's most valued professional friend. Clearly enchanted with Floria's news, she sat eagerly forward in her creaky old lawn chair, eyes wide behind Coke-bottle glasses.

She said, "Do you suppose he thinks he's a revivified corpse?"

Below, down at the end of the street, Floria could see two kids skidding their skateboards near a man who wore a woolen cap and heavy coat despite the May warmth. He was leaning against a wall like a monolith. If corpses walked, some, not nearly revivified enough, stood in plain view in New York.

"I'll have to think of a delicate way to ask," she said. "How did he come to you?"

"He was working in an upstate college, teaching and doing research, and all of a sudden he just disappeared—vanished, literally, without a trace. A month later he turned up here in the city. The faculty dean at the school knows me and sent him to see me."

Lucille gave her a sly look. "So you thought, Ah-hah, do a little favor for a friend, this looks classic and easy to transfer if need be: repressed intellectual blows stack and runs off with spacy chick or something like that—only a little more interesting, looks like."

"You know me too well," Floria said.

"Huh," grunted Lucille. She sipped ginger ale from a chipped white mug. "I don't take panicky middle-aged guys anymore—they're too depressing. And you shouldn't be taking this one, intriguing as he sounds."

Here comes the lecture, Floria told herself.

Lucille got up. She was short, heavy, prone to wearing caftans that swung about her like ceremonial robes. As she paced, her hem brushed at the flowers starting up in the planting boxes that rimmed the little terrace. "You know damn well this is just more overwork you're loading on. Don't take this man; refer him."

Floria sighed. "I know, I know. I promised everybody I'd slow down for a while. But you said it yourself just a minute ago—it looked like a simple favor. So what do I get? Count Dracula, for God's sake! Would you give that up?"

Fishing around in one capacious pocket, Lucille brought out a dented package of cigarets and lit up, scowling. "You know, when you give me advice I try to take it seriously. Joking aside, Floria, what am I supposed to say? I've listened to you moaning for months now, and I thought we'd figured out that what you need is to shed some pressure, to start saying *no*—and here you are insisting on a new case. You know what I think: you're hiding in other people's problems from a lot of your own stuff you should be working on.

"Okay, okay, don't glare at me. Be pig-headed. Have you gotten rid of Chubs, at least?" This was Floria's code name for a troublesome client named Kenny she'd been trying to unload for some time.

Floria shook her head.

"What gives with you? It's weeks since you swore you'd dump him! Trying to do everything for everybody is wearing you out. I bet you're still dropping weight. Judging by the very unbecoming circles under your eyes, sleeping isn't going too well either. Still no dreams you can remember?"

"Lucille, don't nag. I don't want to talk about my health."

"Well, what about his health—Dracula's? Did you suggest that he have a physical before seeing you? There might be something physiological—"

"You're not going to be able to whisk him off to an M.D. and out of my hands," Floria said wryly. "He says he won't consider either medication or hospitalization."

Involuntarily, she glanced down at the end of the street. The woolen-capped man had curled up on the sidewalk at the foot of the building, sleeping or passed-out or dead. The city was tottering with sickness. Compared with that wreck down there and the others like him, how sick could this "vampire" be, with his cultured baritone voice, his self-possessed approach?

"And you won't consider handing him off to somebody else," Lucille said.

"Well, not until I know a little more. Come on, Luce—wouldn't you want at least to know what he looks like?"

Lucille stubbed out her cigaret against the low parapet. Down below a policeman strolled along the street ticketing the parked cars. He didn't even look at the man lying at the corner of the building. They watched his progress without comment. Finally, Lucille said, "Well, if you won't drop Dracula, keep me posted on him, will you?"

He entered the office on the dot of the hour, a gaunt but graceful figure. His name, typed in caps on the initial information sheet that she proceeded to fill out with him, was Edward Lewis Weyland. He was impressive: wiry gray hair, worn short, emphasized the massiveness of his face with its long jaw, high cheekbones, and stony cheeks grooved as if by winters of hard weather. He told her about the background of the vampire incident, incisively describing his life at Cayslin College: the pressures of collegial competition, interdepartmental squabbles, student indifference, administrative bungling. History has limited use, she knew, since memory distorts. Still, if he felt most comfortable establishing the setting for his illness, let him.

At length his energy faltered. His angular body sank into a slump, his voice became flat and tired as he haltingly worked up to the crucial event: night work at the sleep-lab, fantasies of blood-drinking as he watched the youthful subjects of his dream research slumbering, finally an attempt to act out the fantasy with a staff member at the college. He had been repulsed. Then—panic. Word would get out, he'd be fired, blacklisted forever. He'd bolted. A nightmare period had followed—he offered no details. When he had come to his senses he'd seen that just what he feared, the ruin of his career, would come from his running away. So he'd phoned the dean, and here he was.

Throughout this recital she watched him diminish from the dignified academic who had entered her office to a shamed and frightened man hunched in his chair, his hands pulling fitfully at each other.

"What are your hands doing?" she said gently. He looked blank. She repeated the question.

He looked down at his hands. "Struggling," he said.

"With what?"

"The worst," he muttered. "I haven't told you the worst." She had never grown hardened to this sort of transformation. His long fingers busied themselves fiddling with a button on his jacket while he explained painfully that the object of his "attack" at Cayslin had been a woman. Not young but handsome and vital, she had first caught his attention earlier in the year during a "festschrift"—an honorary seminar—for a retiring professor. A picture emerged of an awkward Weyland, lifelong bachelor, seeking this woman's warmth and suffering her refusal.

Floria knew she should bring him out of his past and into his here-and-now, but he was doing so beautifully on his own that she was loath to interrupt.

"Did I tell you there was a rapist active on the campus at this time?" he said bitterly. "I borrowed a leaf from his book: I tried to take from this woman, since she wouldn't give. I tried to take some of her blood." He stared at the floor. "What does that mean—to take someone's blood?"

"What do you think it means?"

The button, pulled and twisted by his fretful fingers, came off in his hand. He put it in his pocket, the impulse of a fastidious nature, she guessed. "Her energy," he whispered, "stolen to warm the walking corpse—the vampire—myself."

His silence, his downcast eyes, his bent shoulders, all signaled a man brought to bay by a life crisis. Perhaps he was going to be the kind of client therapists dream of and she needed so badly these days: a client intelligent and sensitive enough, given the companionship of a professional listener, to swiftly unravel his own mental tangles. Exhilarated by his promising start, Floria restrained herself from trying to build on it too soon. She made herself tolerate the silence, which lasted until he said suddenly, "I notice that you make no notes as we speak. Do you record these sessions on tape?"

A hint of paranoia, she thought, not unusual. "Not without your knowledge and consent, just as I won't send for your personnel file from Cayslin without your knowledge and consent. I do, however, write notes after each session as a guide to myself and in order to have a record in case of any confusion later about anything we do or say here. I can promise you that I won't show my notes or speak of you by name to anyone—except Dean Sharpe at Cayslin, of course, and even then only as much as is strictly necessary—without your written permission. Does that satisfy you?"

"I apologize for my question," he said. "The—incident has left me—very nervous: a condition that I hope to get over with your help."

The time was up. When he had gone she stepped outside to check with Hilda, the receptionist she shared with four other therapists here at the Central Park South office. Hilda always sized up new clients in the waiting room.

Of this one she said, "Are you sure there's anything wrong with that guy? I think I'm in love."

Waiting at the office for a group of clients to assemble Wednesday evening, Floria dashed off some notes on the "vampire."

Described incident, background. No history of mental illness, no previous experience of therapy. Personal history so ordinary you almost don't notice how bare it is: only child of German immigrants, schooling normal, anthropology field work, academic posts leading to Cayslin College professorship. Health good, finances adequate, occupation satisfactory, housing pleasant (though presently installed in a N.Y. hotel); never married, no kids, no family, no religion, social life strictly job-related, leisure—likes to drive. Reaction to question about drinking, but no signs of alcohol problem. Physically very smooth-moving for his age (over fifty) and height; cat-like, alert. Some apparent stiffness in mid-section—slight protective stoop—tightening up of middle-age? Paranoic defensiveness? Voice pleasant, faint accent (German speaking childhood at home). Entering therapy condition of consideration for return to job.

What a relief: now she could defend to Lucille her decision to do therapy with the "vampire." His situation looked workable with a minimum of strain on herself.

After all, Lucille was right. Floria did have problems of her own that needed attention, primarily her anxiety and exhaustion since her mother's death more than a year before. The break-up of Floria's marriage had caused her misery, but not the endless depression now wearing her down. Intellectually the problem was clear: with both her parents dead she was left exposed. No one stood any longer between herself and the inevitability of her own death. Knowing the source of her feelings didn't help: she couldn't seem to mobilize the nerve to work on them.

The Wednesday group went badly again. Lisa lived once more her experiences in the European death camps and everyone cried. Floria wanted to stop Lisa, turn her, extinguish the droning misery of her voice in illumination and release, but she couldn't see how to do it. She found nothing in herself to offer except some clever ploy out of the professional bag of tricks—dance your anger, have a dialog with your young self of those days—useful techniques when they flowed organically as part of a living process in which the therapist participated. But thinking out responses that should have been intuitive wouldn't work. The group and its collective pain paralyzed her. She was a dancer without a choreographer, knowing all the moves but unable to match them to the music these people made.

Rather than act with mechanical clumsiness she held back, did nothing, and suffered guilt. Oh, God, the smart, experienced people in the group must know how useless she was here.

Going home on the bus she thought about calling up one of the therapists who shared the downtown office. He had expressed an interest in doing co-therapy with her under student observation. The Wednesday group might respond well to that. Suggest it to them next time? Having a partner might take pressure off Floria and revitalize the group, and if she felt she must withdraw, he would be available to take over. Of course, he might take over anyway and walk off with some of her clients.

Oh, boy, terrific, who's paranoid now? Wonderful way to think about a good colleague. God, she hadn't even known she was considering shucking the group.

Had the new client, running from his "vampirism," exposed her own impulse to retreat? This wouldn't be the first time that Floria had obtained help from a client while attempting to give help. Her old supervisor, Rigby, said that such mutual aid was the only true therapy, the rest was fraud. What a perfectionist, old Rigby, and what a bunch of young idealists he'd turned out, all eager to save the world.

Eager, but not necessarily able. Jane Fennerman had once lived in the world, and Floria had been incompetent to save her. Jane, an absent member of tonight's group, was back in the safety of a locked ward, hazily gliding on whatever tranquilizers they used there.

Why still mull over Jane? she asked herself severely, bracing against the bus's lurching halt. Any client was entitled to drop out of therapy and commit herself. Nor was this the first time that sort of thing had happened in the course of Floria's career. Only this time she couldn't seem to shake free of the resulting depression and guilt.

But how could she have helped Jane more? How could you offer reassurance that life was not as dreadful as Jane felt it to be, that her fears were insubstantial, that each day was not a pit of pain and danger?

She was taking time during a client's canceled hour to work on notes for the new book. The writing, an analysis of the vicissitudes of salaried versus private practice, balked her at every turn. She longed for an interruption to distract her circling mind.

Hilda put a call through from Cayslin College. It was Doug Sharpe, who had sent Dr. Weyland to her.

"Now that he's in your capable hands, I can tell people plainly that he's on what they call 'compassionate leave' and make them swallow it." Doug's voice seemed thinned by the long-distance connection. "Can you give me a preliminary opinion?"

"I need time to find out more."

He said, "Try not to take too long. At the moment I'm holding off pressure to appoint someone in his place. Some of his enemies up here—and a sharp-tongued bastard like him acquires plenty of those—are trying to get a search committee authorized to find someone else for the Directorship of the Cayslin Center for the Study of Man."

"Of People," she corrected automatically, as she always did. "What do you mean, 'bastard'? I thought you liked him, Doug. 'Do you want me to have to throw a smart, courtly, old-school gent to Finney or MaGill?' Those were your very words." Finney was a Freudian with a mouth like a pursed-up little asshole and a mind to match, and MaGill was a primal yowler with a padded gym of an office.

She heard Doug tapping at his teeth with a pen or pencil. "Well," he said, "I have a lot of respect for him, and sometimes I could cheer him for mowing down some pompous moron up here. I can't deny, though, that he's earned a reputation for being an accomplished son-of-a-bitch and tough to work with. Too damn cold and self-sufficient, you know?"

"Mmm," she said. "I haven't seen that yet."

He said, "You will. How about yourself? How's the rest of your life?"

"Well, off-hand, what would you say if I told you I was thinking of going back to art school?"

"What would I say? I'd say bullshit, that's what I'd say. You've had fifteen years of doing something you're good at, and now you want to throw all that out and start over in an area you haven't touched since Studio 101 in college? If God had meant you to be a painter, she'd have sent you to art school in the first place."

"I did think about art school at the time."

"The point is that you're good at what you do. I've been at the receiving end of your work and I know what I'm talking about. By the way, did you see that piece in the paper about Annie Winslow, from the group I was in? That's a nice appointment; I always knew she'd wind up in Washington. What I'm trying to make clear to you is that your 'graduates' do too well for you to talk about quitting. What's Morton say about that idea, by the way?"

Mort, a pathologist, was Floria's lover. She hadn't discussed this with him, and she told Doug so.

"You're not on the outs with Morton, are you?"

"Come on, Douglas, cut it out. There's nothing wrong with my sex-life, believe me. It's everyplace else that's giving me trouble."

"Just sticking my nose into your business," he replied. "What are friends for?"

They turned to lighter matters, but when she hung up Floria didn't feel cheered. If her friends were moved to this sort of probing and kindly advice-giving, she must be inviting help more openly and more desperately than she'd realized.

The work on the book went no better. It was as if, afraid to expose her thoughts, she must disarm criticism by meeting all possible objections beforehand. The book was well and truly stalled—like everything else. She sat sweating over it, wondering what the devil was wrong with her that she was writing mush. She had two good books to her name already. What was this bottleneck with the third?

"But what do you think?" Kenny insisted, gnawing anxiously at the cuticle of his thumbnail. "Does it sound like my kind of job?"

"What do you feel about it?" she countered.

"I'm all confused, I told you."

"Try speaking for me. Give the advice I would give you."

He glowered. "That's a real cop-out, you know? One part of me talking like you, and then I have a dialog with myself like a tv show about a split personality. It's all me that way, you're off the hook, you just sit there. I want something from *you*."

She looked for the twentieth time at the clock on the file cabinet. This time it freed her. "Kenny, the hour's over."

Kenny heaved his plump, sulky body up out of his chair. "You don't care. Oh, you pretend you do, but you don't really—"

"Next time, Kenny."

He stumped out of the office. She imagined him towing in his wake the raft of decisions he was trying to inveigle her into making for him. Sighing, she went to the window and looked out over the park, filling her eyes and her mind with the full, fresh green of late spring. She felt dismal. In two years of treatment the situation with Kenny had remained a stalemate. He wouldn't go to someone else who might be able to help him, and she couldn't bring herself to kick him out, though she knew she must eventually. His puny tyranny couldn't conceal how soft and vulnerable he was ...

Dr. Weyland had the next appointment. Floria found herself pleased to see him. She could hardly have asked for a greater contrast to Kenny: tall, lean, a fine head that made her want to draw him, good clothes, nice big hands—altogether a distinguished-looking man. Though informally dressed in slacks, light jacket, and tieless shirt, the impression he conveyed was one of impeccable leisure and reserve. He took not the padded chair preferred by most clients but the wooden one with the cane seat.

"Good afternoon, Dr. Landauer," he said gravely. "May I ask your judgment of my case?"

"I don't think of myself as a judge," she said. She decided rapidly to enlist his intelligence by laying out her

thoughts to him as to an equal, and to shift their discussion onto a first-name basis if possible. Calling this
old-fashioned man by his first name so soon might seem
artificial, but how could they get familiar enough to do
therapy while addressing each other as "Dr. Landauer"
and "Dr. Weyland" like two characters in vaudeville?

"This is what I think, Edward," she continued. "We
need to find out about this vampire incident—how it tied
into your feelings about yourself, good and bad, at the
time, what it did for you that led you to try to 'be' a
vampire even though that was bound to complicate your
life terrifically. The more we know, the closer we can
come to figuring out how to insure that this vampire construct won't be necessary to you again."

"Does this mean that you accept me formally as a
client?" he said.

Comes right out and says what's on his mind, she
noted; no problems there. "Yes."

"Good. I, too, have a treatment goal in mind. I will
need at some point a testimonial from you that my mental health is sound enough for me to resume work at
Cayslin."

Floria shook her head. "I can't guarantee that. I can
commit myself to work toward it, of course, since your
improved mental health is the aim of what we do here
together."

"I suppose that answers the purpose for the time being," he said. "We can discuss it again later on. Frankly,
I find myself eager to continue our work today. I've been
feeling very much better since I spoke with you, and I
thought last night about what I might tell you today."

"Edward, my own feeling is that we started out with a
good deal of very useful verbal work, and that now is a
time to try something a little different."

He said nothing. He watched her. When she asked
whether he remembered his dreams he shook his head.

She said, "I'd like you to try to do a dream for me
now, a waking dream. Close your eyes and daydream,
and tell me about it."

He closed his eyes. Strangely, he now struck her as
less vulnerable rather than more, as if strengthened by
increased vigilance.

"How do you feel now?" she said.

"Uneasy." His eyelids fluttered. "I dislike closing my eyes. What I don't see can hurt me."

"Who wants to hurt you?"

"A vampire's enemies, of course—mobs of screaming peasants with torches."

Translating into what, she wondered—young Ph.D.'s pouring out of the graduate schools panting for the jobs of older men like Weyland? "Peasants, these days?"

"Whatever their daily work, there is still a majority of the stupid, the violent, and the credulous, putting their featherbrained faith in astrology, in this cult or that, in various branches of psychology."

His sneer at her was unmistakable. Considering her refusal to let him fill the hour his own way, this desire to take a swipe at her was healthy. But it required immediate and straightforward handling.

"Edward, open your eyes and tell me what you see."

He obeyed. "I see a woman in her early forties," he said, "clever-looking face, dark hair showing gray, flesh too thin for her bones, indicating either vanity or illness, wearing slacks and a rather creased batik blouse—describable, I think, by the term 'peasant style'—with a food stain on the left side."

Damn! Don't blush. "Does anything besides my blouse suggest a peasant to you?"

"Nothing concrete, but with regard to me, my vampire-self, a peasant with a torch is what you could easily become."

"I hear you saying that my task is to help you get rid of your delusion, though this process may be painful and frightening for you."

Something flashed in his expression—surprise, perhaps alarm—something she wanted to get in touch with before it could sink away out of reach again. Quickly she said, "How do you experience your face at this moment?"

He frowned. "As being on the front of my head. Why?"

With a sick feeling she saw that she had chosen the wrong technique for reaching that hidden feeling and had provoked hostility instead. "Your face looked to me just now like a mask for concealing what you feel rather than an instrument of expression."

He moved restlessly in the chair, his whole physical

attitude tense and guarded. "I don't know what you mean."

"Will you let me touch you?" she said, rising.

His hands tightened on the arms of his chair, which protested in a sharp creak. He snapped, "I thought this was a talking cure."

Strong resistance to body-work—ease up. "If you won't let me massage some of the tension out of your facial muscles, will you try to do it for yourself?"

"I don't enjoy being made ridiculous," he said, standing and heading for the door, which clapped smartly shut behind him.

She sagged back in her chair; she had mishandled him. Clearly her initial estimation of this as a relatively easy job had been wrong and had led her to move too quickly with him. Certainly it had been too early to try body-work. She should have developed a firmer level of trust first by letting him do more of what he did so easily and well—talk.

The door opened. Weyland came back in and shut it quietly. He did not sit again but paced about the room, coming to rest at the window.

"Please excuse my rather childish behavior just now," he said. "Playing these games of yours brought it on."

"It's frustrating, playing games that are unfamiliar and that you can't control," she said. As he made no reply, she went on in a conciliatory tone, "I'm not belittling you, Edward. I just need to get us off whatever track you were taking us down so briskly. My feeling is that you're trying hard to regain your old stability.

"But that's the goal, not the starting-point. The only way to reach your goal is through the process, and you don't drive the therapy process like a train. You can only help the process happen, as though you were helping a tree grow."

"These games are part of the process?"

"Yes."

"And neither you nor I control the games?"

"That's right."

He considered. "Suppose I agree to try this process of yours; what would you want of me?"

Observing him carefully, she no longer saw the anxious scholar bravely struggling back from madness. Here was a different sort of man, armored, calculating. She didn't know what the change signaled, but she felt her own excitement stirring, and that meant she was on the track of—something.

"I have a hunch," she said slowly, "that this vampirism extends further back into your past than you've told me and possibly right up into the present as well. I think it's still with you. My style of therapy stresses dealing with the 'now' at least as much as the 'then'; if the vampirism is part of the present, telling me about it is crucial."

Silence.

"Can you tell me about being a vampire—being one now?"

"You won't like knowing," he said.

"Edward, try to tell me."

"I hunt," he said.

"Where? How? What sort of—of victims?"

He folded his arms and leaned his back against the window frame. "Very well, since you insist. There are a number of possibilities here in the city in summer. Those too poor to own air-conditioners sleep out on rooftops and fire-escapes. But often their blood is sour with drugs or liquor. The same is true of prostitutes. Bars are full of people but also full of smoke and noise, and there too the blood is fouled. I must choose my hunting grounds carefully. Often I go to openings of galleries or evening museum shows or department stores on their late nights—places where women may be approached."

And take pleasure in it, she thought, if they're out hunting also—for acceptable male companionship. Yet he's never married. Explore where this is going. "Only women?"

He gave her a sardonic glance, as if she were a slightly brighter student than he had first assumed.

"Hunting women is liable to be time-consuming and expensive. The best hunting is in the part of Central Park they call the Ramble, where homosexual men seek encounters with others of their kind. I walk there too at night."

She glanced at the clock. "I'm sorry, Edward, but our time seems to be—"

"Only a moment more," he said coldly. "You asked; permit me to finish my answer. In the Ramble I find someone who doesn't reek of alcohol or drugs, who seems healthy, and who is not inclined to 'hook-up' right there among the bushes. I invite such a man to my room. He judges me safe, at least: older, weaker than he is, unlikely to turn into a dangerous maniac. So he comes to my hotel. I feed on his blood. Now, I think, our time is up."

She sat, after he'd left, torn between rejoicing at his admission of the delusion's persistence and pity that his condition was so much worse than she had first thought. Her hope of having an easy time with him vanished. His initial presentation had been just that—a performance, an act. Forced to abandon it, he had dumped on her this lump of material, too much—and too strange—to take in all at once.

Her next client liked the padded chair, not the wooden one that Weyland had sat in during the first part of the hour. Floria started to move the wooden one back. The armrests came away in her hands.

She remembered him starting up in protest against her proposal of touching him. The grip of his fingers had fractured the joints, and the shafts now lay in splinters on the floor.

Floria wandered into Lucille's room at the clinic after the staff meeting. Lucille was lying on the couch with a wet rag over her eyes.

"I thought you looked green around the gills today," Floria said. "What's wrong?"

"Big bash last night," said Lucille in sepulchral tones. "I think I feel about the way you do after a session with Chubs. You haven't gotten rid of him yet, have you?"

"No. I had him lined up to go see Marty instead of me last week, but damned if he didn't show up at my door at his usual time. It's a lost cause. What I wanted to talk to you about was Dracula."

"What about him?"

"He's smarter, tougher, and sicker than I thought, and maybe I'm even less competent than I thought too. He's already walked out on me once—I almost lost him. I never took a course in treating monsters."

Lucille groaned. "Some days they're all monsters."

This from Lucille, who worked longer hours than anyone at the clinic, to the despair of her husband. She
lifted the rag, refolded it, and placed it carefully across
her forehead. "And if I had ten dollars for every client
who's walked out on me—tell you what: I'll trade you
Madame X for him, how's that?

"Remember Madame X, with the jangling bracelets and
the parakeet eye make-up and the phobia about dogs?
Now she's phobic about things dropping out of the sky
onto her head. It'll turn out that one day when she was
three a dog trotted by and pissed on her leg just as an
over-passing pigeon shat on her head. What are we doing in this business?"

"God knows." Floria laughed. "But am I in this business these days—I mean, in the sense of practicing my
so-called art? Blocked with my group work, beating my
brains out on a book that won't go, and doing something
—I'm not sure it's therapy—with a vampire . . . You
know, once I had this sort of natural choreographer inside myself that hardly let me put a foot wrong and always knew how to correct a mistake if I did. Now that's
gone. I feel as if I'm just going through a lot of inco-
herent motions. Whatever I had once, I've lost it."

Ugh, she thought, hearing the descent of her voice into
a tone of gloomy self-pity.

"Well, don't complain about Dracula," Lucille said.
"You were the one who insisted on taking him on. At
least he's got you concentrating on his therapy instead
of just wringing your hands. As long as you've started,
stay with it—illumination may come. And now I'd better change the ribbon in my typewriter and get back to
reviewing Silberman's latest best-seller on self-shrinking
while I'm feeling mean enough to do it justice." She got
up gingerly. "Stick around in case I faint and fall into
the wastebasket."

"Luce. This case is what I'd like to try to write about."

"Dracula?" Lucille pawed through a desk drawer full
of paper clips, pens, rubber bands, and old lipsticks.

"Dracula. A monograph—"

"Oh, I know the game: you scribble down everything
you can and then read what you wrote to find out what's
going on with the client, and with luck you end up publishing. Great! But if you are going to publish, don't pid-
dle this away on a dinky paper. Do a book. Here's your

subject, instead of those statistics you've been killing yourself over. This one is really exciting—a case study to put on the shelf next to Freud's own wolf-man, have you thought of that?"

Floria liked it. "What a book that could be—fame if not fortune. Notoriety most likely. How in the world could I convince our colleagues that it's legit? There's a lot of vampire stuff around right now—plays on Broadway and tv, books all over the place, movies—they'll say I'm just trying to ride the coattails of a fad."

"No, no, what you do is show how this guy's delusion is related to the fad. Fascinating." Lucille, having found a ribbon, prodded doubtfully at the exposed innards of her typewriter.

"Suppose I fictionalize it," Floria said, "under a pseudonym. Why not ride the popular wave and be free in what I can say?"

"Listen, you've never witten a word of fiction in your life, have you?" Lucille fixed her with a bloodshot gaze. "There's no evidence that you could turn out a best-selling novel. On the other hand, by this time you have a trained memory for accurately reporting therapeutic transactions. That's a strength you'd be foolish to waste. A solid professional book would be terrific—and a feather in the cap of every woman in the field. Just make sure you get good legal advice on disguising Dracula's identity well enough to avoid libel."

The cane-seated chair wasn't worth repairing, so she got its twin out of the bedroom to put in the office in its place. Puzzling: by his history Weyland was fifty-two, and by his appearance no muscle-man. She should have asked Doug—but how, exactly? "By the way, Doug, was Weyland ever a circus strong-man or a blacksmith? Does he secretly pump iron?" Ask the client himself—but not yet.

She invited some of the younger staff from the clinic over for a small party with a few of her outside friends. It was a good evening; they were not a heavy-drinking crowd, which meant the conversation stayed intelligent. The guests drifted about the long living room or stood in twos and threes at the windows looking down on West End Avenue as they talked.

Mort came, warming the room. Fresh from a session with some amateur chamber-music friends, he still glowed with the pleasure of making his cello sing. His own voice was unexpectedly light for so large a man. Sometimes Floria thought that the deep throb of the cello was his true voice.

He stood beside her talking with some others. There was no need to lean against his comfortable bulk or to have him put his arm around her waist. Their intimacy was longstanding, an effortless pleasure in each other that required neither demonstration nor concealment.

He was easily diverted from music to his next-favorite topic, the strengths and skills of athletes.

"Here's a question for a paper I'm thinking of writing," Floria said. "Could a tall, lean man be exceptionally strong? I mean a man with a runner's build, more sinewy than bulky."

Mort rambled on his thoughtful way. His answer seemed to be no.

"But what about chimpanzees?" put in a young clinician. "I went with a guy once who was an animal handler for TV, and he said a three-month-old chimp could demolish a strong man."

"It's all physical conditioning," somebody else said. "Modern people are softies."

Mort nodded. "Human beings in general are weakly made compared to other animals. It's a question of muscle insertions—the angles of how the muscles are attached to the bones. Some angles give better leverage than others. That's how a leopard can bring down a much bigger animal than itself. It has a muscular structure that gives it tremendous strength for its streamlined build."

Floria said, "If a man were built with muscle insertions like a leopard's, he'd look pretty odd, wouldn't he?"

"Not to an untrained eye," Mort said, sounding bemused by an inner vision. "And, my God, what an athlete he'd make—can you imagine a guy in the decathlon who's as strong as a leopard?"

When everyone else had gone Mort stayed, as he often did. Jokes about insertions, muscular and otherwise, soon led to sounds more expressive and more animal, but afterwards Floria didn't feel like resting snuggled together with Mort and talking. When her body stopped racing, her mind turned to her new client. She didn't want to discuss him with Mort, so she ushered Mort out as gently as she could and sat down by herself at the kitchen table with a glass of orange juice.

How to approach the reintegration of Weyland, the eminent, gray-haired academic with the rebellious vampire-self that had smashed his life out of shape?

She thought of the broken chair, Weyland's big hands crushing the wood. Old wood and dried-out glue, of course, or he never could have done it. He was a man, after all, not a leopard.

The day before the third session Weyland phoned and left a message with Hilda: he would not be coming to the office tomorrow for his appointment, but if Dr. Landauer were agreeable she would find him at their usual hour at the Central Park Zoo.

Am I going to let him move me around from here to there? she thought. Shouldn't—but why fight it? Give him some leeway, see what opens up in a different setting. Besides, it was a beautiful day, probably the last of the sweet May weather before the summer stickiness descended. She gladly cut Kenny short so that she would have time to walk to the zoo.

There was a fair crowd there for a weekday. Well-groomed young matrons pushed clean, floppy babies in strollers. Weyland she spotted at once.

He was leaning against the railing that enclosed the seals' shelter and their murky green pool. His jacket, slung over his shoulder, draped elegantly down his long back. Floria thought him rather dashing and faintly foreign-looking. Women who passed him, she noticed, tended to glance back.

He looked at everyone. She had the impression that he knew quite well that she was walking up behind him.

"Outdoors makes a nice change from the office, Edward," she said, coming to the rail beside him. "But there must be more to this than a longing for fresh air." A fat seal lay in sculptural grace on the concrete, eyes blissfully shut, fur drying in the sun to a translucent water-color umber.

Weyland straightened from the rail. They walked. He did not look at the animals; his eyes moved continually over the crowd. He said, "Someone has been watching for me at your office building."

"Who?"

"There are several possibilities. Pah, what a stench—though humans caged in similar circumstances smell as bad." He sidestepped a couple of shrieking children who were fighting over a balloon and headed out of the zoo under the musical clock.

They walked the uphill path northward through the park. By extending her own stride a little Floria found that she could comfortably keep pace with him.

"Is it peasants with torches?" she said. "Following you?"

"What a childish idea," he said.

All right, try another tack then. "You were telling me last time about hunting in the Ramble. Can we return to that?"

"If you wish." He sounded bored—a defense? Surely—she was certain this must be the right reading—surely his problem was a transmutation into "vampire" fantasy of an unacceptable aspect of himself. For men of his generation the confrontation with homosexual drives could be devastating.

"When you pick up someone in the Ramble, is it a paid encounter?"

"Usually."

"How do you feel about having to pay?" She expected resentment.

He gave a faint shrug. "Why not? Others work to earn their bread. I work too, very hard in fact. Why shouldn't I use my earnings to pay for my sustenance?"

Why did he never play the expected card? Baffled, she paused to drink from a fountain. They walked on.

"Once you've got your quarry, how do you—" She fumbled for a word.

"Attack?" he supplied, unperturbed. "There's a place on the neck, here, where pressure can interrupt the blood flow to the brain and cause unconsciousness. To get close enough to apply that pressure isn't difficult."

"You do it before or after any sexual activity?"

"Before, if possible," he said dryly, "and instead of." He turned aside to stalk up a slope to a granite outcrop that overlooked the path they had been following. He settled on his haunches, looking back the way they had come. Floria, glad she'd worn slacks today, sat down near him.

He didn't seem devastated—anything but. Press him, don't let him get by on cool. "Do you often prey on men in preference to women?"

"Certainly. I take what is easiest. Men have always been more accessible because women have been walled away like prizes or so physically impoverished by repeated child-bearing as to be unhealthy prey for me. All this has been changing recently, but gay men are still the simplest quarry." While she was recovering from her surprise at his unforeseen and weirdly skewed awareness of female history, he added suavely, "How carefully you control your expression, Dr. Landauer—no frown, no disapproval."

She did disapprove, she realized. She would prefer him not to be committed sexually to men. Oh, hell.

He went on, "Yet no doubt you see me as one who victimizes the already victimized. This is the world's way. A wolf brings down the stragglers at the edges of the herd. Gay men are denied the full protection of the human herd and are at the same time emboldened to make themselves known and available.

"On the other hand, unlike the wolf I can feed without killing, and these particular victims pose no threat to me that would cause me to kill. Outcasts themselves, even if they comprehend my true purpose among them they will not accuse me."

God, how neatly, completely, and ruthlessly he distanced the homosexual community from himself! "And how do you feel, Edward, about their purposes—their sexual expectations of you?"

"The same as about the sexual expectations of women whom I choose to pursue: they don't interest me. Besides, once my hunger is active, sexual arousal is impossible. My physical unresponsiveness seems to surprise no one. Apparently impotence is expected in a gray-haired man, which suits my intention."

A Frisbee sailed past them, pursued by a trio of shouting kids. Floria's eye followed the arc of the red plastic disc. She was thinking, astonished again, that she had never heard a man speak of his own impotence with such cool indifference. She had induced him to talk about his problem all right. He was speaking as freely as he had in the first session, only this time it was no act. He was drowning her in more than she had ever expected or for that matter wanted to know about vampirism. What the hell; she was listening, she thought she understood—what was it all good for? Time for some cold reality, she thought; see how far he can carry all this incredible detail. Give the whole structure a shove.

"You realize, I'm sure, that people of either sex who make themselves so easily available are also liable to be carriers of disease. When was your last medical check-up?"

"My dear Dr. Landauer, my first medical check-up will be my last. Fortunately, I have no great need of one. Most serious illnesses—hepatitis, for example—reveal themselves to me by an alteration in the odor of the victim's skin. Warned, I abstain. When I do fall ill, as occasionally happens, I withdraw to some place where I can heal undisturbed. A doctor's attentions would be more dangerous to me than any disease."

Eyes on the path below, he continued calmly, "You can see by looking at me that there are no obvious clues to my unique nature. But believe me, an examination of any depth by even a half-sleeping medical practitioner would reveal some alarming deviations from the norm. I take pains to stay healthy, and I seem to be gifted with an exceptionally hardy constitution."

Fantasies of being unique and beyond fear; take him to the other pole. "I'd like you to try something now. Will you put yourself into the mind of a man you contact in the Ramble and describe your encounter with him from his point of view?"

He turned toward her and for some moments regarded her without expression. Then he resumed his surveillance of the path. "I will not do that. Though I made a poor peasant-with-torch on another occasion, I do have enough empathy with my quarry to enable me to hunt efficiently. I must draw the line at erasing the necessary distance that keeps prey and predator distinct.

"And now I think our ways part for today." He stood up, descended the hillside, and walked beneath some low-canopied trees, his tall back stooped, toward the Seventy-second Street entrance to the park.

Floria arose more slowly, aware suddenly of her shallow breathing and the sweat on her face. Back to reality or what remained of it. She looked at her watch. She was late for her next client.

Floria couldn't sleep that night. Barefoot in her bathrobe, she paced the living room by lamplight. They had sat together on that hill as isolated as in her office—more so, because there was no Hilda and no phone. He was, she knew, very strong, and he had sat close enough to her to reach out for that paralyzing touch to the neck—

Just suppose for a minute that Weyland had been brazenly telling the truth all along, counting on her to treat it as a delusion because on the face of it the truth was inconceivable.

Jesus, she thought, if I'm thinking that way about him, this therapy is more out of control than I thought. What kind of therapist becomes an accomplice to the client's fantasy? A crazy therapist, that's what kind.

Frustrated and confused by the turmoil in her mind, she wandered into the workroom. By morning the floor was covered with sheets of newsprint, each broadly marked by her felt-tipped pen. Floria sat in the midst of them, gritty-eyed and hungry.

She often approached problems this way, harking back to art training: turn off the thinking, put hand to paper, and see what the deeper, less verbally sophisticated parts of the mind have to say. Now that her dreams had deserted her, this was her only access to those levels.

The newsprint sheets were covered with rough representations of Weyland's face and form. Across several of them were scrawled words: DEAR DOUG, YOUR VAMPIRE IS FINE, IT'S YOUR EX-THERAPIST WHO'S OFF THE RAILS. WARNING: THERAPY CAN BE DANGEROUS TO YOUR HEALTH. ESPECIALLY IF YOU ARE THE THERAPIST. BEAUTIFUL VAMPIRE, AWAKEN TO ME. AM I REALLY READY TO TAKE ON A LEGENDARY MONSTER? GIVE UP—

REFER THIS ONE OUT. DO YOUR JOB—WORK IS A GOOD DOCTOR.

That last sounded pretty good, except that doing her job was precisely what she was feeling so shaky about these days.

Here was another message: HOW COME THIS ATTRACTION TO SOME ONE SO SCARY? Oh ho, she thought, is that a real feeling or an aimless reaction out of the body's early-morning hormone peak? You don't want to confuse honest libido with mere biological clockwork.

Deborah called. Babies cried in the background over the Scotch Symphony. Nick, Deb's husband, was a musicologist with fervent opinions on music and nothing else.

"We'll be in town a little later in the summer," Deborah said, "just for a few days at the end of July. Nicky has this seminar-convention thing. Of course, it won't be easy with the babies . . . I wondered if you might sort of coordinate your vacation to spend a little time with them?"

Baby-sit, that meant. Damn. Cute as they were and all that, damn! Floria gritted her teeth. Visits from Deb were difficult. Floria had been so proud of her bright, hard-driving daughter, and then suddenly Deborah had dropped her studies and rushed to embrace all the dangers that Floria had warned her against: a romantic, too-young marriage, instant breeding, no preparation for self-support, the works. Well, to each her own, but it was so wearing to have Deb around playing the empty-headed hausfrau.

"Let me think, Deb. I'd love to see all of you, but I've been considering spending a couple of weeks in Maine with your Aunt Nonnie." God knows I need a real vacation, she thought, though the peace and quiet up there is hard for a city kid like me to take for long. Still, Nonnie, Floria's younger sister, was good company. "Maybe you could bring the kids up there for a couple of days. There's room in that barn of a place, and of course Nonnie'd be happy to have you."

"Oh, no, Mom, it's so dead up there, it drives Nick

crazy—don't tell Nonnie I said that. Maybe Nonnie could come down to the city instead. You could cancel a date or two and we could all go to Coney Island together, things like that."

Kid things, which would drive Nonnie crazy and Floria too before long. "I doubt she could manage," Floria said. "But I'll ask. Look, hon, if I do go up there, you and Nick and the kids could stay here at the apartment and save some money."

"We have to be at the hotel for the seminar," Deb said rather shortly. No doubt she was feeling just as impatient as Floria was by now. "And the kids haven't seen you for a long time—it would be really nice if you could stay in the city just for a few days."

"We'll try to work something out." Always working something out. Concord never comes naturally—first we have to butt heads and get pissed off. Each time you call I hope it'll be different, Floria thought.

Somebody shrieked for "oly"—jelly that would be. Floria felt a sudden rush of warmth for them, her grandkids, for God's sake. Having been a young mother herself, she was still young enough to really enjoy them (and to fight with Deb about how to bring them up).

Deb was starting an awkward good-bye. Floria replied, put the phone down, and sat with her head back against the flowered kitchen wallpaper, thinking, Why do I feel so rotten now? Deb and I aren't close, no comfort, seldom friends, though we were once. Have I said everything wrong, made her think I don't want to see her and don't care about her family? What does she want from me that I can't seem to give her? Approval? Maybe she thinks I still hold her marriage against her. Well, I do, sort of. What right do I have to be critical, me with my divorce? What terrible things would she say to me, would I say to her, that we take such care not to say anything important at all?

"I think today we might go into sex," she said.

Weyland responded dryly, "Might we indeed. Does it titillate you to wring confessions of solitary vice from men of mature years?"

Oh, no you don't, she thought. You can't sidestep so easily. "Under what circumstances do you find yourself sexually aroused?"

"Most usually upon waking from sleep," he said indifferently.

"What do you do about it?"

"The same as others do. I am not a cripple, I have hands."

"Do you have fantasies at these times?"

"No. Women, and men for that matter, appeal to me very little, either in fantasy or reality."

"Ah—what about female vampires?" she said, trying not to sound arch.

"I know of none."

Of course: the neatest out in the book. "They're not needed for reproduction, I suppose, because people who die of vampire bites become vampires themselves."

He said testily, "Nonsense. I am not a communicable disease."

So he had left an enormous hole in his construct. She headed straight for it: "Then how does your kind reproduce?"

"I have no kind, so far as I am aware," he said, "and I do not reproduce. Why should I, when I may live for centuries still, perhaps indefinitely? My sexual equipment is clearly only detailed biological mimicry, a form of protective coloration." How beautiful, how simple a solution, she thought, full of admiration in spite of herself. "Do I occasionally detect a note of prurient interest in your questions, Dr. Landauer? Something akin to stopping at the cage to watch the tigers mate in the zoo?"

"Probably," she said, feeling her cheeks grow hot. He had a great backhand return-shot there. "How do you feel about that?"

He shrugged.

"To return to the point: do I hear you saying that you have no urge whatever to engage in sexual intercourse with anyone?"

"Would you mate with your livestock?"

His matter-of-fact arrogance took her breath away. She said weakly, "Men have reportedly done so."

"Driven men. I am not driven in that way. My sex-urge is of low frequency and is easily dealt with unaided

—although I have occasionally engaged in copulation out of the necessity to keep up appearances. I am capable, but not—like humans—obsessed."

Was he sinking into lunacy before her eyes? "I think I hear you saying," she said, striving to keep her voice neutral, "that you're not just a man with a unique way of life. I think I hear you saying that you're not human at all."

"I thought that this was already clear."

"And that there are no others like you."

"None that I know of."

"Then—you see yourself as what? Some sort of mutation?"

"Perhaps. Or perhaps your kind are the mutation."

She saw disdain in the curl of his lip. "How does your mouth feel now?"

"The corners are drawn down. The feeling is contempt."

"Can you let the contempt speak?"

He got up and went to stand at the window, positioning himself slightly to one side as if to stay hidden from the street below.

"Edward," she said.

He looked back at her. "Humans are my food. I draw the life out of their veins. Sometimes I kill them. I am greater than they are. Yet I must spend my time thinking about their habits and their drives, scheming to avoid the dangers they pose—I hate them."

She felt the hatred like a dry heat radiating from him. God, he really lived all this! She had tapped into a furnace of feeling. And now—? The sensation of triumph wavered, and she grabbed at a next move: hit him with reality now, while he's burning.

"What about blood banks?" she said. "Your food is commercially available, so why all the complication and danger of the hunt?"

"You mean turn my efforts to piling up a fortune and buying blood by the case? That would certainly make for an easier, less risky life in the short run. I could fit quite comfortably into modern society if I became just another consumer.

"However, I prefer to keep the mechanics of my survival firmly in my own hands. After all, I can't afford to lose my hunting skills. In two hundred years there may be no blood banks, but I will still need my food."

Jesus, you set him a hurdle and he just flies over it. Are there no weaknesses in all this, has he no blind spots? Look at his tension—go back to that. "What do you feel now in your body?"

"Tightness." He pressed his spread fingers to his abdomen.

"What are you doing with your hands?"

"I put my hands to my stomach."

"Can you speak for your stomach?"

" 'Feed me or die,' " he snarled.

Elated again, she closed in. "And for yourself, in answer?"

" 'Will you never be satisfied?' " He glared at her. "You shouldn't seduce me into quarreling with the terms of my own existence!"

"Your stomach is your existence," she paraphrased.

"The gut determines," he said harshly. "That first, everything else after."

"Say, 'I resent—' "

He held to a tense silence.

" 'I resent the power of my gut over my life,' " she said for him.

He stood with an abrupt motion and glanced at his watch, an elegant flash of slim silver on his wrist. "Enough," he said.

That night at home she began a set of notes that would never enter his file at the office, notes toward the proposed book.

Couldn't do it, couldn't get properly into the sex thing with him. Everything shoots off in all directions. His vampire concept so thoroughly worked out, find myself half-believing sometimes—my own childish fantasy-response to his powerful death-avoidance, contact-avoidance fantasy. Lose professional distance every time—is that what scares me about him? Don't really want to shatter his delusion (own life a mess, what right to tear down others' patterns?)—so see it as real? Wonder how much of "vampirism" he acts out, how far, how often. Something attractive in his purely selfish, predatory stance —the lure of the great outlaw.

Told me today quite coolly about a man he killed once—inadvertently!—by drinking too much from him. *Is* it fantasy? Of course—the victim, he thinks, was college student. Breathes there a professor who hasn't dreamed of murdering some representative youth, retaliation for years of classroom frustration? Speaks of teaching with caustic humor —amuses him to work at cultivating the minds of those he regards strictly as bodies, containers of his sustenance. He shows the alienness of full-blown psychopathology, poor bastard, plus clean-cut logic. Suggested he find another job (assuming his delusion at least in part related to pressures at Cayslin); his fantasy-persona, the vampire, more realistic about job-switching than I am:

"For a man of my apparent age it's not so easy to make such a change in these tight times. I might have to take a position lower on the ladder of 'success' as you people assess it." Status important to him? "Certainly. An eccentric professor is one thing; an eccentric pipe-fitter another. And I like good cars, which are expensive to own and run." (He refuses though to discuss other "jobs" from former lives.)

We are deep into the fantasy—where the hell going? Damn right I don't control the "games"— preplanned therapeutic strategies get whirled away as soon as we begin. Nerve-wracking.

Tried again to have him take the part of his enemy-victim, peasant with torch. Asked if he felt himself rejecting that point of view? Frosty reply: "Naturally. The peasant's point of view is in no way my own. I've been reading in your field, Dr. Landauer. You work from the Gestalt orientation—" Originally, yes, I corrected; eclectic these days. "But you do proceed from the theory that I am projecting some aspect of my own feelings outward onto others, whom I then treat as my victims? Your purpose then must be to maneuver me into accepting as my own the projected 'victim' aspect of myself. This integration is supposed to effect the freeing of energy previously locked into maintaining the projection. All this is an interesting insight into the nature of ordinary human confusion, but I am not an ordinary human, and I am not confused. I cannot afford confusion."

Felt sympathy for him—telling me he's afraid of having own internal confusions exposed in therapy, too threatening. Keep chipping away at delusion, though with what prospect—it's so complex, so deep-seated.

Returned to his phrase "my apparent age." He asserts he has lived many human lifetimes, all details forgotten however during periods of suspended animation between lives. Perhaps sensing my skepticism at such handy amnesia, grew cool and distant, claimed to know little about the hibernation process itself: "The essence of this state is that I sleep through it—hardly an ideal condition for making scientific observations."

Edward thinks his body synthesizes vitamins, minerals (as all our bodies synthesize Vitamin D), even proteins. Describes unique design he deduces in himself: special intestinal microfauna plus super-efficient body chemistry that extracts enough energy to live on from blood. Damn good mileage per calorie, too. (Recall observable tension, first interview, at question about drinking—my note, possible alcohol problem!)

Speak for blood: " 'Lacking me, you have no life. I flow to the heart's soft drumbeat through lightless prisons of flesh. I am rich, I am nourishing, I am difficult to attain.' " Stunned to find him positively lyrical on subject of his "food," almost hated to move him on. Drew attention to whispering voice of blood.

" 'Yes. I am secret, hidden beneath the surface, patient, silent, steady. I work unnoticed, an unseen thread of vitality running from age to age—beautiful, efficient, self-renewing, self-cleansing, warm, filling—'" Could *see* him getting worked up. Finally stood: "My appetite is pressing. I must leave you." And he did.

Sat and trembled for five minutes after.

New development (or new perception?): he sometimes comes across very unsophisticated about own feelings—lets me pursue subjects of extreme intensity and delicacy to him.

Asked him to daydream—a hunt. (Hands—mine—shaking now as I write. God. What a session.) He told of picking up a woman at poetry reading, 92nd Street Y—has N.Y.C. all worked out, circulates to avoid too much notice any one spot. Spoke easily, eyes shut without observable strain: chooses from audience redhead in glasses, dress with drooping neckline (ease of access), no perfume (strong smells bother him). Approaches during intermission, encouraged to see her fanning away smoke of others' cigarets—meaning she doesn't smoke, health sign. Agreed in not enjoying the reading, they adjourn together to coffee shop.

"She asks whether I am a teacher," he says, eyes shut, mouth amused. "My clothes, glasses, manner all suggest this, and I emphasize the impression—it reassures. She is a copy editor for a publishing house. We talk about books. The waiter brings her a gummy-looking pastry. As a non-eater, I pay little attention to the quality of restaurants, so I must apologize to her. She waves this away—is engrossed, or pretending to be engrossed, in talk." A longish dialog between interested woman and Edward doing shy-lonesome-scholar act—dead wife, competitive young colleagues who don't understand him, quarrels in professional journals with big shots in his field—a version of what he first told me. She's attracted (of course—lanky, rough-cut elegance plus hints of vulnerability all very alluring, as intended). He offers to take her home.

Tension in his body at this point in narrative—spine clear of chair-back, hands braced on thighs. "She settles beside me in the back of the cab, talking about problems of her own career—illegible manuscripts of Biblical length, mulish editors, suicidal authors—and I make comforting comments, I lean nearer and put my arm along the back of the seat, behind her shoulders. Traffic is heavy, we move slowly. There is time to make my meal here in the taxi and avoid a tedious extension of the situation into her apartment—if I move soon."

How do you feel?

"Eager," he says, voice husky. "My hunger is so roused I can scarcely restrain myself. A powerful hunger, not like yours—mine compels. I embrace her shoulders lightly, make kindly-uncle remarks, treading that fine line between the game of seduction she perceives and the game of friendly interest I affect. My real purpose underlies all: what I say, how I look, every gesture is part of the stalk. There is an added excitement—and fear—because I am doing my hunting in the presence of a third person —behind the cabbie's head." Could scarcely breathe. Studied him—intent face, mask-like with closed eyes, nostrils slightly flared; legs tensed, hands clenched on knees. Whispering: "I press the place on her neck. She starts, sighs faintly, silently drops against me. In the stale stench of the cab's interior, with the ticking of the meter in my ears and the mutter of the radio— I take hold here, at the tenderest part of her throat. Sound subsides into the background—I feel the sweet blood beating under her skin, I taste salt at the moment before I—strike. My saliva thins her blood, it flows out, I draw it into my mouth swiftly, swiftly, before she can wake, before we can arrive . . ."

Trailed off, sat back loosely in the chair. Saw him swallow. "Ah. I feed." Heard him sigh. Managed to ask about physical sensation. "Warm. Heavy here" —touches his belly—"in a pleasant way. The good taste of blood, tart and rich, in my mouth . . ."

And then? A flicker of movement beneath his closed eyelids: "In time I am aware that the cabbie has glanced back once and has taken our—embrace for just that. I can feel the cab slowing, hear him move to turn off the meter. I withdraw, I quickly wipe my mouth on my handkerchief. I take her by the shoulders and shake her gently. Does she often have these attacks, I inquire, the soul of concern.

She comes around, bewildered, weak, thinks she has fainted. I give the driver extra money and ask him to wait. He looks intrigued—'What was that all about?' I can see the question in his face—but as a true New Yorker he will not expose his own ignorance by inquiring.

"I escort the woman to her front door, supporting her as she staggers. Any suspicion of me that she may entertain, however formless and hazy, is allayed by my stern charging of the doorman to see that she reaches her apartment safely. She grows embarrassed, thinks perhaps that if not put off by her 'illness' I would spend the night with her, which moves her to press upon me, unasked, her telephone number. I bid her a solicitous good night and take the cab back to my hotel, where I sleep."

No sex? No sex. How did he feel about the victim as a person? "She was food."

This was his "hunting" of last night, he admits afterward, not a made-up dream. No boasting in it, just telling. Telling me! Think: I can go talk to Lucille, Mort, Doug, others about most of what matters to me. Edward has only me to talk to and that for a fee—what isolation! No wonder the stone, monumental face—only those long, strong lips (his point of contact, verbal and physical-in-fantasy, with world and with "food") are truly expressive. An exciting narration; uncomfortable to find I felt not only empathy but enjoyment. Suppose he picked up and victimized—even in fantasy—Deb or Hilda, how would I feel then?

Later: truth—I also found this recital sexually stirring. Keep visualizing how he looked finishing this "dream"—sat very still, head up, look of thoughtful pleasure on his face. Like handsome intellectual listening to music.

Kenny showed up unexpectedly at Floria's office on Monday, bursting with malevolent energy. She happened to be free, so she took him—something was definitely up. He sat on the edge of his chair.

"I know why you're trying to unload me," he accused. "It's that new one, the tall guy with the snooty look—what is he, an old actor or something? Anybody could see he's got you itching for him."

"Kenny, when was it that I first spoke to you about terminating our work together?" she said patiently.

"Don't change the subject. Let me tell you, in case you don't know it: that guy isn't really interested, doctor, because he's a fruit. A faggot. You want to know how I know?"

Oh Lord, she thought wearily, he's regressed to age ten. She could see that she was going to hear the rest whether she wanted to or not. What in God's name was the world like for Kenny, if he clung so frantically to her despite her failure to help him?

"Listen, I knew right away there was something flaky about him, so I followed him home from here to that hotel where he lives. I followed him the other afternoon, too. He walked around like he does a lot, and then he went into one of those ritzy movie houses on Third that open early and show risqué foreign movies—you know, Japs cutting each other's things off and glop like that. This one was French, though.

"Well, there was a guy came in, a Madison Avenue type carrying his attaché case, taking a work break or something. Your man moved over and sat down behind him and reached out and sort of stroked the guy's neck, and the guy leaned back, and your man leaned forward and started nuzzling at him, you know—kissing him.

"I saw it. They had their heads together and they stayed like that awhile. It was disgusting: complete strangers, without even 'Hello.' The Madison Avenue guy just sat there with his head back looking zonked, you know, just swept away, and what he was doing with his hands under the raincoat in his lap I couldn't see, but I bet you can guess.

"And then your fruity friend got up and walked out. I did, too, and I hung around a little outside. After a while the Madison Avenue guy came out looking all sleepy and loose, like after you-know-what, and he wandered off on his own someplace.

"What do you think now?" he ended, on a high, triumphant note.

Her impulse was to slap his face the way she would

have slapped Deb-as-a-child for tattling. But this was a client, not a kid. God give me strength, she thought.

"Kenny, you're fired."

"You can't!" he squealed. "You can't! What will I—who can I—"

She stood up, feeling weak but hardening her voice. "I'm sorry. I absolutely cannot have a client who makes it his business to spy on other clients. You already have a list of replacement therapists from me."

He gaped at her in slack-jawed dismay, his eyes swimmy with tears.

"I'm sorry, Kenny. Call this a dose of reality therapy and try to learn from it. There are some things you simply will not be allowed to do." She felt stronger, better: it was done at last.

"I hate you!" He surged out of his chair, knocking it back against the wall. Threateningly, he glared at the fish tank, but, contenting himself with a couple of kicks at the nearest table-leg, he stamped out.

Floria buzzed Hilda: "No more appointments for Kenny, Hilda. You can close his file."

"Whoopee," Hilda said.

Poor, horrid Kenny. Impossible to tell what would happen to him, better not to speculate or she might relent, call him back . . . She had encouraged him, really, by listening instead of shutting him up and throwing him out before any damage was done.

Was it damaging to know the truth? In her mind's eye she saw a cream-faced young man out of a Black Thumb Vodka ad wander from a movie theater into daylight, yawning and rubbing absently at a sore spot on his neck.

She didn't even look at the telephone on the table or think about whom to call, now that she believed. No, she was going to keep quiet about Dr. Edward Lewis Weyland, her vampire.

· Hardly alive at staff meeting, clinic, yesterday —people asking what's the matter, fobbed them off. Settled down today. Had to, to face him.

Asked him what he felt were his strengths. He

said speed, cunning, ruthlessness. Animal strengths, I said. What about imagination, or is that strictly human? He defended at once: not human only. Lion, waiting at water-hole where no zebra yet drinks, thinks "Zebra—eat," therefore performs feat of imagining event yet-to-come. Self experienced as animal? Yes—reminded me that humans are also animals. Pushed for his early memories, he objected: "Gestalt is here-and-now, not history-taking." I insisted, citing anomalous nature of his situation, my own refusal to be bound by any one theoretical framework. He defends tensely: "Suppose I became lost there in memory, distracted from dangers of the present, left unguarded from those dangers?"

Speak for memory. He resists, but at length attempts it: " 'I am heavy with the multitudes of the past.' " Fingertips to forehead, propping up all that weight of lives. " 'So heavy, filling worlds of time laid down eon by eon, I accumulate, I persist, I demand recognition. I am as real as the life around you— more real, weightier, richer.' " His voice sinking, shoulders bowed, head in hands—I begin to feel pressure at the back of my own skull. " 'Let me in.' " Only a rough whisper now. " 'I offer beauty as well as terror. Let me in.' " Whispering also I suggest he reply to his memory. "Memory, you want to crush me," he groans. "You would overwhelm me with the cries of animals, the odor and jostle of bodies, old betrayals, dead joys, filth and anger from other times —I must concentrate on the danger now. Let me be." All I can take of this crazy conflict, I gabble us off onto something else. He looks up—relief?—follows my lead—where? Rest of session a blank.

No wonder sometimes no empathy at all—a species boundary! He has to be utterly self-centered just to keep balance—self-centeredness of an animal. Thought just now of our beginning, me trying to push him to produce material, trying to control him, manipulate—no way, no way; so here we are, someplace else—I feel dazed, in shock, but stick with it— it's real.

Therapy with a dinosaur, a Martian.

"You call me 'Weyland' now, not 'Edward.' " I said first name couldn't mean much to one with no memory of being called by that name as a child, silly to pretend it signifies intimacy where it can't. I think he knows now that I believe him. Without prompting, told me truth of disappearance from Cayslin. No romance; he tried to drink from a woman who worked there, she shot him, stomach and chest. Luckily for him, small-calibre pistol, and he was wearing a lined coat over three-piece suit. Even so, badly hurt. (Midsection stiffness I noted when he first came—he was still in some pain at that time.) He didn't "vanish"—fled, hid, was found by questionable types who caught on to what he was, sold him "like a chattel" to someone here in the city. He was imprisoned, fed, put on exhibition—very privately—for gain. Got away. "Do you believe any of this?" Never asked anything like that before, seems of concern to him now. I said my belief or lack of same was immaterial; remarked on hearing a lot of bitterness.

Steepled his fingers, looked brooding at me over tips: "I nearly died there. No doubt my purchaser and his friends are still searching for me. Mind you, I had some reason at first to be glad of the attentions of the people who kept me prisoner. I was in no condition to fend for myself. They brought me food and kept me hidden and sheltered, whatever their motives. There are always advantages . . ."

Silence today started a short session. Hunting poor last night, Weyland still hungry. Much restless movement, watching goldfish darting in tank, scanning bookshelves. Asked him to be books. "I am old and full of knowledge, well-made to last long. You see only the title, the substance is hidden. I am a book that stays closed." Malicious twist of the mouth, not quite a smile: "This is a good game." Is he feeling threatened too—already "opened" too much to me? Too strung out with him to dig when he's skimming surfaces that should be probed. Don't know how to *do* therapy with Weyland—just have to let things happen, hope it's good. But what's "good"? Aristotle?

Rousseau? Ask Weyland what's good, he'll say, "Blood."

Everything in a spin—these notes too confused, fragmentary—worthless for a book, just a mess, like me, my life. Tried to call Deb last night, cancel visit. Nobody home, thank God. Can't tell her to stay away —but damn it—do not need complications now.

Floria went down to Broadway with Lucille to get more juice, cheese, and crackers for the clinic fridge. This week it was their turn to do the provisions, a chore that rotated among the staff. Their talk about grant proposals for the support of the clinic trailed off.

"Let's sit a minute," Floria said. They crossed to a traffic island in the middle of the avenue. It was a sunny afternoon, close enough to lunchtime so that the brigade of old people who normally occupied the benches had thinned out. Floria sat down and kicked a crumpled beer can and some greasy fast-food wrappings back under the bench.

"You look like hell but wide awake, at least," Lucille commented.

"Things are still rough," Floria said. "I keep hoping to get my life under control so I'll have some energy left for Deb and Nick and the kids when they arrive, but I can't seem to do it. Group was awful last night—a member accused me afterward of having abandoned them all. I think I have, too. The professional messes and the personal are all related somehow, they run into each other. I should be keeping them apart so I can deal with them separately, but I can't. I can't concentrate, my mind is all over the place. Except with Dracula, who keeps me riveted with astonishment when he's in the office and bemused the rest of the time."

A bus roared by, shaking the pavement and the benches. Lucille waited until the noise faded. "Relax about the group. They'd have defended you if you'd been attacked during the session. They'd all understand, even if you don't seem to: it's the summer doldrums, people don't want to work, they expect you to do it all for them.

But don't push so hard. You're not a shaman who can magic your clients back into health."

Floria tore two cans of juice out of a six-pack and handed one to her. On a street corner opposite a violent argument broke out in typewriter-fast Spanish between two women. Floria sipped tinny juice and watched. She'd seen a guy last winter straddle another on that same corner and try to smash his brains out on the icy sidewalk. What's crazy, what's health?

"It's a good thing you dumped Chubs, anyhow," Lucille added. "I don't know what finally brought that on, but it's definitely a move in the right direction. What about Count Dracula? You don't talk about him much anymore. I thought I diagnosed a yen for his venerable body."

Floria shifted uncomfortably on the bench and didn't answer. If only she could deflect Lucille's sharp-eyed curiosity—

"Oh," Lucille said. "I see. You really are hot—or at least warm. Has he noticed?"

"I don't think so. He's not on the lookout for that kind of response from me. He says sex with other people doesn't interest him, and I think he's telling the truth."

"Weird," Lucille said. "What about *Vampire on My Couch?* Shaping up all right?"

"It's shaky, like everything else. I'm worried that I don't know how things are going to come out. I mean, Freud's wolf-man case was a success, as therapy goes. Will my vampire case turn out successfully?"

She glanced at Lucille's puzzled face, made up her mind, and plunged ahead. "Luce, think of it this way: suppose, just suppose, that my Dracula is for real, an honest-to-God vampire—"

"Oh, *shit!*" Lucille erupted in anguished exasperation. "Damn it, Floria, enough is enough—will you stop futzing around and get some help? Coming to pieces yourself and trying to treat this poor nut with a vampire fixation—how can you do him any good? No wonder you're worried about his therapy!"

"Please, just listen, help me think this out. My purpose can't be to cure him of what he is. Suppose vampirism isn't a defense he has to learn to drop? Suppose it's the core of his identity? Then what do I do?"

Lucille rose abruptly and marched away from her across the traffic, plunging through a gap between the rolling waves of cabs and trucks. Floria caught up with her on the next block.

"Listen, will you? Luce, you see the problem? I don't need to help him see who and what he is, he knows that perfectly well, and he's not crazy, far from it—"

"Maybe not," Lucille said grimly, "but you are. Don't dump this junk on me outside of office hours, Floria. I don't spend my time listening to nut-talk unless I'm getting paid."

"Just tell me if this makes psychological sense to you: he's healthier than most of us because he's always true to his identity, even when he's engaged in deceiving others. A fairly narrow, rigorous set of requirements necessary to his survival—that *is* his identity, and it commands him completely. Anything extraneous could destroy him. To go on living he has to act solely out of his own undistorted necessity, and if that isn't authenticity, what is? So he's healthy, isn't he?" She paused, feeling a sudden lightness in herself. "And that's the best sense I've been able to make of this whole business so far."

They were in the middle of the block. Lucille, who could not on her short legs outwalk Floria, turned on her suddenly. "What the hell do you think you're doing, calling yourself a therapist? For God's sake, Floria, don't try to rope me into this kind of professional irresponsibility. You're just dipping into your client's fantasies instead of helping him to handle them. That's not therapy, it's collusion. Have some sense! Admit you're over your head in troubles of your own, retreat to firmer ground—go get treatment for yourself!"

Floria angrily shook her head. When Lucille turned away and hurried on up the block toward the clinic, Floria let her go without trying to detain her.

Thought about Lucille's advice. After my divorce going back into therapy for a while did help, but now? Retreat again to being a client, like old days in training—so young, inadequate, defenseless then. Awful prospect. And I'd have to hand W. over to somebody else—who? I'm not up to handling him, can't cope, too anxious, yet with all the limitations we do good therapy together somehow. I offer: he's free to take, refuse, use as suits, as far as he's willing to go. I serve as resource while he does own therapy —isn't that therapeutic ideal, free of "shoulds," "shouldn'ts"?

Saw ballet with Mort, lovely evening—time out from W.—talking, singing, pirouetting all the way home, feeling safe as anything in the shadow of Mort-mountain, rolled later with that humming (off-key), sun-warm body.

Then today W. talked mechanics of blood-sucking while I thought cowardly thoughts about giving him notice, calling a halt. Doesn't bite, he says; has puncturing organ under tongue, hence no fangs. Half my mind saying, ah-hah, always wondered why movie vampire's victims have those two little holes in the throat, maybe 1 inch apart, while vampire has these huge canines 3 inches from each other at least. Other half screaming, Lucille's right, one (or both) here is crazy—*Get out!*

Then he says he saw me at Lincoln Center last night, avoided me because of Mort. W. is ballet fan! Started attending to pick up victims, now also because dance puzzles and pleases. "When a group dances well, the meaning is easy—the dancers make a visual complement to the music, all their moves necessary, coherent, and flowing. When a gifted soloist performs, the pleasure of making the moves is echoed in my own body. The soloist's absorption is total, much like my own in the actions of the hunt.

"But when a man and a woman dance together, something else happens. What is it? Sometimes one is hunter, one is prey, or they shift these roles between them. Yet some other level of significance exists—I suppose to do with sex, and I feel it—a tugging sensation, here"—touched his solar plexus— "but I do not understand it."

Worked with his reactions to ballet. The response he feels to pas de deux is a kind of pull, "like hunger but not hunger." Of course he's baffled— Balanchine writes that the pas de deux is always a love story between man and woman. W. isn't man, isn't woman, yet the drama reaches him. His hands hovering as he spoke, fingers spread toward each other. Pointed this out. Body-work comes easier to him now: joined his hands, interlaced fingers, spoke for hands without prompting: "We are similar, we want the comfort of like closing to like." What would it be for him, to find—likeness, another of his kind? "Female?" Starts to tell me how unlikely this is—no, forget sex and pas de deux for now—just to find your like, another vampire. He springs up, agitated now. There are none, he insists.

But what would it be like? What would happen? "I fear it!" Sits again, hands clenched. "I long for it." Silence. He watches goldfish, I watch him. I withhold fatuous attempt to pin down this insight, if that's what it is—what can I know about his insight? Suddenly he turns, studies me intently till I lose nerve, react, cravenly suggest that if I make him uncomfortable he may choose to switch to a male therapist. "Certainly not." More follows, all gold: "There is value to me in what we do here, Dr. Landauer, much against my earlier expectations. Although people talk appreciatively of honest speech they generally avoid it, and I myself have found scarcely any use for it at all. Your straightforwardness with me—and the straightforwardness you require in return—this is healthy in a life so dependent on deception as mine."

Sat there, wordless, much moved, thinking of what I don't show him—my upset life, seat-of-pants course with him and attendant strain, attraction to him—I'm holding out on him while he appreciates my honesty.

Hesitation, then lower-voiced: "Also, there are limits on my methods of self-discovery, short of turning myself over to a laboratory for vivisection. I have no others like myself to look at and learn from. Any tools that may help are worth much to me, and these games of yours are—potent."

Other stuff besides, not important. Important: he moves me and he draws me and he keeps on coming back. Hang in if he does.

Bad night—Kenny's aunt called: no bill from me this month, so if he's not seeing me, who's keeping an eye on him, where's he hanging out? Much implied blame for what *might* happen. Absurd, but shook me up: I did fail Kenny. Called off group this week also; too much.

No, it was a *good* night—first dream in months I can recall, contact again with own depths—but disturbing. Dreamed myself in cab with W. in place of the woman from the Y. He put his hand not on my neck but breast—I felt intense sensual response in the dream, also anger and fear so strong they woke me.

Thinking about this: anyone leans toward him sexually, to him a sign his hunting technique has maneuvered prospective victim into range, maybe arouses his appetite for blood. I *don't want that*. "She was food." I am not food, I am a person. No thrill at languishing away in his arms in a taxi while he drinks my blood—that's disfigured sex, masochism. My sex response in dream signaled to me I would be his victim—I rejected that, woke up.

Mention of *Dracula* (novel). W. dislikes: meandering, inaccurate, those absurd fangs. Says he himself has when needed a sort of needle under his tongue, used to pierce skin. No offer to demonstrate, and no request from me. I brightly brought up historical Vlad Dracul—celebrated instance of Turkish envoys who, upon refusing to uncover to Vlad to show respect, were killed by spiking their hats to their skulls. "Nonsense," snorts W. "A clever ruler would use very small thumbtacks and dismiss the envoys to moan about the streets of Verna holding their tacked heads." First spontaneous play he's shown—took head in hands and uttered plaintive groans: "Ow, oh, ooh." I cracked up. W. reverted at once to usual dignified manner: "You can see that this would serve the ruler much more effectively as an object lesson against rash pride."

Later, same light vein: "I know why I'm a vampire; why are you a therapist?" Off balance as usual, said things about helping, mental health, etc. He shook his head: "And people think of a vampire as arrogant! You want to perform cures in a world which exhibits very little health of any kind—and it's the same arrogance with all of you. This one wants to be President or Class Monitor or Department Chairman or Union Boss, another must be first to fly to the stars or to transplant the human brain, and on and on. As for me, I wish only to satisfy my appetite in peace." And those of us whose appetite is for competence, for effectiveness? Thought of Green, treated eight years ago, went on to be indicted for running a hellish "home" for aged. I had helped him stay functional so he could destroy the helpless for profit.

W. not my first predator, only most honest and direct. Scared; not of attack by W., but of process we're going through. I'm beginning to be up to it (?), but still—utterly unpredictable, impossible to handle or manage—Occasional stirrings of inward choreographer that used to shape my work so surely. Have I been afraid of that, holding it down in myself, choosing mechanical manipulation instead? Not a choice with W.—thinking no good, strategy no good, nothing left but instinct, clear and uncluttered responses if I can find them. Have to be my own authority with him, as he is always his own authority with a world in which he's unique. So work with W. not exhausting—exhilarating too, along with strain, fear.

Am I growing braver? Not much choice.

Park again today (air-conditioning out at office). Avoiding Lucille's phone calls from clinic (very reassuring that she calls despite quarrel, but don't want to take all this up with her again). Also meeting W. in open feels saner somehow—wild creatures belong outdoors? Sailboat pond N. of 72nd, lots of kids, garbage, one beautiful tall boat drifting.

W. maintains he remembers no childhood, no parents. I told him my astonishment, confronted by someone who never had a life of the previous generation (even adopted parent) shielding him from death—how naked we stand when the last shield falls. Got caught in remembering a death dream of mine, dream it now and then—couldn't concentrate, got scared, spoke of it—a dog tumbled under a passing truck, ejected to side of the road where it lay unable to move except to lift head and shriek—couldn't help. Shaking nearly to tears—remembered mother got into dream somehow—had blocked that at first. Didn't say it now. Tried to rescue situation, show W. how to work with a dream (sitting in vine arbor near band shell, some privacy).

He focused on my obvious shakiness: "The air vibrates constantly with the death-cries of countless animals large and small. What is the death of one dog?" Leaned close, speaking quietly, instructing. "Many creatures are dying in ways too dreadful to imagine. I am part of the world; I listen to the pain. You people claim to be above all that. You deafen yourselves with your own noise and pretend there's nothing else to hear. Then these screams enter your dreams, and you have to seek therapy because you have lost the nerve to listen."

Remembered myself, said, Be a dying animal. He refused: "You are the one who dreams this." I had a horrible flash, felt I was the dog—helpless, doomed, hurting—burst into tears. The great therapist, bringing her own hang-ups into session with client! Enraged with self, which did not help stop bawling.

W. disconcerted, I think; didn't speak. People walked past, glanced over, ignored us. W. said finally, "What is this?" Nothing, just the fear of death. "Oh, the fear of death. That's with me all the time. One must simply get used to it." Tears into laughter. Goddamn wisdom of the ages. He got up to go, paused: "And tell that stupid little man who used to precede me at your office to stop following me around. He puts himself in danger that way."

Kenny, damn it! Aunt doesn't know where he is, no answer on his phone. Idiot!

Sketching all night—useless. W. beautiful beyond the scope of line—the beauty of singularity, cohesion, rooted in absolute devotion to demands of his specialized body. In feeding (woman in taxi), utter absorption one wants from a man in sex—no score-keeping, no fantasies, just hot urgency of appetite, of senses, the moment by itself.

His sleeves worn rolled back today to the elbows
—strong, sculptural forearms, the long bones curved
in slightly, suggest torque, leverage. How old—?

Endurance: huge, rich cloak of time flows back
from his shoulders like wings of a dark angel. All
springs from, elaborates, the single, stark, primary
condition: he is a predator who subsists on human
blood. Harmony, strength, clarity, magnificence—
all from that basic animal integrity. Of course I long
for all that, here in the higgledy-piggledy hodge-
podge of my life! Of course he draws me!

Wore no perfume today, deference to his keen,
easily insulted sense of smell. He noticed at once,
said curt thanks. Saw something bothering him,
opened my mouth seeking desperately for right thing
to say—up rose my inward choreographer, wide
awake, and spoke plain from my heart: thinking on
my floundering in some of our sessions—I am aware
that you see this confusion of mine. I know you
see by your occasional impatient look, sudden dis-
engagement—yet you continue to reveal yourself to
me (even shift our course yourself if it needs shifting
and I don't do it). I think I know why. Because
there's no place for you in world as you truly are.
Because beneath your various facades your true self
suffers; like all true selves, it wants, needs to be honored as real and valuable through acceptance by
another. I try to be that other, but often you are beyond me. He rose, paced to window, looked back,
burning at me. "If I seem sometimes restless or impatient, Dr. Landauer, it's not because of any professional shortcomings of yours. On the contrary
—you are all too effective. The seductiveness, the
distraction of our—human contact worries me. I
fear for the ruthlessness that keeps me alive."

Speak for ruthlessness. He shook his head. Saw
tightness in shoulders, feet braced hard against floor.
Felt reflected tension in my own muscles.

Prompted him: " 'I resent—' "

"I resent your pretension to teach me about myself! What will this work that you do here make of
me? A predator paralyzed by an unwanted empathy

with his prey? A creature fit only for a cage and keeper?" He was breathing hard, jaw set. I saw suddenly the truth of his fear: his integrity is not human, but my work is specifically human, designed to make humans more human—what if it does that to him? Should have seen it before, should have seen it. No place left to go: had to ask him, in small voice, Speak for my pretension.

"No!" Eyes shut, head turned away.

Had to do it: Speak for me.

W. whispered, "As to the unicorn, out of your own legends—'Unicorn, come lay your head in my lap while the hunters close in. You are a wonder, and for love of wonder I will tame you. You are pursued, but forget your pursuers, rest under my hand till they come and destroy you.'" Looked at me like steel. "Do you see? The more you involve yourself in what I am, the more you become the peasant with the torch!"

Two days later Doug came into town and had lunch with Floria.

He was a man of no outstanding beauty who was nevertheless attractive: he didn't have much chin and his ears were too big, but you didn't notice because of his air of confidence. His stability had been earned the hard way —as a gay man facing the straight world. Some of his strength had been attained with effort and pain in a group that Floria had run years earlier. A lasting affection had grown between herself and Doug. She was intensely glad to see him.

They ate near the clinic. "You look a little frayed around the edges," Doug said. "I heard about Jane Fennerman's relapse—too bad."

"I've only been able to bring myself to visit her once since."

"Feeling guilty?"

She hesitated, gnawing on a stale breadstick. The truth was, she hadn't thought of Jane Fennerman in weeks. Finally she said, "I must be."

Sitting back with his hands in his pockets, Doug chided

her gently. "It's got to be Jane's fourth or fifth time into the nuthatch, and the others happened when she was in the care of other therapists. Who are you to imagine—to demand—that her cure lay in your hands? God may be a woman, Floria, but she is not you. I thought the whole point was some recognition of individual responsibility—you for yourself, the client for himself or herself."

"That's what we're always saying," Floria agreed. She felt curiously divorced from this conversation. It had an old-fashioned flavor: Before Weyland. She smiled a little.

The waiter ambled over. She ordered bluefish. The serving would be too big for her depressed appetite, but Doug wouldn't be satisfied with his customary order of salad (he never was) and could be persuaded to help out.

He worked his way around to Topic A. "When I called to set up this lunch, Hilda told me she's got a crush on Weyland. How are you and he getting along?"

"My God, Doug, now you're going to tell me this whole thing was to fix me up with an eligible suitor!" She winced at her own rather strained laughter. "How soon are you planning to ask Weyland to work at Cayslin again?"

"I don't know, but probably sooner than I thought a couple of months ago. We hear that he's been exploring an attachment to an archaeology department at a Western school, some niche where I guess he feels he can have less responsibility, less visibility, and a chance to collect himself. Naturally, this news is making people at Cayslin suddenly eager to nail him down for us. Have you a recommendation?"

"Yes," she said. "Wait."

He gave her an inquiring look. "What for?"

"Until he works more fully through certain stresses in the situation at Cayslin. Then I'll be ready to commit myself about him," The bluefish came. She pretended distraction: "Good God, that's much too much fish for me. Douglas, come on and help me out here."

Hilda was crouched over Floria's file drawer. She straightened up, grim-looking. "Somebody's been in the office!"

What was this, had someone attacked her? The world took on a cockeyed, dangerous tilt. "Are you okay?"

"Yes, sure, I mean there are records that have been gone through. I can tell. I've started checking and so far it looks as if none of the files themselves are missing. But if any papers were taken out of them, that would be pretty hard to spot without reading through every folder in the place. Your files, Floria. I don't think anybody else's were touched."

Mere burglary; weak with relief, Floria sat down on one of the waiting-room chairs. But only her files? "Just my stuff, you're sure?"

Hilda nodded. "The clinic got hit too. I called. They see some new-looking scratches on the lock of your file drawer over there. Listen, you want me to call the cops?"

"First check as much as you can, see if anything obvious is missing."

There was no sign of upset in her office. She found a note on her table: Weyland had canceled his next appointment.

She buzzed Hilda's desk. "Hilda, let's leave the police out of it for the moment. Keep checking." She stood in the middle of the office, looking at the chair replacing the one he had broken, looking at the window where he had so often watched.

Relax, she told herself. There was nothing for him to find here or at the clinic.

She signaled that she was ready for the first client of the afternoon.

That evening she came back to the office after having dinner with friends. She was supposed to be helping set up a workshop for next month, and she'd been putting off even thinking about it, let alone doing any real work. She set herself to compiling a suggested bibliography for her section.

The phone light blinked.

It was Kenny, muffled and teary-voiced. "I'm sorry," he moaned. "The medicine just started to wear off. I've been trying to call you everyplace. God, I'm so scared—he was waiting in the alley."

"Who was?" she said, dry-mouthed. She knew.

"Him. The tall one, the faggot—only he goes with women too, I've seen him. He grabbed me. He hurt me. I was lying there a long time. I couldn't do anything. I felt so funny—like floating away. Some kids found me. Their mother called the cops. I was so cold, so scared—"

"Kenny, where are you?"

He told her which hospital. "Listen, I think he's really crazy, you know? And I'm scared he might—you live alone—I don't know—I didn't mean to make trouble for you. I'm so scared."

God damn you, you meant exactly to make trouble for me, and now you've bloody well made it. She got him to ring for a nurse. By calling Kenny her patient and using "Dr." in front of her own name without qualifying the title she got some information: two broken ribs, multiple contusions, a badly wrenched shoulder, and a deep cut on the scalp which Dr. Wells thought accounted for the blood-loss the patient seemed to have sustained. Picked up early today, the patient wouldn't say who had attacked him. You can check with Dr. Wells tomorrow, Dr.—?

Can Weyland think I've somehow sicked Kenny on him? No, he surely knows me better than that. Kenny must have brought this on himself.

She tried Weyland's number and then the desk at his hotel. He had closed his account and gone, providing no forwarding information.

Then she remembered: this was the night Deb and Nick and the kids were arriving. Oh, God. Next phone call.

The Americana was the hotel Deb had mentioned. Yes, Mr. and Mrs. Nicholas Redpath were registered in room whatnot. Ring please.

Deb's voice came shakily on the line. "I've been trying to call you." Like Kenny.

"You sound upset," Floria said, steadying herself for whatever calamity had descended: illness, accident, assault in the streets of the dark, degenerate city.

Silence, then a raggedy sob. "Nick's not here. I didn't phone you earlier because I thought he still might come, but I don't think he's coming, Mom." Bitter weeping.

"Oh, Debbie. Debbie, listen, you just sit tight, I'll be right down there."

The cab ride only took a few minutes. Debbie was still crying when Floria stepped into the room.

"I don't know, I don't know," Deb wailed, shaking her head. "What did I do wrong? He went away a week ago, to do some research he said, and I didn't hear from him, and half the bank money is gone—just half, he left me half. I kept hoping—they say most runaways come back in a few days or call up, they get lonely—I haven't told anybody—I thought since we were supposed to be here at this convention thing together, I'd better come, maybe he'd show up. But nobody's seen him, and there are no messages, not a word, nothing—"

"All right, all right, poor Deb," Floria said, hugging her.

"Oh God, I'm going to wake the kids with all this howling—" Deb pulled away, making a frantic gesture toward the door of the adjoining room. "It was so hard to get them to sleep—they were expecting Daddy to be here, I kept telling them he'd be here—" She rushed out into the hotel hallway. Floria followed, propping the door open with one of her shoes since she didn't know whether Deb had the key with her or not. They stood out there together, ignoring passers-by, huddling over Deb's weeping.

"What's been going on between you and Nick?" Floria said. "Have you two been sleeping together lately?"

Deb let out a squawk of agonized embarrassment, "Mo-*ther!*" and pulled away from her. Oh, hell, wrong approach.

"Come on, I'll help you pack and let's go—let Nick come looking for you. We'll leave word you're at my place." Floria firmly squashed down the miserable inner cry, How am I going to stand this?

"Oh, no, I can't move till morning now that I've got the kids settled down. Besides, there's one night's deposit on the rooms. Oh, Mom, what did I do?"

"You didn't do anything, hon," Floria said, patting her shoulder and thinking in some part of her mind, Oh boy, that's great, is that the best you can come up with in a crisis with all your training and experience? Your touted professional skills are not so hot lately, but this bad?

Another part answered, Shut up, stupid, only a dope does therapy on her own family. Deb's come to her mother, not a shrink, so go ahead and be Mommy. If only Mommy had less pressure on her right now—but that was always the way: everything at once or nothing at all.

"Look, suppose I stay the night here with you?"

Deb shook the pale, damp-streaked hair out of her eyes with a determined, grown-up gesture. "No, thanks, Mom. Look, I'm so tired I'm just going to fall out now. You'll be getting a bellyful of all this when we move in on you tomorrow anyway. I can manage tonight, and besides—"

And besides, just in case Nick showed up, Deb didn't want Floria around complicating things; of course. Or in case the tooth-fairy dropped by.

Floria restrained an impulse to insist on staying: the impulse, she recognized, came from her own need not to be alone tonight. That was an inappropriate burden to load on Deb's shoulders.

"Okay," she said. "But look, Deb, I'll expect you to call me up first thing in the morning, whatever happens." And if I'm still alive, I'll answer the phone.

All the way home in the cab she knew with growing certainty that Weyland would be waiting for her there. He can't just walk away, she thought; he has to finish things with me. So let's get it over.

In the tiled hallway she hesitated, keys in hand. What about calling the cops to go inside with her? Absurd. You don't set the cops on a unicorn.

She unlocked and opened the door to the apartment and called inside, "All right, Weyland, where are you?"

Nothing. Of course not—the door was still open, and he would want to be sure she was by herself. She stepped inside, shut the door, and snapped on a lamp as she walked into the living room.

He was sitting quietly on a radiator cover by the street window, his hands on his thighs. His appearance here in a new setting, her setting, this faintly-lit room in her home place, was startlingly intimate. She was sharply aware of the whisper of movement—his clothing, his shoe-soles against the carpet underfoot—as he shifted his posture.

"What would you have done if I'd brought somebody with me?" she said unsteadily. "Changed yourself into a bat and flown away?"

"Two things I must have from you," he said. "One is the bill of health that we spoke of when we began, though not, after all, for Cayslin College. I've made other plans. The story of my disappearance has of course filtered out along the academic grapevine so that even two thousand miles from here people will be wanting evidence of my mental soundness. Your evidence. I would type it myself and forge your signature, but I want your authentic tone and language. Please prepare a letter to the desired effect, addressed to these people."

He took something white from an inside pocket and held it out. She advanced and took the envelope from his extended hand. It was from the Western archaeology department that Doug had mentioned at lunch.

"Why not Cayslin?" she said. "They want you there."

"Have you forgotten your own suggestion that I find another job? That was a good idea after all. Your reference will serve me best out there—with a copy for my personnel file at Cayslin, naturally."

She put her purse down on the seat of a chair and crossed her arms. She felt reckless—the effect of stress and weariness, she thought, but it was an exciting feeling.

"The receptionist at the office does this sort of thing for me," she said.

He pointed. "I've been in your study. You have a typewriter there, you have stationery with your letterhead, you have carbon paper."

"What was the second thing you wanted?"

"Your notes on my case."

"Also at the—"

"You know that I've already been to both your workplaces, and the very circumspect jottings in your file on me are not what I mean. Others must exist: more detailed."

"What makes you think that?"

"How could you resist?" He mocked her. "You have

encountered nothing like me in your entire professional life, and never shall again. Perhaps someday you hope to produce an article, even a book—a memoir of something impossible that happened to you one summer—you are an ambitious woman, Dr. Landauer."

Floria squeezed her crossed arms tighter against herself to quell her shivering. "This is all just supposition," she said.

He took folded papers from his pocket: some of her thrown-aside drawings of him, salvaged from the waste basket. "I found these. I think there must be more. Fetch whatever there is for me, please."

"And if I refuse, what will you do? Beat me up the way you beat up Kenny?"

Weyland said calmly, "I told you he should stop following me. This is serious now. There are pursuers who intend me ill—my former captors, of whom I told you. Whom do you think I keep watch for? No records concerning me must fall into their hands. Don't bother protesting to me your devotion to confidentiality. My pursuers would take what they want, and be damned to your professional ethics. So I must destroy all evidence you have about me before I leave the city."

Floria turned away and sat down by the coffee table, trying to think beyond her fear. She breathed deeply against the fright trembling in her chest.

"I see," he said dryly, "that you won't give me the notes; you don't trust me to take them and go. You see some danger."

"All right, a bargain," she said. "I'll give you whatever I have on your case if in return you promise to go straight out to your new job and keep away from Kenny and my offices and anybody connected with me—"

He was smiling slightly as he rose from the seat and stepped soft-footed toward her over the rug. "Bargains, promises, negotiations—all foolish, Dr. Landauer. I want what I came for."

She looked up at him. "But then how can I trust you at all? As soon as I give you what you want—"

"What is it that makes you afraid—that you can't render me harmless to you? What a curious concern you show suddenly for your own life and the lives of those around you! You are the one who led me to take chances in our work together—to explore the frightful risks of self-revelation. Didn't you see in the air between us the brilliant shimmer of those hazards? I thought your business was not smoothing the world over but adventuring into it, discovering its true nature, and closing valiantly with everything jagged, cruel, and deadly."

In the midst of her terror the inner choreographer awoke and stretched. Floria rose to face the vampire.

"All right, Weyland, no bargains. I'll give you freely what you want." Of course she couldn't make herself safe from him—or make Kenny or Lucille or Deb or Doug safe—any more than she could protect Jane Fennerman from the common dangers of life. Like Weyland, some dangers were too strong to bind or banish. "My notes are in the work room—come on, I'll show you. As for the letter you need, I'll type it right now and you can take it away with you."

She sat at the typewriter arranging paper, carbon sheets, and white-out, and feeling the force of his presence. Only a few feet away, just at the margin of the light from the gooseneck lamp by which she worked, he leaned against the edge of the long table that was twin to the table in her office. Open in his large hands was the notebook she had taken from the table drawer. When he moved his head over the notebook's pages, his glasses threw off pale glints.

She typed the heading and the date. How surprising, she thought, to find that she had regained her nerve here and now. When you dance as the inner choreographer directs, you act without thinking, not in command of events but in harmony with them. You yield control, accepting the chance that a mistake might be part of the design. The inner choreographer is always right but often dangerous: giving up control means accepting the possibility of death. What I feared I have pursued right here to this moment in this room.

A sheet of paper fell out of the notebook. Weyland stooped and caught it up, glanced at it. "You had training in art?" Must be a sketch.

"I thought once I might be an artist," she said.

"What you chose to do instead is better," he said. "This making of pictures, plays, all art, is pathetic. The world teems with creation, most of it unnoticed by your kind just as most of the deaths are unnoticed. What can be the point of adding yet another tiny gesture? Even you, these notes—for what, a moment's celebrity?"

"You tried it yourself," Floria said. "The book you edited, *Notes on a Vanished People*." She typed: ". . . temporary dislocation resulting from a severe personal shock . . ."

"That was professional necessity, not creation," he said in the tone of a lecturer irritated by a question from the audience. With disdain he tossed the drawing on the table. "Remember, I don't share your impulse toward artistic gesture—your absurd frills—"

She looked up sharply. "The ballet, Weyland. Don't lie." She typed: ". . . exhibits a powerful drive toward inner balance and wholeness in a difficult life-situation. The steadying influence of an extraordinary basic integrity . . ."

He set the notebook aside. "My feeling for ballet is clearly some sort of aberration. Do you sigh to hear a cow calling in a pasture?"

"There are those who have wept to hear whales singing in the ocean."

He was silent, his eyes averted.

"This is finished," she said. "Do you want to read it?"

He took the letter. "Good," he said at length. "Sign it, please. And type an envelope for it." He stood closer, but out of arm's reach, while she complied. "You seem less frightened."

"I'm terrified but not paralyzed," she said and laughed, but the laugh came out like a gasp.

"Fear is useful. It has kept you at your best throughout our association. Have you a stamp?"

He took the letter and walked back into the living room. She took a deep breath. She got up, turned off the gooseneck lamp, and followed him.

"What now, Weyland?" she said softly. "A carefully arranged suicide so that I have no chance to retract what's in that letter or to reconstruct my notes?"

"It is a possibility," he observed—at the window again, always at the window, on watch. "Your doorman was sleeping in the lobby. He never saw me enter the building. Once inside I used the stairs, of course. The suicide rate among therapists is notoriously high. I looked it up."

"You have everything all planned?"

The window was open. He reached out and touched the metal grille that guarded it. One end of the grille swung creaking outward into the night air, like a gate opening. She visualized him sitting there waiting for her to come home, his powerful fingers patiently working the bolts at that side of the grille loose from the brick-and-mortar window frame. The hair lifted on the back of her neck.

He turned toward her again. She could see the end of the letter she had given him sticking palely out of his jacket pocket.

"Floria," he said meditatively. "You were named for a woman in the opera *Tosca*, isn't that so? At the end, doesn't she throw herself to her death from a high castle wall? People are careless about the names they give their children. I will not drink from you—I hunted today, and I fed. Still, to leave you living—is too dangerous."

A fire engine tore past below, siren screaming. When it had gone Floria said, "Listen, Weyland, you said it yourself: I can't make myself safe from you—I'm not strong enough to shove you out the window instead of being shoved out myself. Must you make yourself safe from me? Let me say this to you, without promises, demands, or pleadings: I will not go back on what I wrote in that letter. I will not try to reconstruct my notes. I mean it. Be content with that."

"You tempt me to it," he murmured after a moment, "to go from here with you still alive behind me for the remainder of your little life—to leave woven into Dr. Landauer's quick mind those threads of my own life that I pulled for her . . . I want to be able sometimes to think of you thinking of me. But the risk is very great."

"Sometimes it's right to let the dangers live, to give them their place," she urged. "Didn't you tell me yourself a little while ago how risk makes us more heroic?"

He looked amused. "Are you instructing me in the virtues of danger? You are brave enough to know something, perhaps, about that, but I have studied danger all my life."

"A long, long life with more to come," she said, desperate to make him understand and believe her. "Not mine to jeopardize. There's no torch-brandishing peasant here; we left that behind long ago. Remember when you spoke for me? You said, 'For love of wonder.' That was true."

He leaned to turn off the lamp near the window. She thought that he had made up his mind and that when he straightened it would be to spring.

But instead of terror locking her limbs, from the inward choreographer came a rush of warmth and energy into her muscles and an impulse to turn toward him. Out of a harmony of desires she said swiftly, "Weyland, come to bed with me."

She saw his shoulders stiffen against the dim square of the window, his head lift in scorn. "You know I can't be bribed that way," he said contemptuously. "What are you up to? Are you one of those who come into heat at the sight of an upraised fist?"

"My life hasn't twisted me that badly, thank God," she retorted. "And if you've known all along how scared I've been, you must have sensed my attraction to you too, so you know it goes back to—very early in our work." Her mouth was dry as paper. She pressed quickly on, anxious to get it all said to him. "This is simply how I would like to mark the ending of our time together. This is the completion I want. Surely you feel something too, Weyland—curiosity at least?"

"Granted, your emphasis on the expressiveness of the body has instructed me," he admitted, and then he added lightly, "Isn't it extremely unprofessional to proposition a client?"

"Extremely, and I never do, but somehow now it feels right. For you to indulge in courtship that doesn't end in a meal would be unprofessional too, but how would it feel to indulge anyway—just this once?" Go softly now, he's intrigued but wary. "Since we started, you've pushed me light-years beyond my profession. Now I want you to travel all the way with me, Weyland. Let's be unprofessonal together."

She turned and went into the bedroom, leaving the lights off. There was a reflected light, cool and diffuse, from the glowing night air of the great city. She sat down on the bed and kicked off her shoes. When she looked up, he was in the doorway.

Hesitantly, he halted a few feet from her in the dim-

ness, then came and sat beside her. He would have lain
down in his clothes, but she said quietly, "You can un-
dress. The front door's locked and there isn't anyone here
but us. You won't have to leap up and flee for your life."

He stood again and began to take off his clothes, which
he draped neatly over a chair. He said, "Suppose I am
fertile with you; could you conceive?"

By her own choice any such possibility had been closed
off after Deb. She said, "No," and that seemed to satisfy
him.

She tossed her own clothes onto the dresser.

He sat down next to her again, his body silvery in the
reflected light and smooth, lean as a whippet and as
roped with muscle. His cool thigh pressed against her own
fuller, darker one as he leaned across her and carefully deposited his glasses on the bedtable. Then he turned
toward her, and she could just make out two puckerings
of tissue in his skin. Bullet scars, she thought, shivering.

He said, "But why do I wish to do this?"

"Do you?" She had to hold herself back from touching
him.

"Yes." He stared at her. "How did you grow so real?
The more I spoke to you of myself, the more real you became."

"No more speaking, Weyland," she said gently. "This
is body-work."

He lay back on the bed.

She wasn't afraid to take the lead. At the very least she
could certainly do for him as well as he did for himself,
and at the most, much better. Her own skin was darker
than his, a shadowy contrast where she browsed over his
body with her hands. Along the contours of his ribs she
felt knotted places, hollows—old healings, the tracks of
time. The tension of his muscles under her touch and
the sharp sound of his breathing stirred her. She lived
the fantasy of sex with an utter stranger; there was no
one in the world so much a stranger as he. Yet there was
no one who knew him as well as she did, either. If he
was unique, so was she, and so was their confluence here.

The vividness of the moment inflamed her. His body
responded. His penis stirred, warmed, and thickened in
her hand. He turned on his hip so that they lay facing
each other, he on his right side, she on her left. When she

moved to kiss him he swiftly averted his face: of course —to him the mouth was for feeding. She touched her fingers to his lips, signifying her comprehension.

He offered no caresses but closed his arms around her, his hands cradling the back of her head and neck. His shadowed face, deep-hollowed under brow and cheek-bone, was very close to hers. From the parted lips that she must not kiss his quick breath came, roughened by groans of pleasure. At length he pressed his head against hers, inhaling deeply; taking her scent, she thought, from her hair and skin.

He entered her, hesitant at first, probing slowly and tentatively. She found this searching motion intensely sensuous, and clinging to him all along his sinewy length, she rocked with him through two hot, swelling waves of sweetness. She felt him strain tight against her, she heard him whine through clenched teeth.

Panting, they subsided and lay loosely interlocked. His head was tilted back; his eyes were closed. She had no desire to stroke him or to speak with him, only to rest spent against his body and absorb the sounds of his breathing, her breathing.

He did not lie long to hold or be held. Without a word he disengaged his body from hers and got up. He moved quietly about the bedroom, gathering his clothing, his shoes, the drawings, the notes from the work room. He dressed without lights. She listened in silence from the center of a deep repose.

There was no leave-taking. His tall figure passed and repassed the dark rectangle of the doorway, and then he was gone. The latch on the front door clicked shut.

Floria thought of getting up to secure the deadbolt. Instead she turned on her stomach and slept.

She woke as she remembered coming out of sleep as a youngster—peppy and clearheaded.

"Hilda, let's give the police a call about that break-in, so just in case something comes of it later we're on record as having reported it. You can tell them we don't have any idea who did it or why. And please make a photocopy of this letter carbon to send to Doug Sharpe up at Cayslin.

Then you can put the carbon in Weyland's file and close it."

Hilda sighed. "Well, he was too old anyway."

He wasn't, my dear, but never mind.

In her office Floria picked up the morning's mail from her table. Her glance strayed to the window where Weyland had so often stood. God, she was going to miss him; and God, how good it was to be restored to plain working days.

Only not yet. Don't let the phone ring, don't let the world push in here now. She needed to sit alone for a little and let her mind sort through the images left from—from the pas de deux with Weyland. It's the notorious morning-after, old dear, she told herself; just where have I been dancing, anyway?

In a clearing in the enchanted forest with the unicorn, of course, but not the way the old legends have it. According to them, hunters set a virgin to attract the unicorn by her chastity so that they can catch and kill him. My unicorn was the chaste one, come to think of it, and this lady meant no treachery. No, Weyland and I met hidden from the hunt, to celebrate a private mystery of our own . . .

Your mind grappled with my mind, my dark leg over your silver one, unlike closing with unlike across whatever likeness may be found: your memory pressing on my thoughts, my words drawing out your words in which you may recognize your life, my smooth palm gliding down your smooth flank . . .

Why, this will make me cry, she thought, blinking. And for what? Does an afternoon with the unicorn have any meaning for the ordinary days that come later? What has this passage with Weyland left me? Have I anything in my hands now besides the morning's mail?

What I have in my hands is my own strength, because I had to reach deep to find the strength to match him.

She put down the letters, noticing how on the backs of her hands the veins stood, pale shadows, under the thin skin. How can these hands be strong? Time was beginning to wear them thin and bring up the fragile inner structure in clear relief. That was the meaning of the last parent's death: that the child's remaining time has a limit of its own.

But not for Weyland. No graveyards of family dead lay behind him, no obvious and implacable ending of his own span threatened him. Time has to be different for a creature of an enchanted forest, as morality has to be different. He was a predator and a killer formed for a life of centuries, not decades; of secret singularity, not the busy hum of the herd. Yet his strength, suited to that non-human life, had revived her own strength. Her hands were slim, no longer youthful, but she saw now that they were strong enough.

For what? She flexed her fingers, watching the tendons slide under the skin. Strong hands don't have to clutch. They can simply open and let go.

She dialed Lucille's extension at the clinic.

"Luce? Sorry to have missed your calls lately. Listen, I want to start making arrangements to transfer my practice for a while. You were right, I do need a break, just as all my friends have been telling me. Will you pass the word for me to the staff over there today? Good, thanks. Also, there's the workshop coming up next month . . . yes. Are you kidding? They'd love to have you in my place. You're not the only one who's noticed that I've been falling apart, you know. It's awfully soon—can you manage, do you think? Luce, you are a brick and a lifesaver and all that stuff that means I'm very, very grateful."

Not so terrible, she thought, but only a start. Everything else remained to be dealt with. The glow of euphoria couldn't carry her for long. Already, looking down, she noticed jelly on her blouse, just like old times, and she didn't even remember having breakfast. If you want to keep the strength you've found in all this, you're going to have to get plenty of practice being strong. Try a tough one now.

She phoned Deb. "Of course you've slept late, so what? I did too, so I'm glad you didn't call and wake me up. Whenever you're ready—if you need some help moving uptown I can cancel here and come down—well, call if you change your mind. I left a house key for you with my doorman.

"And listen, hon, I've been thinking—how about all of us going up together to Nonnie's over the weekend? Then when you feel like it maybe you'd like to talk about what you'll do next. Yes, I've already started setting up some free time for myself. Think about it, love. Talk to you later."

Kenny's turn. "Kenny, I'll come by during visiting hours this afternoon."

"Are you okay?" he squeaked.

"I'm okay. But I'm not your mommy, Ken, and I'm not going to start trying to hold the big bad world off you again. I'll expect you to be ready to settle down seriously and choose a new therapist for yourself. We're going to get that done today once and for all. Have you got that?"

After a short silence he answered in a desolate voice, "All right."

"Kenny, nobody grown up has a mommy around to take care of things for them and keep them safe—not even me. You just have to be tough enough and brave enough yourself. See you this afternoon."

How about Jane Fennerman? No, leave it for now, we are not Wonder Woman, we can't handle that stress today as well.

Too restless to settle down to paperwork before the day's round of appointments began, she got up and fed the goldfish, then drifted to the window and looked out over the city. Same jammed-up traffic down there, same dusty summer park stretching away uptown—yet not the same city, because Weyland no longer hunted there. Nothing like him moved now in those deep, grumbling streets. She would never come upon anyone there as alien as he —and just as well. Let last night stand as the end, unique and inimitable, of their affair. She was glutted with strangeness and looked forward frankly to sharing again in Mort's ordinary human appetite.

And Weyland—how would he do in that new and distant hunting ground he had found for himself? Her own balance had been changed. Suppose his once-perfect, solitary equilibrium had been altered too? Perhaps he had spoiled it by involving himself too intimately with another being—herself. And then he had left her alive—a terrible risk. Was this a sign of his corruption at her hands?

"Oh, no," she whispered fiercely, focusing her vision on her reflection in the smudged window-glass. Oh, no, I am not the temptress. I am not the deadly female out of legends whose touch defiles the hitherto unblemished being, her victim. If Weyland found some human likeness in himself, that had to be in him to begin with. Who said he was defiled anyway? Newly discovered capacities can be either strengths or weaknesses, depending on how you use them.

Very pretty and reassuring, she thought grimly; but it's pure cant. Am I going to retreat into mechanical analysis to make myself feel better?

She heaved open the window and admitted the sticky summer breath of the city into the office. There's your enchanted forest, my dear, all nitty-gritty and not one flake of fairy dust. You've survived here, which means you can see straight when you have to. Well, you have to now.

Has he been damaged? No telling yet, and you can't stop living while you wait for the answers to come in. I don't know all that was done between us, but I do know who did it: I did it, and he did it, and neither of us withdrew until it was done. We were joined in a rich complicity—he in the wakening of some flicker of humanity in himself, I in keeping and—yes—enjoying the secret of his implacable blood-hunger.

What that complicity means for each of us can only be discovered by getting on with living and watching for clues from moment to moment. His business is to continue from here and mine is to do the same, without guilt and without resentment. Doug was right: the aim is individual responsibility. From that effort not even the lady and the unicorn are exempt.

Shaken by a fresh upwelling of tears she thought bitterly, moving on is easy enough for Weyland; he's used to it, he's had more practice. What about me? Yes, be selfish, woman—if you haven't learned that you've learned damn little.

The Japanese say that in middle age you should leave the claims of family, friends, and work, and go ponder the meaning of the universe while you still have the chance. Maybe I'll try just existing for a while, and letting grow in its own time my understanding of a universe that includes Weyland—and myself—among its possibilities.

Is that looking out for myself? Or am I simply no longer fit for living with family, friends, and work? Have I been damaged by him—by my marvelous, murderous monster?

Damn, she thought, I wish he were here, I wish we could talk about it. The light on her phone caught her eye; it was blinking the quick flashes that meant Hilda was signaling the imminent arrival of—not Weyland—the day's first client.

We're each on our own now, she thought, shutting the window and turning on the air-conditioner.

But think of me sometimes, Weyland, thinking of you.

THE HAUNTING

by Mary C. Pangborn

Although Mary C. Pangborn started writing over sixty years ago (in collaboration with her brother Edgar, the late and much lamented author of such science fiction classics as *Davy* and *A Mirror for Observers*), her first story was published only last year, in *Universe 9*. Between those early efforts and now she worked as a research biochemist for the New York State Health Department and returned to writing after her retirement in 1970. "The Haunting" is her second professional sale.

What follows is a tight and tiny gem, a time-travel story with an unexpected and beautifully realized twist. Ms. Pangborn has said, in correspondence with the editors, "I sometimes think it is rather absurd for me to be turning to writing in my second childhood." After reading "The Haunting," we think you'll agree that we should all, in our second childhoods, be so lucky.

been a couple of years later, and the book was at least two

THAT HOUSE HAS BEEN GONE FOR FORTY YEARS, but I can see it, all of it, exactly the way it was. Ever notice how a mere place can leave sharper-edged memories than the people in it? The living faces you try to recall were always changing from minute to minute, going their own way; but the shape of a room shows you the same face day after day, so the picture goes on printing itself in your head till it's there for keeps.

Damn silly waste, tearing down a good solid house to build a shopping center. I've never been back, I wouldn't want to see a parking lot where our garden was. It wasn't an old house; my father built it a few years before I was born, somewhere around 1900. No history; not the sort of place you'd expect to be haunted.

No, of course I don't believe in ghosts. Spooks, table-rapping, witches, flying saucers, the lot—you can have 'em. Doesn't make sense. Anyway it wasn't a ghost.

Away off in the country it was, twenty-odd miles from New York, a reasonable distance for a gentleman to travel to his office by train. But not rustic—we had modern inventions, electricity and a telephone. A huge coal-burning iron range in the kitchen. Fireplaces. A garden, chickens, always a cat or three or six, depending on circumstances—plenty of room for kittens. Hm? why, yes, there must have been a few automobiles around, but I don't recall seeing them at the time I'm talking about. It must have been a couple of years later that my father got his first auto; never liked the damn thing, kept grumbling he wished he'd kept the horses.

When the wind blew from the west it smelled of pine woods. Clean and sweet.

This isn't ancient history, you know. One lifetime, that's all. Time for two wars, time for a world to change like a film running too fast, blurred—change into a fragile playtoy we keep tossing in our hands while we figure out which way to smash it. I don't expect I'll be around when the smash comes; it looks now as if they've maybe put it off for a while; but you might be. You were born into this brave new world, you don't know any other, you take the sword of Damocles for granted; it's tough for an old man to imagine how that could feel. Must be a bit like coming of age in the year one thousand, when Judgment Day was due any minute. They had an advantage over us, though; they had old man Jehovah in charge of the show, and they figured He knew what He was doing.

But there *was* another world back there, my world. I'm not saying it was "better," you understand, that's not the point, no, there never was a Golden Age, but it had one thing we've lost forever. It was solid. No one doubted we had plenty of time.

Sorry. Where was I? Oh, I promised to tell you about the haunting.

Yes, I could draw you an exact map of that house. My room was over the library; it had one big window looking toward the stable, and another into the garden. The stairway: down six steps to the first landing, a square turn, twelve more steps to another broad landing—those square turns made it hard to slide down the banister. The big hall with the Oriental rug. Then the long living room where the Christmas tree was.

I know it was Christmas because of the tree, but I'm not sure which year it was; I was either six or seven. A splendid big tree all glittering with colored balls and tinsel, presents and torn wrappings strewn about, a children's party in full blast—the usual noise and ice cream and cake and so on. I looked up from some ecstasy over presents and saw the old man.

He was just standing there, sort of mixed up with the Christmas tree, but not misty, the way they say ghosts are; more as though there wasn't any reason why he and the tree shouldn't be using the same space. And I know my first thought was "Santa Claus!" (or rather, Daddy dressed up as Santa Claus—oh yes, I knew all about *that,* but it never spoiled the fun). Then right away I could tell it wasn't, because Santa Claus would have a white beard, not a gray one, and he'd be wearing a red suit; so then I yelled "Grampa!" Knowing all the time, as I'd often been told, that Grampa died long ago, before I was born (the other one, Mother's father, had to be called *Grandfather,* starchy-polite, and he didn't even have a beard). So it had to be Grampa, because how else could I be so sure I knew him? I guess that'll show you how clearly my mind was working, young as I was. And I had time to figure they must have made a mistake about his being dead, because I could tell this wasn't a ghost. I think it did puzzle me a bit that he was wearing such sloppy-funny clothes, like an old tramp, not even a proper necktie, but it had to be him, so I hollered again, "Daddy, look, Grampa's come to see us!" Then there were grown-up noises and Mother saying "Oh dear, too much candy," and I suppose I was put to bed early. I don't remember any more. All that while the old man was standing there, until suddenly he wasn't.

What—? well, I don't know how long. It was a while. Long enough that I could watch him looking around the room, turning his head, trying to find something; looking right at me too, but not seeing me. And that's a true memory, for I can't see the child when I look around that room now, only a small moving blur over yonder where he must have been—not so strange, for I suppose I never did really see him. Small boys don't spend much time looking in mirrors.

No, I don't think any of the other children saw the old man; why would they?

But I did; I saw him just as clearly as I'd see if I'd bother to get up and look in that mirror now. Same gray hair, gray beard, same old sweater and jeans. An old man looking for something lost. Not childhood certainly (though I know that's what the shrinks would say) and not any silly fantasy of a golden age. Only a world that wouldn't shiver and rumble under your feet at every step; one that would surely last out more than your own time. I saw him as I'm seeing the room now; it could have been this same moment of seeing. Time, a serpent taking its tail in its mouth?

Well, you say, rivers don't run uphill, time only flows one way, right? Right. But rivers may have eddies in them . . .

Doesn't make any sense? No; I told you it wouldn't.

THE EROS PASSAGE

by Scott Sanders

This is Scott Sanders' first appearance in *New Dimensions*, although it is our fond hope that it will not be the last. Sanders has written only a handful of science fiction stories, the first appearing in the *Magazine of Fantasy & Science Fiction* in 1979, but has accumulated an impressive list of credits outside of the field, ranging from historical novels to books of literary criticism. From an early bent to physics and mathematics he turned to literature and fiction, is the fiction editor for the *Minnesota Review,* is passionately interested in botany and geology, builds houses in the summers, is a professor of literature at Indiana University, has a wife and two children, and occasionally takes time off to create evocative stories like the one that follows.

A psychological barrier to faster-than-light travel is not a new concept to science fiction, but we think you'll agree that in Sanders' imaginative and persuasive hands, the subject becomes unexpected, fresh and exciting.

ON THE MORNING OF HIS THIRTEENTH BIRTHDAY, Hoagy Dillard woke to find an eros couch installed in his bedroom. The screen was small and the range of neuro-stimulation was skimpy. But the Freud, as his mother called it, or the Orgasm Express, as his friends called it, was versatile enough for a beginner.

With helmet strapped on, Hoagy soon learned to project his desires onto the overhead screen. Unlike the eros couches he had used at friends' apartments or at public arcades, where tapes made by virtuoso eroticists generated the sensations of loving, this couch allowed Hoagy to dictate the sensory material. Meshing his brain-waves with the simulator proved no more difficult than the bio-feedback he already practiced for controlling his metabolic rate.

At first the images of video stars and nubile school-mates were fuzzy, and they dazzled upon the screen in full costume. With practice, Hoagy sharpened the focus. Undressing his visitors took longer. He was slow in overcoming the fear that these women who mooned down at him from the screen could actually see him.

Embarrassed, he would conduct long conversations with his primly-dressed sirens. "Do you like to watch the skate races?" he might ask.

"They're my favorite," the current beauty would confess.

"And do you hope there's blood?"

"Always. I pray for great crack-ups on the hairpin turns."

Lulled by these agreeable chats, in which he dictated both sides of the dialogue, Hoagy eventually allowed a strap to glide free of a shoulder on his lady, then permitted a streak of thigh to show through a slit in her moodgown. Once the undressing was begun, it hastened forward until the woman's body lolled upon the screen as naked as the sun on a cloudless noon.

Since his knowledge of female anatomy, despite seven years of sex education, was more theoretical than practical, he called upon the Freud's memory to put the finishing touches on his visions. The resulting images were considerable improvements—or at least modifications—on the girls he knew from school, the actresses he studied on the video, the women he trailed through the streets of Oregon City. No female living or dead ever approached the erotic perfection achieved by the beauties whom Hoagy conjured upon his screen. Their breasts and buttocks paid scant attention to gravity, refusing to sag as mere flesh would do. Their skin, no matter how closely examined, showed no pores. Their joints and limbs assumed any posture that Hoagy imagined, including ones that would baffle a master yogi. Their eyes never said anything except what he wanted them to say.

As his mother had hoped when she decided to install the Freud, Hoagy soon lost interest in flesh-and-blood women. He quit mentioning the new facepaint that Veronica had worn at school. He no longer recited the words that Sharon had whispered to him during halftime at the ion shootout. Instead of riding about the city on pedbelts, slathering after women, now he came directly home from school and buckled himself onto the eros couch.

By programming the Freud according to a plan developed at the Pacific Behavioral Institute, Ingra Dillard subtly influenced the drift of her son's fantasies. The machine did not originate the images he saw, but instead reinforced a powerful strain of imagery that he generated on his own. First came the prim maidens chit-chatting about inanities, then strumpets cavorting in black negligees, then austere nudes rehearsing the *Kama Sutra*. Each in turn relieved his adolescent lust. But they were only preliminary enticements, weaning him away from earthly females.

One red-haired visitor haunted him for weeks. Veins showed like a netting of blue through her translucent skin.

"Where do you live?" he asked.

"California City," she murmured. "Or maybe Alaska City. Maybe on the fifth planet of Epsilon Eridani. Anywhere and nowhere."

Ashamed by his confusion, as if this seductive phantasm could actually dwell in the Pacific Cities or in a stellar system conveniently placed just eleven light-years from Earth, Hoagy let her evaporate from the screen. But he soon conjured her back again. And when she returned he supplied her with a landscape of ferns, waterfalls, and benevolent unearthly beasts. Why not put her on the fifth planet of Epsilon Eridani, or some other inhabitable globe? If she was impossible on Earth, why couldn't she wait for him elsewhere? Real or not, this red-haired woman with translucent skin set up a tide in him that he could not resist.

By the time Hoagy turned fifteen, and graduated to the next more sophisticated model of the eros couch, all his projections had grown otherworldly in their beauty. Instead of rushing him straight to orgasm, as they had done in their early days of acrobatic postures and exotic lingerie, now his lovelies entranced him for entire evenings. His desire spread out from the women to encompass entire planets. Adrift on the Freud, he sculpted mountain ranges that mimicked the nobbed ridge of the woman's spine, lakes that shimmered at him with the same blue longing he saw in her eyes. Sometimes he would postpone climax for several days in order to pursue his visions through refinements of splendor, like an alchemist in search of the philosopher's stone.

As the behavioral engineers had promised, Hoagy soon neglected everything but the eros couch and school. While other sixteen-year-olds were gawking at automated beasts in the disney, or mangling themselves in ion shootouts, or smooching behind the desalinization works, Hoagy was poring over texts in exobiology. One night Ingra Dillard watched her son contemplating a numerical display on the microfiche reader.

His face glowed faintly orange with light reflected from the reader's screen.

"What are the tables?" she asked him, gingerly testing how far his passion had carried him in the direction she had chosen.

"Probable distribution of life forms within a million-light-year radius of Earth."

"How many have we actually contacted?"

"By drone or in the flesh?" said Hoagy.

"In the flesh."

"One half of one percent."

The mother hummed. "It makes you wonder about the other ninety-nine point five percent."

"It sure does."

Hesitantly, not wanting Hoagy to feel his secrets were suspected, Ingra added: "Imagine the elegant adaptations to bio-niches out there. Think of all the beauty that's possible."

"Possible" was all Hoagy replied. Scrooched over the reader, his face aglow with the statistics of near-universe life, he tracked his speculations beyond reach of words.

Ingra studied the boy, her ninth birthing, the only one she had chosen to raise. He was no more her genetic offspring than the other eight had been. Only the Eugenics Board knew whose ovum and sperm had been implanted in her womb. But by rearing Hoagy, feeding him, teaching him when he was a child, she had left her thumbprint on his character, and that mattered more than genetics. He was the only mark she was likely to leave on the world.

He did not glance up from his statistics when she wished him good night and closed the door.

Hoagy emerged from bouts on the eros couch or at the microfiche reader with haggard lines in his face and a hungering gleam in his eyes. Even though the psychiatrists had warned her, Ingra was not fully prepared for this transformation in her son. He was possessed by his otherworldly women, as the mystics must have been possessed by their own visions in the old God-days. He scarcely spoke to her anymore. His eyes never seemed to fix on anything in front of him. At meals, fork lifted half-way to his mouth, he would stare off into no-space while the algae patties cooled on his plate.

Shortly before his eighteenth birthday, when it came time to replace Hoagy's eros couch with the most sophisticated model, Ingra suffered anxious second thoughts and fifth thoughts and ten-to-the-power-of-tenth thoughts about her long-ago decision to start him on this ascetic journey into space. She knew that within his own mental sphere he was enjoying a life of exalted pleasures and longings; but he was sealed in that sphere, and it had nothing to do with friends, Oregon City, planet Earth, or Ingra Dillard.

From Hoagy's infancy onward, every government test had shown him to be extraordinarily gifted at abstract thinking and even more gifted at using complex imagery. Eidetic vision, the examiners called it. This fusion of concrete and abstract imagination was so rare that a Project Viva psychiatrist, hearing of Hoagy's case, had eventually persuaded Ingra to enroll him in the pre-space program. The specially programmed eros couch was the key instrument in weaning him away, not merely from the women of Earth, but from Earth itself. The psychiatrist put it bluntly: Your son will give up the chance of leading a normal life for a chance to escape the timeshell. Better he should pay this price, Ingra decided, and be able perhaps to slip through the warp undamaged, than to be trapped earthside forever as she was.

She knew that neither money nor fame nor curiosity had proved a strong enough motivation to carry astronauts through the mind-wrenching agonies of warp passage. The life-contact program, Project Viva, was stymied by a difficulty that no one could have foreseen in the pre-warp days: bodies passed through the timeshell unscathed, but minds were severely damaged. When the early warp-ships returned at all, their crews were insane. Ingra knew about these early casualties, but she had never been allowed to visit the space hospital in California City, where the wrecked veterans sat in catatonic stupors or drooled mumbling on benches. Imagining the psychic dangers that Hoagy would encounter if he passed through the warp, she thought only of curable phobias, an eye twitch, a stutter. She never allowed herself to dream of this permanent vegetable idiocy.

After the first disastrous flight, doctors tried drugs,

sleep-freezing, sound therapy, anything to ease the explorers through the warp. Nothing worked. Funding agencies grew queasy. Qualified volunteers for Project Viva were almost impossible to recruit.

Many people, including a scattering of scientists, began calling the timeshell an impassable barrier, as the speed of light had been described in the previous century. Just when the IASA was on the point of shelving Project Viva, declaring the human costs too high, the seventh flight brought back the hint of an answer. Against all rules of medical ethics, a psychiatrist acting on a hunch had approved for flight a woman whose records showed her to be a paranoid schizophrenic. She returned just as insane as the rest of the crew, just as incapable of reporting her experiences—but with her original psychosis intact. Her paranoia had passed twice through the warp without altering.

For experimenting with a patient in this way, the psychiatrist was stripped of his license. But his findings were eagerly used to remodel Project Viva. If some mental fixation less crippling than the woman's paranoia could be induced in the astronauts, perhaps they would preserve their sanity through the warp. Ships number eight through fourteen bore crews who had been trained with mandalas, mantras, and focal objects of every imaginable sort. The returned astronauts were mad in novel ways, but mad nonetheless. Again there was a saving exception—a twenty-year-old hydroponics specialist who brought back snatches of sanity. For minutes at a time he could speak sensibly about the chlorophyll-based, planet-encircling organism his flight had observed. Most of the time he raved. He was the youngest person ever to dare the warp, and by far the youngest to undertake the program of fixation-training.

Perhaps, the psychiatrists reasoned, adults were the wrong candidates for training. Perhaps children or adolescents, with their fierce attachments, their irrational cravings, were more likely subjects. And what cravings were more fierce or more easily manipulated than those of sex? Cautiously, after prolonged debate in scientific and governmental circles, the Project Viva psychiatrists were empowered to recruit twenty adolescents for the special eros training.

Over two thousand parents were interviewed before

wenty of them, including Ingra Dillard, could be per-
uaded to enroll their children. On the eve of Hoagy's
eighteenth birthday Ingra was reminding herself, with a
mixture of guilt and nostalgia, of all the arguments the
psychiatrist had used: money first, of course, for which
she cared nothing; fame second, for which she cared
little more; service to humanity third. The boy's eidetic
quotient places him in the top tenth of a percentile,
they told her, and his abilities would be wasted on earthside work. If he survives the warp with mind intact,
they told her, humanity will have broken out of the
timeshell. Your son will be honored as Lindbergh and
Armstrong were honored, as Stravik and Noyson and
Franno have been honored.

Ingra had nodded politely at the psychiatrists. But
they had never touched on her deepest reason for en-
rolling Hoagy: she wanted him to escape the smothering
cities in which she had been doomed to lead her life;
she wanted him to discover a free space for himself
beyond all this ruck of people. Near-space was available, of course, without the trauma of warp passage.
But every planet and asteroid and moon that circled
within reach of real-time ships already budded with
miniature imitations of the domed cities of Earth. Only
through the warp could Hoagy travel to a landscape
where *Homo sapiens* had never meddled. In order to
deliver him there, Ingra was willing to abandon him to
his visions and to possible insanity.

So Hoagy returned from the Institute for Exobio-
logical Research on the afternoon of his eighteenth
birthday to find a state-of-the-art Freud newly installed
in his bedroom. Instead of projecting images onto a
domed screen, as the old eros couches had done, this
one stimulated the visual cortex directly. Lying naked
in the machine's webbing, with helmet in place, Hoagy felt
weightless. Eyes closed, mind alive to the tingling electronic fingers, he entered deep trance immediately. Whatever he envisioned in this charmed state became more
vivid for him than anything he experienced in the waking world.

Women of almost catastrophic beauty were still the
focus of his visions. Now they dallied in landscapes
whose exotic life-forms surpassed in variety even what

Hoagy knew of from his textbooks. They no longer merely offered impossibly silken bellies and antelope-graceful feet. Now they shone with a radiance that had nothing to do with any biology Hoagy could understand. Making love with such a woman was to seep beyond the confines of his own chemistry, to merge through the woman into the life-rhythms of her planet.

These women mesmerized him. Even without the electronic blandishments of the eros couch, he carried their images with him now wherever he went. By comparison the actual people he saw every day seemed mere echoing shells. The sculptured avenues of Oregon City, compared to his visionary landscapes, seemed like flimsy diagrams of reality. He meandered from home to Institute, from Institute to home, in a perpetual daze of desire.

His instructors were not privy to the secrets of Project Viva. So they did not know why Hoagy's curiosity about alien life-forms was so insatiable. All they knew was that he proved gifted and fanatical in his studies. The curriculum that should have kept him busy until age twenty-three he finished at eighteen. The next five years' worth of material he devoured in two. By age twenty-one, he was encamped on the frontiers of the discipline, facing outward onto the unknown.

He soon became a leading theoretician for the Seedling Theory of life-distribution. According to the rival Discretist Theory, life had originated separately on each of the billions upon billions of inhabited planets. If that theory were valid, then no matter how Earth-like the planet, the chances of even a vaguely humanoid creature evolving elsewhere were infinitesimal. The Seedling Theory—which Hoagy in his first monograph buttressed with fragmentary evidence from the few returned warp-ships—argued that some Ur-species had sown families of organisms on hospitable planets. Perhaps there were millions of such races, perhaps each had scattered life upon millions of planets. What interested Hoagy, what obsessed him, was the special case of the genus *Homo*: a few glimmerings of evidence suggested that an Ur-species had seeded many planets, and Earth among them, with humanoid animals. If the Seedling Theory were valid, then one who traveled to enough Earth-type planets would stand a good chance of encountering variations on *Homo sapiens*. One might even find, if one searched long enough, the infinitely desirable women who tantalized Hoagy in daylight and dream.

Logic counseled him to be pessimistic. But his heart— or whatever primitive organ it was that kept generating these unearthly desires—would not surrender to logic.

At the age of twenty-one, Hoagy lived so little in the everyday world that he did not realize his decision to enlist as an astronaut in Project Viva would come as no surprise to his mother.

"You approve?" he asked in puzzlement.

"It's the only path for you," Ingra insisted. "You were born to it. I've seen you headed into space for years."

"You know the dangers?"

"Forget dangers. Everything worth doing is dangerous."

"The timeshell—" he began.

"Maybe you'll be the one to break through it with your mind intact," she continued vehemently. "I know you'll do it, Hoagy. Just think of it—breaking out."

Even Hoagy, rarely attuned to other people, could hear the urgency in her voice. It took him several days of brooding to comprehend that she had been pointing him toward this decision for years. It took him several more days to persuade himself that the eros couches had been programmed to manipulate his desires. Rage gathered in him as he groped through his memories of the past eight years. It had all been a puppet show, a jerking of strings.

With a lampstand he methodically hacked the Freud to pieces, scattering electrodes and filaments all through his bedroom. It took him three careful blows to crack the helmet, a dozen more to reduce it to a heap of shards. No matter how brutally he pounded, the steel mirrors and glass walls of his room would not shatter.

When his mother peered in through the doorway, he flung the lamp at her. Seeing it narrowly miss her astonished face, he slumped down in a corner.

"It's all lies!" he cried, rocking back and forth. He squeezed one fist into his mouth to keep from howling.

Ingra took a few seconds to survey the wreckage. The eros couch was a snarl of fused wiring and shredded gossamer bands. No one would ever dream again in its embrace. Keeping one hand on the door panel, in case her son should grow violent again, she said, "What lies?"

"All the junk up here." He drummed with fists on his skull.

"Your visions?"

"Lies!"

"What you've imagined—"

"Not what I've imagined! What that machine's invented!"

"What *you* have imagined. You and you alone. The Freud only reinforced tendencies that were already in you. It gave flesh to your own desires."

"It gave me awful hungers."

"It gave you nothing!" she snapped. "We've all got hungers for things our life can't provide. Most of us just suffer them in frustration. But you," she said, her voice rising passionately, "you're one of the rare ones who can do something about the hunger. Your imaginings are so strong they can deliver you."

"To what?"

"To the universe. To a larger future. What kind of dumb question is that? Do you want to be bottled up here in the cities of Earth forever? You want to feel you and your kind are stuck for always in an evolutionary blind alley? You want that?"

Her fury made Hoagy lift his head to gaze at her. Quietly he said, "No, I don't want to be stuck here." Then, as the vision of otherworldly women and mountains and waterfalls swept over him again, he added bitterly, "But I don't want to fritter my life away on a trillion-light-year wild goose chase."

"Why a wild goose chase?"

"Do you really think I'll find what I'm looking for out there, even if I survive the warp?"

"Why not? The universe is big enough to create anything you're capable of imagining."

"Even if the Seedling Theory is valid, the chances of ever finding a people and place to match my vision are—"

"Slim," she broke in. "Of course they're slim. Were you expecting a written guarantee? The only things left to do that a thousand people haven't already done are risky. But at least you've got a chance to find what you're hungering for, a chance, even if it's a slim one.

And that's more than I—than anyone—can usually expect."

Slumped against the wall, hands uncurling in his lap, Hoagy looked searchingly at his mother, something he had not done since he was a child. Her face was pinched, eyes creased, as if she had spent years treading water, searching for specks on the horizon. Suddenly he felt he understood her anger, her restlessness, her frenzied encouragement of his space-hunger. Frightened by her intensity, he would not trust himself to ask what unappeasable hungers had been gnawing at her. He could only bring himself to say, "I'll go through the warp. I'll go searching for other creatures so long as I'm able."

Ingra's smile was only half-hidden from him as she turned away. "The Freud—" She nodded at the snarl of printed circuits and webbing.

"I don't need it anymore," he answered. "The vision never leaves me now."

Training for warp passage took him three more tortuous years. While his conscious mind was attending to the technicalities of flight, cross-species communication, bio-surveys and the like, his unconscious mind was elaborating the details of his visionary planet. Even though infinitely desirable women still meandered through his dreaming, their sexual aura had spread outwards to encompass an entire bio-sphere. Now he thought on a planetary scale. When he imagined loving, it was still loving through a woman, but now the loving opened out beyond her into nature. Not a female nature, nor a male, but a nature that was the matrix of all life. The woman he entered was herself, and also a doorway.

The fever of desire kept a half-smile on Hoagy's face wherever he went in the Project Viva complex. The other half of the smile was a grimace. When he brought himself to notice other people, he thought he saw, in the handful of recruits who were also training for warp passage, the same mixture of pleasure and anguish.

The engineers who lectured to him about the operation of landers, the psychiatrists who monitored him while he was in trance-state, the linguists who instructed him in the idiosyncracies of computer translation—all these women and men were a blur of faces to him, a stutter of voices. He learned what they had to teach, because he would need it for his journeying. Otherwise, they did not exist for him.

The only faces and voices that became personal for him belonged to his two partners, Jaffa Marx and Blake Polo. Together, the three of them made up Alpha Trio, the first mind-conditioned group scheduled to venture out through the warp.

Soon after the three had been introduced, Hoagy cautiously asked, "How old were you when you started on the Freud?"

"Fourteen," Blake answered.

"Twelve," said Jaffa.

"And how long before you were—?" He let his voice trail off, uncertain how to phrase the question.

"Possessed?" Jaffa slipped the word into the air between them. As soon as her lips were still, the three of them felt an immediate affinity. Her green-eyed stare skipped from Hoagy to Blake, then back to Hoagy. "I was possessed within a few months," she said.

"Me, within a year," Blake said. "And this thing I see—it makes me feel—you know, turned inside out."

Hoagy nodded. "I know, I know."

"Like a crater, a vast aching want," Jaffa said.

The ache bound them together. The yearning for a material counterpart to their imaginings had driven Jaffa into the study of astrophysics, Blake into exolinguistics. They also had come to feel like puppets. Outraged, they had accused parents or friends of planting unfulfillable desires in their minds. And, like Hoagy, they had eventually acknowledged the hungers as their own.

"Maybe these wants in us are a genetic inheritance," Jaffa suggested. Her hands spidered through the air as if climbing invisible webs.

"Sort of a racial memory," Blake said.

"A memory of our biological past—life in other environments—other human possibilities—" Hoagy added.

"Or maybe all life everywhere generates a field, and we can detect glimmerings of it." As she spoke, Jaffa seemed to be delicately tracing field-lines with her fingers.

Blake seized the idea. "So we navigate in a sea of being, with a kind of sense for simultaneity of being, the way birds navigate in electromagnetic fields."

"Biological gravity," Hoagy said.

"Maybe the brain—"

"—preserves a buried sense for—"

"Other life," Hoagy said excitedly. "Then myths of the golden age and tales of gods and nightmares might not be inventions at all. They might be reports, reports about what life is doing elsewhere. Our visions—"

"Our visions," Jaffa interrupted him, "might be glimpses of places and creatures as real as this meat," she said, stubbing a finger into his chest.

And so the three of them talked breathlessly, finishing one another's sentences, discovering they each secretly held the same bizarre ideas. Even their visions of lovers and landscapes matched closely.

"Behold the loonies meet again," Jaffa would say during their pre-flight conferences, "to foist our madness onto the cosmos."

If he was mad, Hoagy found madness easier to bear in the company of these other visionaries. Blake argued that language formed a net throughout the universe, and that all life forms, with their myriad languages, were unknowingly engaged in weaving this net tighter and tighter. Eventually, he believed, consciousness would be able to journey from galaxy to galaxy on a web of signs. Consciousness was already doing pretty well, according to Jaffa, who speculated that pulsars and globular clusters and other more complex structures were actually forms of mind, with a subjective interior as well as a physical exterior. "Matter thinks," she said flatly. "Just look at the brain. If the brain, why not a nebula?"

Compared to their speculations, Hoagy's work on the Seedling Theory appeared to be a commonsensical endeavor. Sensible or not, he kept at it, devising methods of testing the hypothesis on their warp-journey. The answer might come at once, through contact with an intelligent species that had already discovered whether parallel life-forms had been sown on many planets. More likely the answer, if it came at all in Hoagy's lifetime, would come slowly, after a painstaking search of many worlds.

He realized that he and his partners might be concocting theories to avoid despair. If their theories were only the vapors of diseased minds, well then, they would be failures. And failure was the most common fate for all ideas. But if any of their wild speculations proved true, then that would be a triumph, something worth living for.

Through their daily talks the Alpha Trio cut themselves off still further from other people. No one understood their obsessions, their ideas, their argot. Hoagy vaguely sensed this estrangement when he found himself unable to talk with his mother on the videophone.

"Are you excited about the launch?" she asked. "Only two weeks."

"Mmmm," was all he could answer.

"They won't let me come. Said it would break your concentration. Can't even call you again." Her face was a white smear on the viewer. No matter how much he blinked, he could not bring it into focus. "Until after the passage," she added hastily, covering over his silence. "Then I can visit you all I want. After—" Her voice died. A few seconds later she said, "Sweetheart, if what I did was wrong—if you don't—if you don't ever break out—" Again her voice faltered.

The pain came through the blurred video face, the fuzzy electronic voice. He wanted to answer the pain, say something to his mother. But he could not think of any words she would understand.

"I'm sorry," he said, and her face vanished from the screen before he could recall any of the formulas that people used to keep pain at bay. For an instant he felt toward her a glint of that overwhelming love he felt toward his visionary planet. She also was a doorway, he thought, a way in.

During the last two weeks before launch, the Alpha Trio were kept apart, each one secluded in a full-scale mockup of the warp chamber. Murmuring to them through headphones, the psychiatrists coaxed them into deeper and deeper trance states, then urged them back to real-time.

Leaping into trance was easy for Hoagy. The struggle was in coming back. When the psychiatrist whispered, "T-state . . . *now*," Hoagy immediately envisioned the planet. For a few seconds he still felt the Earth under him, and the visionary planet seemed a remote crescent of blue. But the Earth quickly dwindled away behind him, until he could scarcely feel its pull. And at the same time his imaginary globe swelled until it occupied his whole field of vision. He recognized the landmasses, the oceans, the mountain ranges. He traced the sinuous flow of rivers. Hovering down toward the surface, he smelled the fruity ground mosses, the ozone from waterfalls, and he knew he was approaching a forest clearing where his dream-folk lived. And if he were allowed to go on, he would come to a woman, give himself to her, and scatter into the cells of her body.

But each time, just as he was about to reach the point of orgasmic release, the metallic voice would clatter in his ear: "R-state . . . *now!*" Return was torture. He fought against the pull of his vision, fought until he could sense the tug of Earth again. On the return his eyes were closed, all his senses shut down. Real-time gradually invaded his mind. Eventually he found himself in the warp chamber again, and he heard the metallic voice soothing, "Good, good. R-phase is down to forty-three seconds. We need another thirteen seconds off for cushion. So again: T-state . . . *now.*"

Again and again they forced him through the round-trip, driving him out further and back faster. "Psychic marathoning," Jaffa had called it, back before the Alpha Trio had been sequestered.

By the time the sleep hypodermic arrived each night, Hoagy screamed inwardly from the pain.

On many visionary trips during those two weeks, Hoagy was tempted to ignore the whispering voice that called him back. He ached to burst through the frail skin that separated him from consummation. But that climax was being saved for the warp passage—he knew that. Dissipating the psychic charge beforehand might be suicidal. From what little the doctors understood about the psychology of warp transfer, the only defense against the fragmenting effects of temporal dislocation was a powerful mental fixation. "Like nuclear bonding," Blake had described it, "to keep the center from whirling apart."

Beginning three days before launch, the schedule of visionary calisthenics was relaxed. Protein and hormonal injections quickly brought Hoagy's body up to peak strength. He suffered the final injections of memory enhancers and neuro-stimulators in silence. How much of this had the broken astronauts, the mad ones, received? He would not let himself brood on madness.

Whenever his thoughts drifted in that direction, he sum-
moned up his visionary planet and clung to it fiercely.

On the morning of the launch the Alpha Trio were
reunited in the warp chamber. Three faces with skin
stretched taut, three pairs of inward-staring eyes. Now
there was no swapping of cosmologies, no talk of lunacy.
The only business was to survive the passage with mind
intact. There would be time for speculation on the other
side.

Harnessed in, shoulders touching in the cramped
chamber, the three went through pre-flight checks by
rote. Stroking the switches, reading the dials, calling out
measurements was a formality made unnecessary by
computers, but a formality that steadied the mind. They
each double-checked the targeting instructions: third planet
of K-47 in Messier 13, constellation Hercules, 25,000 light-
years away. Time elapse was set at .001 seconds. For
reasons that the temporal physicists still could not explain,
zero-elapse passage disintegrated machines as well as
minds. Yet time elapses much longer than a thousandth of
a second—also for reasons no one had yet explained—
greatly accelerated the rate of fatigue in silicon-based
materials. So the elapse meter was set carefully at .001, and
each of the astronauts read the setting aloud.

Hoagy knew the contours of the warp chamber more
intimately than he knew the surface of his own body.
As he listened to the final whispered instructions from
the mission coordinator, his hands played over the instrument panel, and he regretted for a moment how little
he had lived in his body, how little he had ever felt or
known besides the visionary planet. Later, he promised
himself, after he'd found it, then he would live there
in the flesh.

A faint whine told him the warp projectors were
warming up. Instinctively, he gripped the arm-rests,
bracing for a super-G acceleration he knew would never
come. The force tearing at him a few seconds from now
would not be so gentle or predictable as gravity. And it
would yank him in a thousand directions at once.

"Ready to center," a voice called through the headphones. "Counting from sixty."

On the arm-rest to the right, Blake's hand squeezed
until the skin was bloodless. To the left Hoagy saw

Jaffa's hands spidering in the air above her lap, playing among the force-lines that only she could detect. That was his last outward glimpse before the headphones ordered, "Center."

Immediately the blue-swirled globe filled his inner field of vision.

"Prepare for deep trance."

A fragment of his mind registered the oscillation in the projector's whine, the mild tingle of electricity along his skin as the warp vector strengthened.

"T-state . . . *now*."

Warp chamber, partners, real-time vanished as he flung himself into visionary space. This time he met violent turbulence on his mental flight. Storms tumbled him around. He kept losing track of his planet, had to fight to center himself on it again. Gales ripped at him, loosened his joints, stretched his nerves to the point of snapping. Blackness crept into the waters of his cells, squeezed membrane apart from membrane, exploding him in slow-motion, thinning him out toward the emptiness of space. But he kept fighting his way back around. Gradually the planet loomed before him, massive, familiar, and its gravity drove the blackness out of his cells, welded his fragments together again. Soon the blue globe filled all space. Its tug was all he could feel, pulling him downward, inward. As he settled into a favorite meadow, beasts sauntered out of the woods, then men carrying food, then women chanting. One among them signaled to him, a red-haired woman with green eyes and a catch in her breathing, an intimate from many visionary journeys. She sang to him, undressed him, laid him down upon the spongy turf. When she spread herself on him he became a seed, buried in the dirt of this world. The energies so long bottled inside him burst free, into the woman, into the planet, and he was at peace.

A noise clawed at his ears: "R-state . . . *now!*" A pause, then the same clawing message. Again. Again.

Hoagy dragged himself from beneath the woman, tore himself from the soil. Return to real-time left him aching in every fiber.

Taped orders kept chattering through his headphone. He punched a button to silence them.

"Are you back?" It was Blake's groggy voice.

"Most of me."

"Jaffa hasn't returned yet."

As Blake spoke, the woman's body twitched violently in her restraining harness, a twitching rendered grotesque by zero-G. Then she grew still, and her eyes slicked open. At first only the whites were visible, then the green irises. Leaning around to peer at her, Hoagy saw the tiny green diaphragms tighten as Jaffa focused on him. "Back?" he said gently.

"What?"

"Are you back?"

Her head swiveled around, surveying the warp chamber, as if she had never seen it before. "Where is 'back'?"

Staring into those dazed eyes, Hoagy suddenly glimpsed that green-eyed woman who had spread herself over him like a breathing mountain. He felt suspended, half in real-time and half in trance-time. "Jaffa, listen to me carefully. You are part of Alpha Trio, Project Viva. We are through the warp. Do you understand that?"

Grudgingly, she nodded.

And so he coaxed her back.

Meanwhile Blake checked the real-space coordinates. "Dead perfect," he concluded. "That's Messier Thirteen," he said, pointing through the port at a massive orange star that seemed to amble across the blackness as the warp-ship slowly revolved on its axis.

Jaffa came fully alert when she gazed at the flaring ball. "There's life out here."

"We hope," said Blake.

"Life, life. Can't you feel it?"

Hoagy eased himself away from her. A burning in his chest puzzled him until he remembered she had once prodded him there, weeks before, with one of her life-sensing fingers. "First we have to convince the computer to let us land," he said.

Each one took the psychometric exam, to prove that he or she had survived the warp with faculties intact. When the green lights blinked on all three screens, the Alpha Trio cheered. The timeshell was broken. They had made it through sanely, at least in the machine's estimation.

According to the flight plan, now the plasma engines

hould begin nudging them into the orbital path of K-47.
nstead of the characteristic pulse of the engines, how-
ver, they heard the start-up whine of the warp pro-
ector. An instant later the computer voice buzzed through
heir headphones: "Five minutes until transfer."

"Destination?" Hoagy demanded.

"Earth," the computer answered.

"Something wrong with the tests?" said Jaffa.

"You have passed the test, and now you and the
sycho-monitoring records will be returned for study."

"No landing?" Hoagy said sharply.

"You were never meant to land, not on this flight."

"We were meant to prove transfer is possible without
mind-destruction," Jaffa angrily finished the explanation.

"Correct."

"Puppets," Hoagy moaned.

Blake said nothing, only laughed softly, then more
and more hysterically, until his laughter hammered
nside the warp chamber.

"Blake?"

The man writhed in his harness, shaken by explosions
of laughter.

"You okay?"

"Three minutes," the computer announced.

Jaffa and Hoagy looked at one another helplessly.
They could not risk sedating him so soon before pas-
age.

"Two minutes."

There was no time for nursing the linguist back from
wherever it was the brutal disappointment had driven
him. Perhaps he was skittering out across his cosmic net
of language. There was no time for rage against the
Project Viva directors, no time for fear, no time except
for Hoagy to gather himself toward his own center.

"Ready to center," the headphone purred. "Counting
from sixty."

His hand crept over to touch Jaffa's wrist. "Make it,"
he cried, loud enough for her to hear above the taped
nstructions, above Blake's maniacal laughter. "Make it
through. Next time we'll land. We'll get there."

Her reply was a shout. "I'll make it."

On order, he leapt into trance. Blake's giddy squealing
was the last sound he heard.

The spiral back to real-time, to Earth, was a familiar agony, easier to control because of its familiarity. When the trance released him, Hoagy found himself in a dazzling white room. A man with a long-chinned face he vaguely recognized was staring into his eyes through a lighted tube. Behind him, a woman called out numbers in a husky voice as an electron scanner swept back and forth above his skull.

"Congratulations," the woman said as his eyes blinked open, "you've made it through twice without damage."

"The others?" Hoagy asked weakly. She did not answer, and he was too exhausted to beg for her attention. A pinprick inside his left elbow quickly silenced all his questions about Jaffa and Blake. This trance was a chemical one, gentle, empty of vision.

Jaffa sidled up to him at the debriefing, sat in the next chair. "Zero damage," she confided.

"Same here."

Neither spoke of Blake, not in front of these officials who were gathered in the circular council room. How could these strangers understand the agony of passage or the bitterness of return?

After ritual congratulations, after apologies for having deceived the Alpha Trio with the promise of landing— "We were afraid no weaker bait could have lured you safely through," the director explained, "and yet we couldn't risk letting you actually land on K-47"—the debriefing became a discussion of the psychology of warp transfer.

Psycho-electronic recordings of each crew-member's vision played on an overhead screen. Superimposed on these images were the electron scans, showing changes in brain chemistry corresponding to the various stages of trance. Hoagy did not mind this naked display of his vision, because the numbers and the holographic simulation were far removed from the overwhelming experience of the vision itself. Yet it seemed to him somehow an invasion to show Blake's. From what he could make out of Jaffa's vision, she was seeking a world very like his own.

Within an hour the audience of psychiatrists and brain-chemists and behavioral engineers agreed on the fundamental pattern implicit in the recordings: in all three tapes for the voyage out, and in two tapes for the voyage back, the peak moment of the trance, when mind slipped without harm through the warp, corresponded to a precise distribution of catecholamines, principally serotonin and epinephrine.

"Similar to the distribution we aim for in schizophrenia therapy," observed one of the psychiatrists.

"You can train someone to reproduce it through biofeedback in, say, two weeks," another voice said.

"If they're mandala-trained first."

"Sure. But what are we talking about? Another month? We can still have astronauts mentally ready for warp transfer within six weeks."

Excited talk quickly led them to the conclusion which Hoagy, with relief and infinite sadness, had already reached. It seemed likely that self-induced shifts in brain-chemistry, coupled with modest fixation training, could produce trance states as invulnerable to warp as his own. No one else ever need be consumed by impossible visions. No one else ever need give up Earth and flesh in order to leap through time.

The test would come soon, with a crew whose members had never sweated in the electronic embrace of a Freud, had never been possessed by desire for otherworldly beauty.

"We can still fly?" Jaffa demanded. "And *land?*"

"Of course," the Director replied. "That's why we've trained you."

"Can we name the target planets?" Hoagy asked.

"Within reason. You know the bio-parameters that most interest us."

"And also interest us," Hoagy said. Jaffa was looking at him. The hardness in her eyes kept him from crying. The search would be long, perhaps endless. The pain might decrease with each warp passage, but it was not likely to disappear. He began writing the astronomical labels of Earth-type planets on his scratch pad. Leaning across the gap between their seats, Jaffa added names to the list.

A SUNDAY VISIT WITH GREAT-GRANDFATHER

by Craig Strete

Craig Strete is not new to *New Dimensions*, having appeared in *New Dimensions 8* with a story called "Three Dream Woman," written in collaboration with Michael Bishop. In addition, Strete has appeared in such diverse publications as *Scholastic, Orbit, Ellery Queen's Mystery Magazine,* and *Galaxy*.

Strete is of Cherokee blood and has brought his keen Native American background into play in his fiction. Here, he takes an off-center look at the time-honored Invasion by Aliens theme and comes up with something new and strange and hilarious. Bug-eyed monsters will never be the same.

GREAT-GRANDFATHER STARED AT HIS GIFT WITH a sharply critical eye. Great-grandmother gnashed her teeth like she always did when great-grandfather was about to make a social error.

"This tobacco stinks!" said great-grandfather. He held the pouch away from his nose. "As usual, my cheap great-grandson has shown his respect by bringing me cheap tobacco."

Great-grandmother kicked great-grandfather in the shin, as she had been doing in such instances as long as she could remember. Not that it did any good. Great-grandfather had grown old and independent and it took something of the magnitude of an earthquake to change his ways.

Great-grandson sighed. He knew that no matter what kind of tobacco he brought or how much it cost, great-grandfather would always say it was cheap.

"You are looking well, Great-grandfather," he said.

"A fat lot you know!" said great-grandfather irritably.

"It's the vapors. It gets him in the back," said great-grandmother. "And he hasn't got enough sense to come in when the cold clouds are out. Not him. He stands out in bad vapors and rain looking for a demi-god or trying to remember where he's supposed to be, as if one rock didn't look like another, as if one burial rack didn't—"

"Some day your tongue will go crazy and beat you to death!" roared great-grandfather.

Great-grandmother gave her great-grandson a sympathetic look and shrugged.

"How are the white people treating you in away school?" asked great-grandfather. He shifted his position upon the hard rock so that the sun did not shine directly into his weak, old eyes.

"As badly as usual, revered one. Those white people are crazy."

"And what kind of things are they learning you? Healing arts? Better ways of hunting? Surely these white men are teaching you many things?" said great-grandfather.

"No, great-grandfather," answered great-grandson. "They are not teaching me any of those things. I am learning science. I am learning how lightning is made and what rocks are made of and what stars are and how fast light travels."

"Spells! Most excellent! These white people are smarter than I thought. But what was that you said about light traveling? I have never heard of such a thing! Of what use is it?" great-grandfather asked.

"They are not spells," explained great-grandson patiently. "And the traveling of light is mathematics."

Great-grandfather nodded his head wisely. "Ah yes! Mathematics." A shadow darkened his face and he scowled. "What the hell is mathematics?" growled great-grandfather.

"Counting and measuring. Adding and subtracting the number of things one has," said great-grandson.

"Sending you to away school has turned you into a wise nose! Why didn't you say that the first time! Mathematics! Any fool knows how to count on his fingers! You went to away school to learn a four-dollar word for counting on your fingers? This is the kind of a thing you are learning?"

"You don't understand. We learn more than just how to count on our fingers. We've learned how to measure great distances. For instance, I know how far away the stars are."

Great-grandfather shook his head. He looked at his wife. They both shrugged. "That is very interesting," said great-grandfather. "And what is that used for?"

"I don't know," admitted great-grandson. "They only told me how far away it is."

"What other kinds of things have they told you?" asked great-grandmother. "These things sound as crazy as eating rocks."

"Well, I have learned that man was once an ape, that the earth flies in the air around the sun, and that when people die their bodies rot and their souls go to heaven. Also I learned that—"

Great-grandfather jumped off the rock. "What? What?" he shouted. "What is this craziness! Has my great-grandson fallen upon his head too many times?"

Great-grandmother tried to quiet great-grandfather down but he jumped around like a frightened horse. He paced back and forth, cursing loudly.

"They also told me the Great Spirit is superstition," said great-grandson.

"What is this superstition?" roared great-grandfather. "Is that another of those city funnies you picked up at away school? If I wasn't so old I'd flatten you with a rock! I never heard such foolishness!"

"But, great-grandfather," protested great-grandson, "I am only telling you what they are teaching me at away school. It isn't my fault that the white people are all crazy. They even told me that it was impossible to talk with people after they are dead."

"They have gone too far!" shrieked great-grandfather. "They have gone too far! There will be no more away school!"

Great-grandfather beat his scrawny chest with his fists in a defiant gesture which sent him into a fit of coughing.

Great-grandmother patted him on the back as his face swelled up and turned red.

She looked disgusted. "You shouldn't have told him all those terrible things," she said, pounding great-grandfather's back vigorously. "You know this happens every time he gets upset."

Great-grandson looked properly apologetic and helped great-grandmother sit him back on his favorite sitting rock. The coughing fit passed, leaving great-grandfather weak and gasping for breath.

"It's the vapors," said great-grandmother. "If he had enough sense to come in out of the—"

Great-grandfather scowled so ferociously that she stopped speaking. She knew when she was well off.

"No more!" gasped great-grandfather between gasps. "No more away school!"

"But, great-grandfather," the boy protested. "I will be arrested and thrown into the white man's jail if I do not go to away school."

The old man folded his arms across his chest. He raised his head, tilting it at a defiant angle. He sucked his scrawny stomach in and pushed his thin chest out. It was his warrior's stance, which had once put fear into the hearts of many a comely woman. When great-grandfather did this, it meant that his mind was made up. It meant that there would be no further discussion. It meant that there would be no more away school. It also meant another coughing spell for great-grandfather, who was always forgetting his condition.

Great-grandmother began whacking him on the back again with the practiced ease of one who has done it many hundreds of times. She sighed. "He never learns."

"Or else he never remembers," suggested great-grandson.

Great-grandmother shook her head wearily. "I think it is a little of both," she said.

The letter from away school came three weeks later. The boy carried the letter to his great-grandparents. "I told you they were going to throw me into the slammer if I didn't go to away school," he said after reading them the letter. The letter said they were going to throw him into the slammer.

Great-grandfather started to go into his warrior's stance, but the old woman had anticipated that very thing and she whacked him on the back before he could get a decent start at it. He was taken completely by surprise and fell forward off his favorite sitting rock. This saved him from another coughing spell.

"What happens is that they are going to come and get me and throw me in the slammer," said great-grandson, looking unhappy about the whole thing.

"Something will have to be done about this thing," said the old man solemnly from his seat upon the ground. "I will not take this thing lying down." He got up as if he meant it literally and started to sit back down on his favorite sitting rock. His dim eyes betrayed him and he almost sat down on great-grandmother.

"The rock is two feet to your left," said great-grandmother.

"I knew that all along," said great-grandfather indignantly. "I was only trying to get you to guess my weight."

He moved over to the rock, stared at it carefully, judging its exact location, and sat down. He missed the rock by three inches.

"It is good to sit upon the ground once in a while," reflected the old man as he rubbed his hip. "It gives a man a whole new perspective on things."

Great-grandmother snickered to herself. In an aside to the boy, she said, "Boy! He's in lousy shape, ain't he?"

It was but one day later that great-grandson rushed up to his great-grandparents. "They've come," he cried, gazing over his shoulder fearfully. There was a loud whining noise in the direction from which he had just come. Great-grandfather was asleep in the sun with his mouth open. He jumped awake, thinking he had been shot. He felt all over his chest, not that it would have made any difference in his condition.

"Who? What?" he said.

"The white men have come to throw your one and only great-grandson into the slammer!" shouted great-grandson.

Great-grandfather yawned and closed his eyes again. "That's nice," he said. "I always liked buffalo sou—" He was asleep again.

"Wake up, great-grandfather!" shouted great-grandson.

"Boy, he really is in lousy shape, ain't he?" said great-grandmother.

"Who? What?" said great-grandfather.

"We already covered that already!" groaned great-grandson.

Grudgingly, great-grandfather awoke. He rubbed his eyes. From a distance, there was a strange whooshing noise.

"Who's that whooshing around my place of business!" roared the old man.

"It's the white men come to throw me in the slammer!" yelled great-grandson for the third or fourth time.

"No kidding," said great-grandfather. He didn't seem

particularly concerned. "By the way," asked the old man, "what the hell is a slammer?"

"That's a white man's jail," replied the boy.

"Well! Why the hell didn't you say so in the first place! You idiot! I thought a slammer was a—"

Great-grandson was never to know what the old man thought a slammer was because the white men arrived in a strange vehicle without wheels.

"It's the white men come to throw our one and only great-grandson into the slammer," said great-grandmother. But as she said it she had doubts. For one thing, they had tentacles and were blue. She'd seen some ugly white people in her day, but none quite as ugly as the two specimens who had just come into view.

Great-grandson threw his hands up in the air, screamed at least once, and ran like hell. He disappeared behind an outcropping of rock.

"What's wrong with him?" asked great-grandfather. "Did he sit on a cold worm? Where's he going?"

"It's the white men come to throw our one and only great-grandson into the slammer," repeated great-grandmother, and she motioned at the aliens embarking from the vehicle. He followed her arm with his weak eyes and saw them vaguely.

Great-grandfather snorted. "You think I don't know what they are? I got eyes, you know." He blinked his eyes uncertainly. For some reason the blurry forms in front of him seemed suspiciously blue. He attributed this to indigestion.

The aliens advanced on the seated couple. The aliens were six feet tall, covered with blue scaly armor. They had eyebulbs on each side of their face, thin slit mouths, red eye membranes across red pupiled eyes. They were clothed in a superior smirk.

"So you think you're going to throw my one and only great-grandson into the slammer, do you?" roared great-grandfather. He immediately went into a coughing fit. Great-grandmother began pumping his back in the usual fashion.

"What's a slammer?" said the first alien. He eyed the old man, who was bent over double, gasping and coughing with his tongue hanging out. "Boy, he's really in lousy shape ain't he?" commented the first alien.

"Yeah," said the second alien. "This is going to be easier than making candy out of babies."

The first alien took a hand weapon out of a pouch strapped below his chin. He set the gauge on stun. "This is going to be the easiest one yet. No technology worth shaking a quantum at. No force fields, no personal power packs, no weapons. Clothes made out of animal skins. Primitive." He aimed the weapon at great-grandfather and shot him in the head, laughing to himself all the while.

It had absolutely no effect on the old man. He just kept coughing. The first alien turned and stared at the second alien. "Wow!" he said.

"Yeah," agreed the second alien. A good stun shot was strong enough to cripple a five-ton herbil.

Great-grandfather coughed, great-grandmother pounded his back, and great-grandson hid in the rocks viewing the whole proceedings with alarm.

"My stunner must be out of whack. Lemme use yours," grunted the first alien.

The second alien handed it over to him. The first alien set it on stun and shot the old man again. Nothing happened. The old man didn't even blink an eye. He was too busy trying to get his breath back.

"Hey!" said the first alien, whipping his tentacles in a confused circle around his shoulders. "Hey!"

The second alien nodded his head. "Yeah."

"Am I gonna get him now!" threatened the first alien, setting his tentacles determinedly around the hand weapon. He set the stunner on full charge, moved the power setting to overload, and blasted away at the old man again. The only thing that happened was that the weapon overheated and melted into a shapeless hunk of hot metal. It burned the alien's tentacle. He yelped and threw the useless weapon away. He waved his stinging tentacle in the air. He looked madder than hell. He looked at the second alien, who looked right back at him.

"We didn't get the wrong planet, did we? I mean, I've seen technology and I've seen technology, but this is beyond me. How come he ain't dead, is what I want to know?"

"I can't understand it either," said the second alien. "We flew over the missile base. They had atomic weapons. Real kid stuff. No force fields, no anti-matter weapons. Pre-pubescent technology. So how come this one is so hard to kill?"

"I'll nail him with my molecular disruption gun," said the first alien, as he took a small metal tube out of his neck pouch. "He won't know what hit him." He smirked, but his smirk lacked conviction.

Great-grandfather sat weakly on his favorite sitting rock. He'd got his breath back finally. Great-grandmother had her eyes on the ugly white men. She couldn't understand anything they were saying. None of it made any sense. This helped convince her that they were indeed white people.

"Stop burping me!" growled great-grandfather. She stopped whacking his back.

The gun in the alien's tentacle erupted in a silvery-red flash and a brilliant beam of energy passed through great-grandfather and completely destroyed his favorite sitting rock. It disappeared in a shimmering cloud of vaporized molecules. Great-grandfather fell flat on his back. He was so shocked he almost went into another coughing fit.

"Hey!" shouted the first alien, whipping tentacles in all directions, entangling two of them in his confusion. "Hey!"

The second alien was too shocked to even say yeah.

"That does it!" shouted great-grandfather, struggling to get off the ground. "I'm going to teach you crazy white people to mess with me! Throw my one and only great-grandson into the slammer, will you?"

"What's a slammer?" said the first alien. "Are we talking the right language or what?"

"I'm going to hit you with the dreaded curse of Cheroboa! I'll knock your rooty-tooty eyes out!" exclaimed great-grandfather, dangerously close to another coughing fit.

Great-grandmother covered her eyes. "Oh no! Not that old song and dance again!"

"Maybe they put up that missile base to fool us," suggested the second alien. "Maybe those radio broadcasts we picked up twenty years ago, are true? Maybe this guy is Superman?"

"Hoogma nuba toot!" roared great-grandfather, and he made a mystic pass through the air with his hands. He looked around expectantly. Nothing happened.

"Nuts!" he said. "I was sure I had it right."

"Who is kidding who?" asked the first alien. He eyed the old man critically, studying him first with one eye-bulb and then the other.

"Where's his cape? Superman got to have a cape," said the first alien. "How we gonna find out if he's Superman?"

"Hoogma toot nuba." It began raining in downtown Los Angeles. "Ah, come on now!" complained great-grandfather. "I know I had it right that time!" He stared at the sky expectantly.

The second alien pulled a handful of weapons out of his pouch, rummaging frantically for something at the bottom of the pouch. He pulled out a hunk of kryptonite and threw it at the old man. They had prepared for everything, even Superman. It passed right through him and fell to the ground.

"He must be the Green Hornet!" said the first alien, all his tentacles agog at the prospect. "Or Captain Marvel! Or all of them!"

"Well, toot hoogma nuba!" roared great-grandfather without much conviction. Suddenly the sky opened up and it began raining frogs.

"Nuts!" said great-grandfather, thoroughly disgusted with the whole business. Frogs pelted off the heads of the aliens. They were too stunned by this sudden turn of events to even duck.

"I give it one more try," said great-grandfather. Great-grandmother, who had been crouching behind her sitting rock, poked her head up from behind the rock and looked rather dubiously at the sky. "He never learns and he never remembers either," she muttered under her breath.

A frog bounced off great-grandfather's head, almost knocking him to the ground.

"And, boy, is he in lousy shape," she added.

"I heard that," roared great-grandfather, and he went into a violent coughing fit.

The second alien began packing up his weapons meekly. "I think I just better go home and forget about the whole invasion. I think we better leave before he notices we're here and does something to us we'll regret. Did we ever get the wrong planet!"

The first alien was staring at a frog resting on his

shoulder. He was scared to death to touch it. He'd heard about warts. The frog returned his stare and then hopped off his shoulder. The alien almost collapsed with relief.

The sky stopped dropping frogs.

"This ain't no technology to be fooling with! Let's get the hell out of here! Man! Am I glad we decided to hit the sticks first!"

"I can't understand it. It should have worked. I can't figure out what went wrong. That curse always worked on chickens," said great-grandfather.

"It could have been worse," said the first alien. "We could have landed in Cleveland."

"Or met the Lone Ranger," added the other alien, a look of pure horror on his face.

The aliens turned in full flight and ran to their vehicle. They jumped in, dropping weapons carelessly in their haste to get away.

"Take a good look," said the first alien as he slammed the power bar into gear. "Sure doesn't look like a super-technology, does it? I'd swear there wasn't a weapon or self-defense mechanism on any of them. They'll never believe it back home." He stared at great-grandfather with absolute terror. Great-grandfather was looking up into the sky, still expecting the curse of Cheraboa to materialize. "You wouldn't think—" said the first alien, thinking about the energy beams passing through the old man, without hurting him at all, thinking about the frogs. "No. No. You wouldn't think—" he paused. "He sure—"

"Is in lousy shape, ain't he?" finished the second alien.

"Yeah," said the first alien. "I should be in such lousy shape!"

They returned to their spaceship and left the Earth as fast as they could travel. They never came back.

"You can come out now!" yelled great-grandmother to great-grandson. "The crazy white men are gone."

"They are?" asked great-grandfather, looking disappointed. "Nuts! Just when I had the curse down pat, too."

Great-grandmother rolled her eyes.

Great-grandson came out from behind a rock. Great-grandfather stared at the rock. "He's putting on weight, ain't he? White man's school has made him fat and weak."

Great-grandmother sighed. It had been a long day. Every day was a long day that was spent with a rascal like great-grandfather.

"It's time we got some sleep," said great-grandmother.

Great-grandfather yawned.

Great-grandson came up to them and looped his arms in theirs. Lifting them to their feet, he walked them across the sacred ground to the burial rack. Tenderly, he helped them climb back onto the burial rack.

"You're a good great-grandson," said great-grandmother. "Will we see you next Sunday?"

"Same time as always," said great-grandson.

"He's such a good great-grandson," said great-grandmother.

"He brings me cheap tobacco," muttered great-grandfather.

Great-grandmother would have kicked him but he was already snoring.

CRIERS AND KILLERS

by Pat Cadigan

Pat Cadigan is in the enviable position of having won an award for fiction before the sale of her first professional story. "Death from Exposure," published in the semiprofessional magazine *Shayol,* won the first Balrog Fantasy Award in 1979. Her first professional sale follows: a precise, implacable view of a strange and plausible future.

Cadigan attended the University of Amherst before transferring to the University of Kansas, where she secured what she calls "a Bachelor's Degree in nothing in particular" and did graduate work under James Gunn. She also worked for Tom Reamy until shortly before his untimely death, and "Criers and Killers" is an excellent commendation of these two fine teachers. In addition, Cadigan has worked as a rectory housekeeper, clock case sander, disc jockey for a radio station for the blind, belly dance teacher, and typesetter—as satisfying a list of strange author-jobs as any we've seen recently. To that list, she can now add professional fiction writer, for while the following may be her first professional sale, it is sure not to be her last.

THE GRIM REAPER WAS HAVING IT OUT WITH a baby-faced Teddy-boy and a crowd had gathered. I was on my way to stare at a cup of coffee and a cigarette, but there was no hurry. So I paused on the edge of the crowd behind three glitterbabies. They were betting among themselves on who would get whom, or would have been, except that all three of them wanted to put money on the Reaper. Well, there was no disputing the psychological impact of the sight of Death himself, and a scythe is a formidable weapon. But long black robes aren't for fighting—one of the Reaper's sleeves was in tatters from the Teddy's switchblade, and the kid wasn't even that good with it. A bike chain was probably more his style, and I wondered why he didn't have one. Then, over one glitterbaby's shoulder, I saw a ferrety-looking girl holding one. She was standing just outside the fighting circle, trying to get the chain to the Teddy. But every time he tried to reach for it, the Reaper would whip the scythe between them and the girl would snatch her hand back barely in time to keep it from being cut off, to a breathy, one-syllable chorus from the spectators.

After about the fourth time this happened, the glitter-baby in the electric puce shorts (with fingernails to match) began to get restless. He was bored. So was I. Except for the times the Reaper tried to cut the girl's hand off, the fight was pretty damned dull. Besides, he was supposed to be fighting the Teddy, not her. Why didn't the Reaper just cut the Teddy's hand off and be done with it?

I did a close-up on each of the fighters. If either one of them had been really applying himself, he would have found dozens of openings; it would have been over in a matter of minutes. But fights were getting longer and longer these days—everyone loves to play an audience. I was hoping the glitterbabies might get bored enough to leave so I could leave with them. Glitterbabies—the real ones, not the faddists—can be pretty gamy, and I thought I could have a lot of fun with these three. They clashed superbly, and all of them were quite beautiful in a glitzy type of way, especially the bald-headed one with the sequins glued to her scalp. Most people don't have the bone structure to carry that off, but she was striking.

None of them moved except to shift their weight on their twinkly platform boots. I gave up on them and moved on, heading for Ike's Coffee. Too bad. The number of real glitterbabies was beginning to dwindle.

Crossing the street to the next block, I heard several raw shrieks followed by some booing, scattered applause, and then louder booing. I didn't bother doing a cut back to see what had happened. Later there'd be another fight with the winner of the one I'd been watching taking on all comers. If I was around, I could check it out and see who had won. But I didn't much care.

Ike's was empty. I took the counter seat nearest the cash register and waited. The waitress was down at the other end trying to charm the only other customer, a Desperado who was absorbed in getting an omelette all over the ends of his mustache. I knew he was a stranger—Desperadoes don't abound in eastern cities. The waitress was really working on him with the chitchat. When she glanced in my direction, her pleasant smile drooped into a sour line. None of the waitresses at Ike's were ever particularly glad to see me. I made the other customers twitchy. Even the loopiest ones had some trouble with the sight of me. I played on it, of course. I can't claim to ever having emptied the joint, though. That distinction belongs to a glitterbaby formerly of my acquaintance, now deceased. He was even gamier than usual.

I guess she decided that if she ignored me, I'd go away, and went back to trying to charm the Desperado. I did a zoom down the length of the counter. He didn't look up at her once, no matter how close she leaned. He hadn't even taken off his hat, for that matter, and I couldn't see much of his face at that angle, just one side of the mustache all those types wear. Finally, the waitress gave up on him and came over to me.

"Well?" Her crazy blonde hair was practically bristling. Glitterbaby in her off-hours, probably.

"Coffee," I said, trying to make my filtered voice sound sweet. "And a doughnut. I'm splurging today." She could have cared.

She poured me half a cup of coffee and reached for the doughnut nearest her on the rack behind the counter.

"Just a moment, please," I said. She looked at me through narrowed eyes, her lower lip pushed up so far that it seemed to threaten her nose. "Not that one. I want one of the cream filled. And I want a full cup of coffee. I take it with milk. Please," I added, knowing it wouldn't help.

She went a little white, but did as I asked. Then she hurried back to the Desperado before he could finish up and leave. I did an extreme close-up on the doughnut she'd given me. There was dust all over it. Disgusting, I thought, and considered calling her back to ask for a clean one. Not that I'd be able to get one—the dirt in the air settles into everything. She was frustrated enough not making any headway with the Desperado and having me there to watch. I decided to give her a break and amused myself by watching the powdered cream dissolve in the coffee.

". . . time you're in the city, stop in and visit. We're *always* open." The Desperado was folding his napkin. I turned up my directional to catch his reply, but all he did was belch (thunderous at the volume). His stomach rumbled with incipient indigestion, which I found hilarious, especially because he couldn't hear that himself. I put my hearing back to normal and tracked him as he slid off his stool and came toward the cash register.

What was it about Desperadoes, I wondered, that excited some women. I wasn't particularly excited myself, but then I'm a rather atypical woman in that respect. Still, it did strike something favorable in me when he stared at me openly as he paid his check. I stared right back at him, medium close-up, although he didn't know it. From his view, I seemed to be focused on the coffee.

He handed the waitress his check without looking at her. I did a quick cut to her face—sour as ever—and went back to him.

It was all plastic surgery, I saw, but it was damned good. His eyes were deep-set (*that* must have cost him), his nose was ever so slightly hooked over the thick, golden-brown mustache. It was meant to be gringo with a hint of Spanish—very effective and aging quite well with him. Probably he'd had it done in England before it closed.

He kept staring at me while she counted change into his hand. Then he stuffed it into his pocket, pulled back his leather vest to scratch his ribs (some people really play a part to the hilt) and leaned a hand on the counter.

"Come back real soon," said the waitress.

"I'm not gone yet." His voice was surprisingly smooth; it belied his appearance. I hadn't tried to estimate his age, but by the sound he was younger than I was.

"Well, then, can I do anything else for you?" The waitress was hopeful.

"Sure. You can tell me how she"— he jerked his chin at me— "is gonna drink coffee."

"She's not," said the waitress and stumped down to the other end of the counter to clear away his dishes. It would probably be best for me not to come in while she was working, I thought. I'd never get served.

"Have you got a cigarette?" I asked him, swiveling around so I faced him.

"Yeah."

"Would you mind lighting one for me?"

I had expected to see him take out a bag of tobacco and some rolling papers from his shirt pocket, but he had a pack of the usual horrid things everyone was smoking these days. He offered it to me.

"You *do* have to light it for me, I'm afraid," I said, running one hand down the smooth surface of the metal shell that covered me from the neck up.

"I'll have to smoke it for you, too, then, won't I?"

I took the cigarette from his lips. "No thanks. This is just something I do with my hands." I tried to chuckle, but my hook-up made it sound like white noise. Someday they may work the bugs out of that. "You can drink my coffee if you want."

He hesitated and then reached over to pick up the cup.

"Want a doughnut? Or are you full?"

He shook his head.

"Don't blame you, actually. You can't see it, but it's covered with dirt. Dust in the air. Settles everywhere."

When he put the cup down it was empty. "Thank you," I said, tapping the cigarette over an ashtray.

"So what are you supposed to be?"

"*Supposed* to be?" I wished for eyebrows, just so I could raise them at times like this.

"Everybody's something. A glitterbaby, a Teddy-boy . . ."

"Or a Desperado," I put in. He shrugged. "There are still people around who don't indulge in being Colorful Characters—did you know that? Some people don't have an image. I hope you stick with yours for a while. Get your money's worth from that job you've had done on yourself. It's very nice."

"It was off-season for Desperadoes. The surgeon gave me a deal."

"No one can pass up a bargain."

"What about you? What are you?"

I got off the stool and pulled back my jacket. He looked grudgingly appreciative.

"And that's all real. No body-carving. No silicone. No off-season. Just diet and exercise. My way of compensating, see."

He didn't understand and I didn't feel like explaining it to him, so I just sat down again.

"More coffee for this lady," he called to the waitress.

"Just a moment," I said. "If *you* want more coffee, buy your own."

"Not for me." He smiled, mustache spreading like a caterpillar. "I just want to leave you with a full cup. So someone else can drink it for you."

The reflection he was getting from my shell of his nasty smile would have to serve for the one I would like to have given him. "Always nice to meet an understanding soul who's a real Desperado," I said cheerfully. He was still smiling as he walked out.

The waitress came with the coffee pot and held it over my cup. "Do you really want this?"

Instead of answering her, I tossed several coins on the counter and got up. Her voice stopped me at the door.

"I'm going to have you barred for annoying the customers."

"Forget it. He didn't want to stay. What would you want with a Desperado anyway?"

She tried to keep her face expressionless and failed. I couldn't help giggling, even if it did sound like a few wires had come loose. "That's probably all plastic, too."

I thought she was going to throw a cup at me. The old-fashioned ceramic cups they use in there could have done my unit a lot of damage, so I beat a hasty retreat, trying not to look like I was hurrying.

On my way back up the street, I passed the three glitterbabies from the fight and was tempted to turn around and follow them. They barely glanced at me; they knew what I was supposed to be. Most of the locals did. If the Desperado hung around long enough, he would too. I turned off my speaker so I could think out loud without anyone hearing.

Thinking out loud was how I'd gotten into the shell in the first place. Not that it was my fault, or anyone else's. But the thinking had been too loud. It went beyond being a public nuisance to a public menace, and there wasn't anything I could do about it. So something had been done for me. The year after that, the Good of Society Death Bill had passed, but it was not retroactive. My shell was on to stay. I was watched, provided for, and regulated, in exchange for letting a scientist perform a test or two once in a while. I would most definitely live, under penalty of law.

A couple of city men were cleaning the spot where the Grim Reaper and the Teddy-boy had been at it earlier, pouring buckets of cleanser over a large, bloody spot and running a miniature streetcleaner over it. The ferrety-looking girl was leaning against a building watching them, swinging the bike chain in a small arc. I stopped beside her.

"What happened?" I asked. "Did your Teddy get it?"

She didn't pay any attention to me and I realized I still had my speaker switched off. I turned it on and repeated myself.

"Neay," she sneered nasally. "They got each other. *Mess*. Everybody lost money. I lost a *bundle*." She lashed the chain against the building.

"You'll make it back on the next fight."

"Yeah, but I lost Roger, too. He was my best. I coulda swore he'd get that Reaper. Man, I hated that sumbitch. All the handlers did. He's gone, but so is my boy. I'm gonna be on the dole suckin' my toes if I don't get another fighter half as good as him. You see it?"

"Some. I missed the climax."

She twisted her mouth hatefully. *"Messy.* That *scythe."*

"So you need another fighter now."

She lashed the chain against the wall again, harder. "Ah, *you* care, right? *You* don't fight. Why are you even talking to me? I only want to talk to fighters. Skin off, leave me alone."

"There's a new Desperado in town," I said, as though I were actually offering her something.

"Desperado, *shit!"* She let fly with her chain again. "Desperadoes don't fight, they fuck. I'm not a pimp!" She wrapped the chain around her fist and shook it at me. "All I know about is a good killer. All I *need* is a good killer. The rest of you—sloppin' around town, looking for your next thrill, the next fight to bet on, blood to smell, cry over the money you lose when some poor bastard like Roger gets it—you just skin off when it's over. The only good people left are the killers. They're the only ones who really do anything. They're the only ones who are really alive anymore. Everybody else on the dole, nothing to do . . ."

"Killers don't live long."

"Yeah, but they work at being alive, don't they? Don't talk Desperado to *me.* A Desperado couldn't even kill *himself.* All he could do is cry about it." She unwound the chain and began swinging it again.

I decided to make her happy by moving on. I tried to keep an eye on her from behind as I walked away, but I'm not good at that unless I'm doing just a quick cut. It's too much like walking backwards while walking forward: I nearly knocked over a Holy Family in the process. They were very nice about it and gave me a blessing, in unison. I wanted to put my fist through their serene smiles. There are times when living among these people in their chosen pigeonholes makes me want to take a can opener to my shell. I wondered a lot what it would be like to live someplace where people didn't have to be Characters. In this part of town, though, I could be a commonplace enough sight to be left to myself. Being the only shellhead

certainly made me a Character's Character. It was pref-
erab'e to living sixty miles away from everything without
the shell, which was how far my thoughts could travel before fading. The government couldn't spare the land or the
expense, anyway.

I did a zoom shot through a store window across the
street to a wall-clock. 3:30. Too early to start hitting the
bars—the only people in them now were people who
really liked being helpless. It was no fun getting one of
them to drink for me. I had an empty afternoon on my
hands for the first time in a long time. Normally, I could
fill several hours at Ike's or any number of places like it,
getting people to consume a meal or two for me before I
switched to the bar circuit. Maybe I had milked my
routine dry and ought to give it a rest for a while. Or
maybe it had been the fight that had soured everyone for
the afternoon. Perhaps the arena mentality that had
passed the Public Fight (to the Public Finish) Bill was on
the wane, and people were ready for a little good old-
fashioned gang violence again.

Waning or not, halfway up the block I could see a
crowd gathering for another fight. A surprising number of
them were glitterbabies, but when I did a close-up on
them I could see that most of them were phonies in costume for the day. They were easy to spot; a real glitterbaby goes in for skin bleaching. Rotten voyeurs; I hate
nothing worse than a professional audience member.

I went around the edge of the crowd, not to see the
fight, but to look for a couple of phonies to victimize. I'd
done it before, it was easy. I'd pick two together and stand
behind them, doing close-ups on the backs of their necks,
switching from one to another. Eventually, they'd begin
to feel odd and turn around. The sight of a faceless
metal head with strange apparatus mounted on top would
be too much for them and they'd skin off in a hurry.

After I found a couple, a man and woman who were
together but didn't clash—another giveaway for fake glitterbabies—I waited to watch the fighters square off. This
time a Christ with a cat-o'-nine-tails was taking on a
Prince Valiant with a broadsword. The Prince started
waving the blade over his head in showy, wide circles,
but before I could go into my routine, I felt a hand on
my arm.

The Desperado wasn't smiling now. For a moment, I

thought he was going to hold me up or something inane like that. But he simply pulled me away from the crowd and began to steer me up the street.

The weak feeling in my legs told me that it was about time to go home anyway and plug some food into my vein. Once I went too long without and fainted. The city carted me home, fed me, and docked my dole for transportation and handling. Expensive. The way I ate was nothing to hurry home for—very little was. No real food, no smoking, no sight or hearing that didn't come through a camera or microphone: count-your-sorrows-it-could-be-better time. I get that way when I'm hungry. But what the hell, I thought, doing a close-up of the Desperado's profile. There was still sex.

"Anything you want to do for me, first?" I asked. "Want to go to a bar and drink for me?"

"I want to know what the hell you are."

"I thought you wanted to know what I was supposed to be."

"Maybe."

"But mostly you'd just like to fuck?"

He didn't answer that one.

"What does it cost, my money or my life?"

He jerked us both to a halt and pushed back his hat with his free hand. "Just how much is something like that worth to you?"

My knees buckled and I sat down hard on the sidewalk. The weight of the shell pulled me backwards, but I managed not to fall over and damage it. The Desperado stood over me with his hands on his hips. He had a pretty fair erection.

"Sure, sure," I said. "Right here. Now. Hop to it. For you I'll lay right on the sidewalk."

He put his hands under my armpits and pulled me to my feet. "Where do you live?"

Ferret-face was right, I thought, and told him. All Desperadoes did was fuck. Maybe that was the fascination for women, that ever-ready randiness. Hell, maybe there was even a smell, which would explain why I wasn't fascinated. I can't smell.

I had left the bed down in my one-room apartment; unless I do, there's no furniture at all. He sat down on it and started taking off his boots.

"Wait a minute, bandito," I said and lurched into the

kitchenette to get a bag out of the refrigerator. He followed, watching as I hung the bag up on the rack over the sink and slid the needle into my vein, making sure the tube was straight and not feeding too fast.

"A cup of coffee just isn't enough to keep me going," I said, trying to sound apologetic.

"You eat like that all the time?"

"All the time."

"You must love needles."

"No. I just play my part to the hilt."

"What's your part?"

"After lunch, we'll discuss it in detail." I adjusted the tube so that it fed a little more slowly, to give myself time to work into something.

There was still sex, and there were enough men and women willing to help me indulge in it, even if most of them were more than a shade on the other side of what passes for normal. I hoped he didn't like to smoke afterward, so I could get him to have a cigarette for me.

I would have been smiling as I finally slid the needle out of my arm and tossed the bag into the trash compactor. "Before we begin," I said, bending my arm up, "I must tell you there is a severe penalty for damaging the unit. Read the notice on the wall next to you."

He started to read the official-looking government document I had tacked up for the benefit of my lady and gentlemen callers, but he lost interest. "What the hell is that?"

I rapped my knuckles on the shell. "This. There is no penalty for damaging me. I'm willing to run the risk to experience it first-hand."

He unbent my arm to look at the small red dot where the needle had gone in. "I don't want to damage you." His face was appreciative again and I let my jacket slide off my other arm onto the floor.

"There *is* the bed," I told him as he unbuttoned my shirt.

"Later."

He didn't even take off his pants, just dropped them some. I managed to get one leg out of mine before we were down on the floor. His leather vest stuck to my skin clammily. I kept trying to move it out of the way and he thought I was pushing him off. He pulled away, kneeling between my legs.

"Make up your mind." His voice was low and dangerous. Between his own legs, his cock was bobbing around,
waiting for further instructions. If it was plastic, it was
exceptional. I didn't do a close-up on it to find out.

"Just take off your vest, will you?"

"A little while ago you were going to lay on the sidewalk. Now you want a bed and all the comforts." He
leaned forward again.

I did an extreme close-up of a spot on the ceiling while
he tried. After a minute, he went soft and pulled back
again.

"It's a brick wall," he growled.

"I'm dry, you imbecile." I sat up clumsily, holding my
shell between my hands to keep it from wavering around.
My head moves awkwardly when it moves at all. "If you
really want in, you'll have to make a few concessions." I
stood up, kicked off my pants, and went into the main
room to lay down on the bed. He followed, holding his
pants up with both hands.

"Okay, What does it take?"

"Strip," I commanded. "Everything."

He didn't much like that, but he started pulling off his
vest.

"The hat, too, Desperado. If you want it so bad, get
desperate."

I think I expected him to leave at that point, but apparently he wanted it enough. He left the hat for last,
though. It should have looked ridiculous, a naked man in
a sombrero, but I suppose it was no more ridiculous
than a nude woman with a steel shell on her head. When
he finally tossed the hat on the floor, I opened my legs.

"Don't get overanxious, and don't make any sudden
moves."

He moved slowly; there was satisfaction in seeing his
erection return as he settled between my thighs, resting
his weight on his hands.

"Kiss me," I said.

He moved his head down toward my breasts.

"Not there. Not yet. Kiss me."

He began to slide down further. I grabbed his arm and
pulled him back up. "I said, kiss me."

"*Where,* goddamn you?" He was angry and going soft
again.

"Kiss *me*." I fondled the smooth surface of the shell. "All over my face. As it were."

"Then take off that contraption."

"No. Didn't you read the notice? Kiss me."

He started to get up, but I still had a good grip on his arm and I'm physically very powerful. "What the hell's wrong with you? Don't you kiss your women?"

"You're not my woman. And I don't kiss *things*."

"You don't think so?"

"I'll kiss your body all you want—any part of it."

I couldn't repress a chuckle, even if it did come out as a burst of static. "You may kiss my ass after you kiss my face."

He grabbed the shell with both hands. "Why the hell is this so important to you?"

"It isn't, not to me. It's important to you, and everyone else in this town. But right now it is extremely important to you alone. So kiss it. Kiss me."

I couldn't feel how tightly he was holding it, but by the look of him, he could have wrenched it off my head and killed me. Ferret-face remained ever correct, though; Desperadoes aren't killers. His face went out of camera range as he leaned close for a moment and then drew back again.

"Happy?"

I raised up on my elbows. "You can do better than that."

"Not with something that doesn't kiss back. Or is that what you like? Sure." He leaned forward again. I could see the top of his head moving back and forth as he rubbed his mouth against the metal. "Sure. You're kissing the other side. Sure." He pushed me down, putting his weight on me as he ran his fingers over the shell. I could feel the vibrations.

"And you said you couldn't do better."

"This isn't better."

"Sure it is."

"Don't talk. You can't talk if you're kissing."

"I'm not kissing. You're kissing."

Then it was all business again, and again he went soft. He clamped his hands on the unit and rolled it from side to side. The bare room wagged like a tail, and I thought he might actually twist my head off. "What does it take for you? What does it take?" he was yelling.

"It doesn't take *that!*" I pried his fingers off the shell. "I warned you about damaging the unit, you dumb fuck!"

He had his fist cocked before either one of us knew it. It hung in the air, white-knuckled, ready; he hesitated.

"You want that?"

I didn't answer.

"Huh? You want that? Right in your soft little belly? I can hit a woman."

"And here I thought you didn't want to damage me."

"I'd call it self-defense. No man alive would argue with me."

"If that's what you want, go find a man."

He was staring at the distorted reflection of himself with his fist up in the shell; I can always tell when some-one's doing that. Facial expression will go a little loose, as though the person in question were under hypnosis. He let his hand drop. "Look. I did what you wanted. I kissed your lousy metal *thing*. I thought that was what it took—"

"It *takes* what it *takes* for anyone. Kissing. Hugging. Caressing. Licking. Sucking. Jesus Christ, do I have to talk you through it? Are you a virgin?"

"I offered to do that."

"Then shut up and do it."

This was not a gentle man, even if he was no killer. He left teeth marks. And he didn't like it. He didn't like one bit of it, but there was no going soft this time. He loomed up over me, staring directly into the camera lens on top of the shell. The deep-set eyes looked like fighters', when they die with them open (they usually do).

"What are you?" There was a loud smack of skin on skin. "What are you?"

I adjusted my vision to stare beyond his head to the ceiling, but he sensed it and moved up higher. My other lenses were buried in the pillow. He brought his face closer, filling my vision.

"What do you do in there?" Smack. Harder. "Make faces? Grit your teeth? No staring at the ceiling this time." I felt the shell bump against the headboard and I pressed my palms to it to prevent damage. "What are you?" Smack. "What are you?"

It went on and on, going nowhere. If this was the fas-cination of Desperadoes, it was a bigger cheat than the street fights. He didn't even play the audience in the end.

His face became as blank as the ceiling, his movement as even as though he were counting the beats.

Then he stopped suddenly. It surprised me so much, I half sat up.

"There *is* some way to get a reaction out of you," he said and flicked a finger against the shell, making it ring.

"That hurts."

He flicked his finger again. "That hurts?"

"The vibrations inside."

"Other vibrations." He was moving again, with the same expression the Reaper had worn before he had brought his scythe down between the Teddy and Ferret-face. But he was no killer. "Does that *thing* cover your whole body? Do I have to *eat* and *drink* and *smoke* and *come* for you, too?" Flesh hit flesh on each word.

"That's right!" I blared, jacking up the sound as far as it would go. "You have to come for me, too. And then when you've had it for me, you can have it for yourself!"

The volume startled him so much that he lost control and he did come. There was no pleasure in it for him. He simply waited for it to stop, holding his position and watching me.

"All right. That was for you." He began moving again. "This one's for me. It's not over yet. Not yet."

Under his voice, I began picking up other voices. I aimed my directional toward the one window across the small room. There was a crowd gathering almost right under it. Nothing was over yet. There was going to be still another fight before evening.

"You're not going to steal this one from me." Smack. "This one's mine."

"This is gonna be a good one for a change," said a woman outside. "Even if it takes forever."

"They always do," said another woman. "Theatrics. Showing off."

Smack. Smack.

"I've never seen *this* combination before."

His face filled my vision again. "Is this what you're supposed to be?"

"I hope I don't lose a bundle like I did this morning!"

"You won't lose it," I said.

"What?" He couldn't hear the people outside. "You bet I won't. This one's mine." Smack. *"Mine."* Smack.

"Oh, *good!*" a woman squealed. "That's g*ood!*"

Smack. Smack. Smack. It stung and burned. The crowd gasped.

"Excitement," I murmured. "Lots of thrills."

Smack. Smack. His face contorted, every muscle pulling away from every other one. His breath was coming in raw gasps through his open mouth. The crowd was yelling.

"What are you?" he rasped. "What are you?" Smack. Smack.

The crowd was applauding. There was a definite favorite.

"What the hell are you!" Bone hit bone under skin, bruising. "What are you!"

Smack. Smack. There was a chopping noise and the crowd groaned.

"What are you?" He reared up, straining. "What are you?" Smack. Smack.

Outside, several bones broke so loudly they must have ripped through flesh. The crowd loved it.

"What are you? *What are you?*"

The crowd was hollering.

"What are you?"

I could no longer hear the sound of his body slamming against me. The crowd was roaring. The fight was too good to be true; the kill was coming at any time.

"What are you!" It carried him over the top. This time he loved it, every moment. It held him up, arched back, gasping loud, dry sobs for an interminable time before it finally released him and let him collapse. Surprisingly, even deadweight, he was not very heavy. The crowd screamed louder, pleased and shocked all at once. He dragged himself out of me, clambering over my legs to sit slumped at the edge of the bed.

"Finish her!" someone screamed over the crowd. The Desperado's head snapped up, and he frowned.

"Fight outside," I explained. "I've been listening to it."

His features relaxed dully. "And did it help?"

I sat up carefully, drawing my legs together. "Questions. Nothing but questions. If you're so concerned——"

His hand whipped out and clamped onto my arm, pulling me to him. His eyes seemed to bore into the shell, as though they could see the ruins of my face through the metal.

"I thought it was obvious," I said. "I'm a woman."

He got up and began to pull on his clothes languidly. The crowd was going crazy.

"That's it. That's the whole thing," I said. "No special attachments."

He zipped up his pants. "What's that steel trap on your head for?"

"For me. For a while. For good. Or for bad. For you, protection."

He shrugged on his vest and swept his hat up from the floor. "I don't know much about protection, and I don't know about you. What the hell was this?"

"This was the earth, moving. You don't believe it? *Eppur si muove.*"

He put on his hat and waited. I should have known he was not a scholar. The crowd below the window peaked, the screams tearing their throats. Finished.

"You," he said, "are a crazed bitch."

"If that is what a woman is, I am that."

He caressed his vest tenderly, his hands much gentler on it than they had been on me. "Screw it, *woman*. Be something else."

I made a show of cleaning my fingernails of his skin. "There is nothing else."

"There's everything else."

"There's nothing else!" I blared at him, getting up on my hands and knees.

"Look at you," he said. "You crazed thing. You like this. You like it all. Go into a restaurant, someone drinks coffee for you. Eats a meal. Has a drink. Smokes a cigarette. Later on you come here and he screws you and he screws himself." He walked over to the bed and squatted down to look directly at me. "I'd rather have me some stupid little glitterbaby, a Holy Virgin, a Teddy-girl. They aren't real, but they *do*. They don't just watch."

I sat back. "You deserve to be screwed. You have an asshole where your brain should be." White noise. My laughter. "Desperado. You and all of them. Acting out your fantasies as a way of life. Is that your best fantasy? Is it your best one? Because if it is, it's piss-poor compared to some of the ones I've got? You're all like desperation machines on repeat cycle. You've got a way out and you don't take it. You don't take it!" The sheet tore under my digging fingers. I yanked as hard as I could, jacking up my hearing so that the ripping noise became an orgy of sound. I must have done a zoom on his eyes because they filled my vision, but I couldn't tell how far away he was. They moved away suddenly and I heard the door open and close like thunder. Stumbling as though I were drunk, I went to the window and looked down at the crowd ten feet below. It was breaking up. Money was changing hands over the body of a Jungle Woman. Her arms were missing, the blood forming fans of darkening red around her shoulders. She looked as if she were pinned to the ground by the ice pick in her belly. I could tell by the phony jewels in the handle it belonged to the glitterbaby in the scream-blue leotard. Coils of electric green hair stood out from his head like spiky springs. He was expressionless as he took his share of the winnings from his handler.

The Desperado appeared among the stragglers, ghosting his way through them until the glitterbaby with gilded nipples stopped him. She put out a twinkly-nailed hand to feel his crotch. He grabbed her wrist, pulling her arm up. But he didn't push her away.

So you all go, I thought, leaning against the window. The glass was cold on my arms. If anyone noticed me, they gave no sign; a naked woman in a window isn't noteworthy. *So you all go. You live as though you have no way out. As though you were locked into boxes marked 'Glitterbaby,' 'Teddy-boy,' 'Jesus Christ,' 'Desperado.' But I'm the one in prison and you're free and you turn your painted backs on it. I have a shell on my head. What's your excuse?*

The Desperado let go of the glitterbaby and turned his head to look up at me. I did a close-up on his face, and I realized he had heard me.

The glitterbaby tugged at him, pulling him away with her as I stepped back from the window and went to sit on the bed.

I had wondered sometimes, after I disconnected my cameras and microphones, before I went to sleep, if the day would come when the force of my thoughts would be stronger than the metal that locked them in. How miraculous is life. At that range a Desperado had heard them, the first one to hear my thoughts for—how long had it been? It didn't matter. They would know soon and come for me.

I thought again about going among the Normals, ignoring their stares and discomfort, making my own solitary way. No doubt there were as many criers and killers among them as among the Characters. But the Characters were easier to find—they were moving targets with "Stick it here" printed on their bodies. Besides, if I was to be cut off by a steel cage on my head (would they make it stronger? Could they?), it was as well to be cut off from a glitterbaby as from a normal person. If there really was such a thing. I wondered.

They didn't come to take me to the laboratory under the city by the time I had gotten dressed, so I went out. It was about time to be hitting the bars, and I felt like getting someone to do some heavy drinking for me.

I took the long way around to my first stop of the evening, walking slowly in the dying day and thinking, with greatest concentration, *Come and get me.*

THE FOUR

≈≈≈≈≈≈≈≈≈≈≈≈≈≈≈≈≈≈≈≈≈≈

by Gary Woolard

Gary Woolard, in the great tradition of science fiction folk, discovered his brother's stack of *Weird Science* comics at the age of five and invaded said brother's stack of *Astounding* at the age of ten; he claims that things have not been the same since. He currently lives in Los Angeles and works for the aerospace industry, a profession which, he says, "simply demonstrates that you must use imagination to apprehend reality." The application of that principle is gloriously obvious in the following story, his first professional sale.

First-contact and first-invasion stories are not unknown, but we think you'll agree that Woolard has applied his strange imagination to the concept and developed a treatment entirely new.

THE FIRST PIECE I SAW WAS ONE OF STARK'S. It was just thirteen lines, written in that semi-sonnet form of his that's become so familiar by now, with the extra beat at the end. It's in his first collection, *Empty Graves,* if you're interested. But I saw its first publication in the back pages of one of the "little" magazines. That was before the *re:Views* cover, before anybody had heard of Alan Stark, or Andros Niarchos, or Oglesby, or Lyenko. Before Ticketron handled their readings and kids wore them on their T-shirts. Before they became superstars.

They didn't do it alone. They had help. I was the one who put together the article for *re:Views.* I was the one who lumped them together and called them simply "the Four."

Alan Stark. A lyrical Thomas Wolfe, they call him. Dark and burly, with T-shirts and a tattoo on his arm. A New York taxi-driver who is always walking across the nighttime skylines of his city.

I took a photographer and followed him one night. We caught up with him at the Brooklyn Bridge, just in time to catch the end of his *Death Song*—

"... sung in the blood,
and whispered in the marrow,
that Cain slew his brother at the Olduvai Gorge"

—when the sun came up. The photographer had a field day.

Jefferson Oglesby, the West Coast Kid. All red hair and green eyes, always laughing, always partying. He keeps a weather eye out for West Coast plastic society as he makes his motorcycle runs up and down the coast highway, past the Naugahyded coffee shops and the institutes of human awareness. Wears striped sweatshirts and tuxedos alike as if they were some sort of outlandish costume.

Andros Niarchos. The Greek from Florida. They said he'd been a sponge diver till he became too old too soon, crippled by the bends. Now he sits on the pilings and spins his folk rhymes in his head. And it's true enough that you can hear the cool wash of water in his words, and the comforting pressure.

Christina Lyenko. Eurasian and exotic. Her father was a White Russian adventurer, her mother a caste Indian. Long dark hair, almond eyes, and those high slavic cheekbones. Peasant dresses and earrings that jingle-jangle at her ears. And a voice that sounded like rusty wind. "She has brought lyric romance back to poetry," I wrote for the article, "and made it respectable." I thought she was beautiful.

That's how I put the article together, and marveled at it. They fit the archetypal mold so well! I knew already that they would become a phenomenon; feted, discussed, and dissected.

But something was missing. Whatever it was that had led me to group them together in the first place. I knew I was right, but nothing in the article answered the question. Why were they "the Four"? I sat with pieces of the article spread around my desk, some in paste-up, some already in galley form, and worried at it.

We had some good Ansel Adams–type photos to run over excerpts of Niarchos' poems. A silhouette of Stark against the sunrise of the Brooklyn Bridge. An interview with Oglesby that wound up as a stream of word association, entertaining if slightly bizarre—

—but nothing to get a handle on Christina Lyenko. A couple of photographs, looking rather posed, a stiff smile on a beach. Excerpts of some of her more romantic work. And an interview that gave little more than the humble artist refusing to judge. I leafed through the raw interview transcript.

*Q: But don't you find it difficult being a romantic
    in this cynical, twentieth-century culture?*

*A: No, the trappings are different, maybe. The
    way of . . . going . . . of communicating may. ,
    sometimes be more difficult. But the feelings,
    the needs, are always the same.*

Q: Universal, would you say?

A: Whatever size that universe may be.

Q: Could you explain that?

*A: If I write a poem. If you read it. Together, we
    constitute a universe.*

*Q: So there are a myriad of universes for each re-
    lationship between poet and reader?*

*A: Or lover and lover. Lover and hater. Or even
    lover and one indifferent.*

I flipped through until I found the section I was looking
for—the standard question I had asked each of them.

*Q: Miss Lyenko, three other poets, beside yourself,
    have suddenly found the public eye; Oglesby,
    Niarchos, and Stark. Are you aware of their. .
    work? And can you see any commonalities?. .*

*A: (a pause) I have read some of their material,
    yes. And found it refreshing. But each, all of us.
    write in different styles, after all, and about
    different kinds of things. I don't really see any
    common link.*

*Q: Yet each of you has been able to use the tools
    of poetics in a new and, as you said, refreshing
    manner. And at the same time your work has
    been understandable and meaningful to the lay-
    man—a public language. Perhaps you share
    the same muse?*

A: (a smile) Perhaps.

To the standard question the same indifferent answer
that each had given.

But Christina in herself was a contradiction. The
most emotional, most open of the four in her work, she
kept the lowest profile of any of them. She wrote of lovers,
but was seen always by herself. Her poems were filled
with empathy, but she kept aloof, reserved, in conversation. It was as if she saved it all to put on paper. If I

could somehow get a tag on her, find out what made her tick, I thought, I could discover what made each of them tick. Or find that I was wrong.

I caught the next flight to San Francisco.

She lived on a houseboat in Sausalito—typical image of the American poet. Paint peeling off in wide strips, leaving sections of planking open to rot. It was a hulking driftwood sculpture.

There was no answer when I knocked on the cabin door, so I walked on around the deck till I came to a narrow window on the other side. It was filmed over with dust; I wiped a spot clean and peered through.

There wasn't much to see. A single bed was pushed up against one wall, with a footlocker next to it. There was a kitchenette area, which looked immaculate. No dirty towels, no dishes in the sink.

And no pictures on the walls. No calendar, no grocery list tacked to a bulletin board. Less than a hotel room would have. It was more like a monk's cell, or the bower of a virgin queen. And no sight, no sound, of activity.

A desk and chair were tucked into the far corner of the room. A small globe, perched on the edge of the desk, threw a subdued light over its surroundings. I took it for some sort of night-light. The desk itself had no cubbyholes, no drawers—just a flat black surface with a pad of paper and a pen on it.

And the top sheet of paper had writing on it—a "work in progress." At least that was something.

I backed away from the window and went to lean against the railing. A gasoline slick floating on the surface of the water reflected colors in the afternoon sun, and the boat rocked gently in the tide.

She was a paradox. A Gordian knot of contradiction, waiting to be loosed.

A single bed. She wrote of breath giving way to breath, of hair tangle-spread across a pillow, of shift of limbs, of mind-tossing night visions that sprawl your body across the sheets. Yet she slept in a single bed, stiff and unforgiving.

Her poetry, full of power and emotion, and the interview, with all answers reasonable and self-contained.

And she lived in a void, created in a void. I couldn't

understand it. She had to have some source, some well-spring of that power.

It was becoming something much more than a magazine article. I wanted to know what she smiled at and what she was frightened of. What kinds of things she invested her care in, what kinds of artifacts, if any, she invested with her own soul. What brought out the little girl in her, all giggles and innocence.

I wanted to know what made her grind her teeth. If she spent a lot of time trying on clothes in the morning. If she saw a quality in the morning light unshared by the afternoon. If she liked the wind, or if it made her nervous.

And of all of these, how she could translate their human sensibility into a poem. Again and again, my mind kept spinning back to that sheet of paper on the desk. If I couldn't tease the knot apart, that work in progress was a proffered sword.

Suddenly I was very itchy.

To catch the act in process. To see what she left out, as well as in. The pain of meanings missed and lines slaughtered. An idea yammered at the base of my skull and refused to let go. I had to see that paper.

I walked back and stared hungrily through the window. She might be back soon, she might not be back tonight. But the article had to be set up the next day to make the printing run, and I could just make it if I caught the evening flight and spent the night recomposing.

I told myself I'd just take a quick look. I told myself it would make for a better article. But my palms were damp and my throat was tight, and I didn't give a damn about the article. What I wanted was a way in.

I found it on the upper deck which formed the cabin's ceiling; a trap-door which was held by a simple latch on the inside. A solid shove tore the latch right out of the soft wood, and I dropped down into the room below.

The trap-door let a narrow shaft of light fall through, as if from a church casement, and left the rest of the cabin in darkness. The place smelled slightly of mold. I blinked hard, trying to adjust my eyes to the darkness.

A quick glance around revealed nothing I hadn't seen from the window, so I went immediately to the desk and picked up that top sheet of paper. I felt like a voyeur as I brought it closer to the light globe.

And found chicken tracks. The characters weren't any

kind of Latin script, or Cyrillic, or anything like Chinese ideographs or hieroglyphs. Not even cuneiform wedges. They were nothing I'd ever seen before.

But they were beautiful chicken tracks. Rich and complex characters, done with obvious care and patience; there was nothing random or disharmonious about them. Bird wings. Asterisk-looking things, some with loops falling off at the bottom. Pie segments cut from a rainbow. French rococo snowflakes. And minute architectures of dots.

The characters were grouped close in neat, vertical columns. There was a column of seven characters. Next to it, a group of three. Another of seven, then a column of five. Then the pattern would begin again. The lines seemed to carry an almost readable organization with them, a feeling of sensibility.

But it was just a feeling. For all their beauty, for all their form, all I could see were chicken tracks. I plopped down into the chair, disgusted, and just sat there for a moment, staring into the globe. I couldn't figure it out. And I felt as if I were being cheated.

When you're in the dark, and there's just a single source of light, that light seems to grow, seems to fill your whole universe as your pupils expand to accept the illumination. That's what happened as I stared into the lamp, or globe, or whatever it was. Slowly, though, another thing began to happen.

A globe. A crystal ball. A cloud of milk-white fire. Stare at it, and it seems to have the bleak hardness of all the loneliness in the world. Stare at it a little longer, and you fall into it; it seems to carry the depth of all the world. It seems to carry all the answers. It seems to carry the Stained Glass Capital A Answer.

The all-encompassing, plug-everything-in, multimodular equation. Beginnings and ends, causes and effects. Universal balance sheets. Snakes chasing their tails. Secret magics of life and death. Pentode tubes speak of Aristotle with crystal purity. Aristotle speaks of causes, first, final, and efficient, and the final cause is Zeus. Zeus wrestles with Jacob on the floor of the Sinai desert, and has changed his name to Yahweh.

Freud called it "the oceanic feeling," and described it as neurosis. Nowdays, neurologists call it a "synaptic explosion," and liken it to an epileptic fit. Whatever, it's a marvelous camera, focused at infinity, and all the little truths become facets of a single, shining gem.

It wasn't just a waking dream anymore, not just that teasing incomplete fragment of a second. I had hold of it, and I did not doubt. I could have told you why Man created God, why God created Man, and erased any contradiction. I could have told you why Mona Lisa smiled, and what the statues of Easter Island said with granite tongues. I could have completed "The Unfinished Symphony" or Coleridge's "Kubla Khan." I could write about the butterfly.

When I was about four or five, I found a cocoon. My parents clipped it off the twig for me, and put it in a jar by my bed. Finally one morning, I woke up and saw that cocoon start to split. In my pajamas and cowboy hat, I carried the jar out to the front yard and watched as it opened. Saw the butterfly crawl up to the rim of the jar. Saw the wings unfold, slowly, and spread out to dry in the sun, becoming hard and shiny with color.

It stayed that way for about five minutes; an eternity— then it made a first, cautious flap of wings, and suddenly it was gone, in a long bright glide across the lawn.

I'd thought often about the cocoon, the butterfly, and that child in pajamas and cowboy hat. Now that pulsing globe gave me the power to write it down. Every nuance, all the emotional context, could be put into words, into a structure as fragile, as precise, as a butterfly's wings. I grabbed the pen, the sheet of paper—

And looked again at the page of chicken tracks. But this time I could read them:

You	*(identity marker, sibling brother's nest)*
see the first	*(primal light, first vision of seed from the mud)*
way,	*(process, procedure, line. The thin [thread] of a [spider])*
I the second.	*(identity marker, self) (In process, continuance—tension across the middle of the thread)*
The third way	*(full cycle, completion)*
lies	*(inert, a dead thing)*
Between us,	*(bipolar tension, not transitive, sadly irremovable)*

a sword	*(general marker, tool, modifier destructive, waiting, a barrier)*
across	*(separation, breaking of tension, the [spider] [thread] cut)*
our bed	*(first shared nesting, unsanctified sibling incest)*

And reading, I could understand, as if it were some half-forgotten memory. A memory of a place where time ran in atom sands. Where a fecund wind brought intangible blends of sweats and perfumes, exotic odors that stuck at the back of my throat. Where another sun than mine peaked a few angstroms higher in the blue. Where the night's sky was pasted over with colors, and its constellations described other beasts than mine, and played out other myths.

This was the common denominator; this was what made them the Four. I'd been trying to find a human essence, a human commonality, and it wasn't there. They fit the archetypes, the expectations, because they'd tailored themselves into them. They wore our dreams.

Then the light went out. That pulsing, immediate illumination that made all things understandable, all things expressible, was gone from the globe. A hand was resting on its dark surface.

It was Christina Lyenko.

I rose from the chair, and saw Jefferson Oglesby standing near the cabin door, looking at me without expression. The two of them together.

Lyenko was the first to speak. "Please," she said, "give me the paper."

I discovered that I still had in my hand the sheet of chicken scratches. It could be the beginning of a bargain.

"Look," I said, "I don't care who you people are or where you came from. But let me use the globe, just once, and I'll go. I have a poem too . . . about a butterfly." I was reaching for words, and they all sounded so dead and foolish now, without the light.

She turned to Oglesby, and he bird-whistled at her. He didn't purse her lips together, the sound came from down in his throat. But what I heard was a shrill, rapidly modulated bird whistle. She bird-whistled back at him, then said to me, "I'm sorry. It would be dangerous for you. It's not . . . attuned properly."

"Dangerous! Damm it, I understood, I nearly had it all!" I was almost screaming now. I held the paper up in front of me. "And I'll tell them! It's not fair that you should—"

That's when Oglesby came at me in a running dive.

The force of his tackle threw us both against the deck, knocked the breath out of me. I managed to kick him away as we fell, and he crashed backwards into Lyenko, which brought her down as well. I saw something fly away from her face as she fell.

And I'd lost the sheet of paper. It went flying sometime during the tussle to land on the cabin floor. Oglesby scrambled across and grabbed it.

That was it, the end of the game. We all sat on the floor, staring at each other like embarrassed children. They had the paper, I had nothing.

Christina Lyenko had lost a contact lens.

Something was wrong with her eye.

She didn't say anything, she just swept her hair away from her face, tucked her feet underneath her, and looked at me. One eye was the almond I had known, the other was—

Trifurcate. An iris split like a cat's, but with three sections instead of two. It made a three-pointed star out of the pupil. I could see a membrane darting across the eye, and thought of a nervous insect, a praying mantis.

She reached out a hand to me then. Maybe in supplication, maybe to help me up. I don't know. But I wouldn't believe that that eye could see any vision that mine could; that she and I could share any commonality of experience. Not right then.

So I got off the floor and got myself the hell out of there. They didn't try to stop me.

I called the *re:Views* office and tried to get the story killed. All I got was an "extended leave of absence." They ran the story with what I'd already put together.

That was the last I saw of the Four. The last I read of their poetry. The last I had anything to do with them.

I keep thinking, nowadays, about something Plato said of the poets—how you have to watch them. They get you marching along to a certain rhythm, a certain way of going, he said, and then they'll change the scansion on you. You can't trust them.

Maybe that's what the Four are trying to do—to slowly

change our poetry, the beat of the drum. To change, oh so slowly, the way we speak and think of ourselves. To what end, I wonder?

And I had a dream last night. One of those pre-dawn visions with all the answers. It was a poem-dream about the butterfly; just the way to say it, all the truth about childhood wisdom and aged innocence. But there was no way to record it, no way to repeat it. I dreamt it all in bird's wings and rococo snowflakes, and asterisks with loops falling off the bottom.

Who could have thought that for the first wave they'd have sent their poets?

COMSTOCK

by Alan Ryan

Alan Ryan began writing in 1977 and has since sold and published an impressive number of stories, appearing in four editions of *Chrysalis,* in *Other Worlds,* the *Magazine of Fantasy & Science Fiction,* and the *Berkley Science Fiction Book,* among others. In addition, he has completed work on his first novel (*Panther!,* scheduled for publication by NAL/Signet in 1980) and has two further novels in progress. "Comstock" represents his first appearance in *New Dimensions,* but it will surely not be his last.

Ryan was born, and currently lives, in New York City. He was a Graduate Fellow in English at U.C.L.A. for two years, after which he spent nine years teaching English, drama, creative writing, and dance criticism. He has also been Director of Audience Development for an off-Broadway theater and has reviewed books for a number of national publications.

"Comstock" is a sensitive, carefully detailed story which, we think, will quietly take up permanent residence in your mind, much as it has in ours.

THE FAMILIAR VOICE WAS STILL TALKING, asking the impossible, when Comstock hung up the telephone. His trembling fingers made plastic clatter against plastic.

"Leave me alone," he said to the now silent instrument. The sound of his voice bounced off the wooden floor and walls of the cabin. It made the room feel hollow. The only other sound was the rattle of rain gusts against the window.

He stood rock still, watching the telephone, fearful it would ring again, but unwilling even to let that thought form clearly in his mind.

He waited in the silence, hearing the rain, feeling a nerve twitch in the back of his neck.

Finally, after waiting long enough to know it would not ring again, not now, not for a while, he let his gaze wander from the telephone. Beside it was a cup, a heavy ceramic mug, half filled with coffee that had now grown cold. He watched, as if from outside himself, as his right hand reached for the cup, picked it up, held it out over the bare floor for a moment, then dropped it.

It was not a violent act, more like a speculative gesture, one performed to see what would happen. He watched as the cup spilled its brown liquid onto the floor, then hit with a solid thud. The handle snapped off clearly and lay in the pool of coffee. The cup rolled in half a circle, rocked, then lay still.

Comstock squatted beside the stain on the floor, looking into the patterns of dark coffee on light wood, and waited

157

for the voices. They were coming. He could hear them now, again, even after all this time. He had known they would come. He had known all along they would come.

Davey!
Yeah!
Ready to check? Check to check?
Ready!
Turn around. Hold still, for God's sake.
Love your suit. Who's your tailor?
Guy I met on Earth. Met him in my worldwide travels. Does all my suits. White, he'll only do them in white. Gotta break him of the habit.
Yeah, maybe a nice dark gray, double-breasted . . .
I could use something double-breasted.
Go nice with your plastic hat.
Hey, pipe down, you guys.
Martians don't have breasts. Don't need 'em.
Shut up. Just check me out.
Check. Check. Check.
Zipper. Snaplock. Velcro. Check. Hurry.
Come on. Hurry up.
Got a date?
Double-breasted Martian.
I told you, they . . .
Hurry up! That's a whole planet out there. A whole virgin planet.
See? Double-breasted virgin Martians!
Saturday night leave on Mars.
Shut up and check.
You're done. Okay. Hurry up with me.
Turn around.
Like doing a goddamn minuet in here.
After you, sir.
You better believe it.
Sand.
Red, pink, red.
Mars.
No moon, no dead rock. A planet, a world.
Race you to the rocks.
Don't . . .
Take it easy, you two.
Pink, goddamn pink.
Race you to the rocks.

Hey . . .
Run, red, rocks, run, red, rocks, run, red . . .
Davey!
Oh . . .
Jesus!
JESUS!

Nothing happened for three hours. The phone call had come early on Monday morning. That meant, Comstock knew, that McQueen had gone home Friday evening to think about calling him, asking him. McQueen would do that. So he had thought about it and made up his mind and then first thing Monday morning he had called. And asked the impossible.

McQueen should know it was impossible. He should, Comstock kept thinking, he should. But he doesn't. Nothing McQueen ever set out to do was impossible. Maybe, Comstock thought, with a mixture of admiration and bitterness, that was because McQueen only set out to do the *possible,* and only after weighing all the facts. So if he's calling now and asking me to do this, to go back there, he must think . . .

The mountain path leveled out here for a stretch and Comstock's lithe and powerful body fell into a regular rhythm of long strides. It was calming to walk the trail again. It was calming to be away from the telephone too. Then the trail twisted and turned sharply upward again. The irregular ruts left by the morning's rain were filled with rocks and he had to concentrate on each step. He was close to the top. Another five minutes of hiking would bring him to the top, to the fire tower, and a view out over the Catskills with the Hudson River in the distance. Maybe he would climb the tower and visit Culley. Maybe.

Then the trail grew better again and required less attention and he heard the telephone ringing again in his head. So if McQueen is calling me now and asking me to go back there, back there where I can't go, where he knows, God damn it, where he knows I can't go . . . Or does he? What in the hell *does* McQueen know? Hasn't he ever heard of Thomas Wolfe? Doesn't he know you can't go home again?

Go home to another man's grave? Christ, leave me alone, McQueen, please just leave me alone.

He was panting for breath when he reached the flat

area at the top. There was a weathered picnic table and bench under a tree and he walked toward them slowly, trying to steady the rate of his breathing. He knew he shouldn't be out of breath from a short hike like that.

In the six years since he had come to the cabin, the six years he had been climbing this trail two or three times a week, he had seldom seen anyone using the picnic table. Occasionally in the spring or summer there might be somebody there, but more often than not he had it all to himself, as he did now. It had become a familiar and favorite place to stop and think before starting up the tower.

He lay down on his back on the table and stared up through the thick leaves. The wood of the table was still wet from the rain and he could feel the wetness against his back, mixing with the sweat from his climb. The leaves above him stirred gently in a silent breeze, revealing glimpses of bright blue sky. He closed his eyes for a moment and thought he felt the dappled shade brush lightly across his eyelids.

Go home to another man's grave.

The thought slid into his mind unlooked for, unprepared for. He was suddenly conscious of lying on his back. He jerked upright stiffly, open mouth sucking in air, booted feet planted firmly on the bench for balance.

Go home to another man's grave.

God, it was getting to him. He had sworn, promised himself, he would not let it get to him. All these years, two in Switzerland, six here in the Catskills, all these years he had repeated that promise to himself. He had made himself ready for it because all along he had known that someday it would come, in one form or another, a telephone call or a letter or a knock at the door, wherever the door might be, but it would come sooner or later and he would be ready for it.

And finally it had come and he had hung up the telephone and now he was sitting here sweating and gasping for air and wondering when McQueen would call back. Because McQueen *would* call back. When Anson McQueen wanted something, he didn't stop reaching until he got it. And now he wants *me,* Comstock thought. And I don't know if I want to let him have me. I don't know.

At least he was thinking about it more calmly, he realized, and that made him feel better. With a sigh, he pushed himself off the table and walked toward the base of the fire tower, one hand twisted behind him, plucking the wet shirt away from his back.

The tower was tall, taller than seemed necessary to Comstock. It was on the top of the highest mountain in that part of the Catskills and the view from the base of it extended for miles. The tower looked even taller than it was, perhaps, because it looked so fragile, even flimsy. He had climbed it many times and been rewarded each time with a couple of hours of quiet conversation with Culley, who spent all day, every day, watching out over the forests, waiting for disaster and hoping not to find it. He was used to climbing the tower but every time Comstock climbed it he was afraid.

It was too tall, too fragile. It swayed in the slightest breeze. His own weight, climbing the steel steps, swaying around the platforms to go up another flight, made the whole tower move. Culley must be able to tell when someone even leans against the base of the tower, Comstock thought. He made a note to ask him about it, then threw his head back and looked up to the top where the tiny hut was perched. With a sharp intake of breath, he placed a foot on the bottom step and began the climb. All the way up, around and around each flight of stairs, he kept one hand on each of the thin railings.

Halfway up the tower, the breeze that had been warm and whisper-soft down below sent a cold chill up his back where the wet shirt clung to it. Imagine going all the way to another planet and coming all the way back and still being afraid of heights, certain heights, anyway, heights that . . . He pushed the thought away, as he always did, and kept climbing. He slid his hands along the thin pipe railings so he wouldn't have to let go.

Finally, holding tight with one hand, he raised the other and knocked at the trapdoor above his head. Before his knuckles touched it, the door flew open and Culley's hand reached down to hoist him up. In another moment he was sitting, breathing heavily, on the floor of the hut. In the whole climb, he had not once allowed himself to look down.

Culley Grant had few visitors in the tower and he felt very possessive of those he did have. Nothing was different this time. In half an hour, most of which was spent silently looking out over the dark green hills, he managed to find out what little there was new to learn about Comstock's life since he had been there five days earlier. That was the routine. Long stretches of silence, of watching the unmoving hills, punctuated by a few brief questions, even briefer answers, the pop of a soda can from the small cooler. It suited both of them that way.

At last, after a long stretch of silence during which Comstock could feel the tower swaying beneath his feet, he found his voice and the silence tore and fell away.

"They want me to come back."

Culley swung his head slowly in a wide arc, surveying the portion of the earth for which he was personally responsible, but said nothing for a long time. His gaze never left the green hillsides.

"Where?" he said at last.

So he had said it and it was out in the open. Now Comstock knew he would have to think about it, talk about it. If they had been in an ordinary room in a house on the ground, instead of up here in this hut so far above the mountaintop, Comstock thought he might have changed his mind and walked out of the room.

There was no walking out of this room and perhaps, murmured some indistinct voice in his head, that's why you came here. And now he had to talk about it.

"They want me back in the space program," he said. "They want me to join the team for the Mars Mission."

Culley nodded, as if only half listening, eyes still roaming over the hills. But Comstock knew that he was listening and thinking. In previous visits he had told Culley enough, slowly and bit by bit as trust grew between them, for Culley to understand what this meant for him. And why he was afraid he couldn't go back. Or at least couldn't go back to Mars. Not to Mars.

Culley rubbed the back of one hand against the bristle of beard on his chin. A bird flew past outside, battling some invisible current of air. Comstock watched it and waited for Culley to say something.

"I've sat up here by myself for eleven years. Spring and summer and fall, anyway. End of summer's the worst. It's dry then. Most danger of fire. You sit and you watch and you wait."

At first Comstock could make no sense of Culley's

words. The man was talking about himself, not about him, Comstock, and not about space or Mars or . . . Davey. He was talking about himself, his voice soft and musing, the memories of all the lonely springs drifting quietly back through his mind, carried on gentle breezes, breezes that could just as well fan a spark into a flame. Comstock remained silent, listening, wondering.

". . . you wait," Culley was saying. "You just sit and wait. Mostly, nothing happens. Oh, you watch the seasons and the colors, the leaves come and go, the clouds change, things like that. But mostly nothing happens. You just sit and watch and wait. Not too many people come by, either. You and a few others but not many, really. So mostly it's just me up here by myself, watching the hills."

Culley stood up suddenly and his chair scraped on the wooden floor. He stretched his back, then slowly made a circuit of his small hut, studying the rolling hills all around the tower and its mountain. Then, satisfied that they were safe, at least for the moment, he returned to his seat. Comstock hadn't moved.

Culley folded his arms on the map-covered surface in front of him and leaned forward. "I watch the hills and wait for a fire," he said.

Comstock noted the change in his voice, the more personal tone. He was sitting stiffly but didn't change his position; there was something about Culley that could not be interrupted. The straight chair he was sitting on felt hard beneath him.

"That's all," Culley said. "I . . . love these hills, I guess you could say, and I spend my life sitting here waiting for them to go up in flames. Hell of a way to spend your life." He shook his head slightly from side to side. "I read," he said, "I listen to the radio, I daydream. Good for daydreaming up here. But mostly I just sit up here and watch for fires." He shook his head again.

Comstock closed his eyes and felt his own head nodding.

"Some seasons, nothing happens at all. Not a single fire, not even an alarm. Those are the longest seasons for some reason. But I have to watch and wait anyway. Have to."

Comstock's eyes were still closed. One of his legs was numb; he knew he would feel pins and needles when he moved it. He waited for Culley to go on, but the other man remained silent. Slowly Comstock opened his eyes.

"And when you spot a fire?" he said quietly.

Culley's shoulders stiffened. He unfolded his arms, still leaning forward, and one finger traced slow lines over the plastic-covered maps in front of him. The locations of past fires? Comstock wondered. Old scars in the earth, grown over now and healed?

"I sit here," he said. "I call it in and then I sit here and watch the fire eat up the hills." His voice had grown very matter-of-fact. "That's why I'm here. To spot fires."

There was another long silence and this time Comstock felt uncomfortable, almost embarrassed by it. Something in Culley's voice told him that this was almost the limit, this was about as far as intimacy of a sort could go.

He waited a little longer and still Culley said nothing. Finally Comstock broke the silence.

"I better be going."

Culley responded by standing up. Comstock stood too. They carefully avoided looking into each other's eyes. Then the awkward moment had passed and they both knelt beside the trapdoor.

Culley hooked a finger into the ring in the door and pulled it up. "Fires have to be spotted," he said and shrugged.

Comstock lowered himself carefully through the opening in the floor until his feet found a secure footing on the steps below. When his head was just below the floor of the hut, he stopped and looked up. Despite the warmth of the sun, the breeze at this height felt like a cold wind. He kept his hands clasped firmly on the railings.

"I'll let you know," he said.

Culley nodded, said, "Careful with the steps," then let the trapdoor fall solidly back into place.

The wind caught at Comstock's shirt, alternately flapping it against his back and billowing it out, as he cautiously made his way down the swaying steps. When he finally reached the bottom, the solid rock felt good beneath his feet.

Without a pause, although one knee was trembling, he headed immediately for the point where the trail started downward, the trail that would take him home to the telephone and the wait until it rang again.

But the telephone did not ring.

He spent the rest of that day starting chores and projects but dropping them after a short while. Nothing seemed quite as necessary as it had before. He had gotten used to directing his own time, his own life, and he had been satisfied. But now there were other factors to consider, outside forces that were crowding back into his life, other considerations to be weighed. He had been meaning to plant some flower seeds today but now the seed packet lay untouched on the kitchen table as he sipped a cup of coffee. Flowers somehow had lost their importance, their immediacy.

It was late afternoon now and the telephone still had not rung.

He should read. He hadn't gotten any reading done today and he couldn't afford to fall behind. He stood up from the table, crossed to the sink, and rinsed out the cup. He wondered if he would be able to concentrate. Better give it a try, he thought.

The cabin was small. He didn't have far to go to what he thought of as his office. The tiny bedroom had been converted to a working space, much to the puzzlement of the local carpenter, who had never built floor-to-ceiling bookshelves before. He would have been even more puzzled by the small home computer that now filled one corner of the room.

Comstock paused before sitting down at the desk. His eyes traveled around the room, the shelves of books, the stacks of journals. His gaze lingered on the piles of minutes and reports on two of the shelves. They had started coming to him shortly after he returned to the United States and moved into the cabin. He had been glad to have them, all these words and pieces of paper that were the lifeblood of the country's space program. If something so crippled could be said to have any lifeblood at all. They were marked CLASSIFIED, many of them. He wasn't supposed to have them, he knew that, but still they came in the mail. It had to be Anson McQueen who was sending them, breaking the law by doing so, but sending them nevertheless. And Anson McQueen never did anything without a reason.

When you withdrew from the space program you might be a hero or a celebrity, however little deserved that recognition might be, but you weren't privy to information like this. Comstock knew he should have looked into it, should have called Anson, should have done it six years ago. He hadn't. He wanted them, all the classified reports. He needed them.

Sometimes during the last six years he had thought he must be out of his mind. How could you keep up with all the developments in the field when you lived in a lonely cabin in the woods, far away from the scientists, the machines, labs, computers, hardware. Away from the ideas. Away from the dream.

But he wasn't away from the dream. He hadn't been separated from it since he was fourteen years old. After college he had made it come true and then, later, reached the culmination of the dream, or what seemed like it at the moment, for that oh so brief moment, Jesus, that brief moment, that short flash of freedom and exhilaration on the pink sand, the first man to touch . . .

The distant voices swirled through his head and he sat down quickly at the desk. No, no voices, please, not now. Please!

But it wasn't a voice. This time it was a picture. Anson McQueen's face peering at him through a helmet and his own face reflected in Anson's faceplate. And between them a shallow grave with rivulets of pink sand trickling into it. And Davey.

His hands gripped the edge of the desk and pushed and suddenly he was standing. He knocked against a yellow pad at the edge of the desk and it fell to the floor with a clatter, pages curled and crumpled under the cardboard. He left it there and walked unsteadily out to the one large room that served as living room, kitchen, and bedroom for him. Forcing himself to keep his mind blank, he pulled his clothes off, turned on the television, and climbed into bed. He stared unmoving at the flickering screen for hours, sometimes almost physically shoving a painful thought out of his mind, not caring what was on the television screen, not knowing. Hours later, as he was finally drifting off to sleep, he realized that he had forgotten to eat.

Paul! Paul?
What do you want, Davey?
Race you to the rocks.
Davey . . .

Hey, Anson, what's the matter with him, anyway? He says he won't race to the rocks when we get there. I think he's getting fat and lazy.

Who says there'll be rocks?

Gotta be rocks. Red rocks. Great big mothers of rocks.

All right, sonny boy, if there are any rocks there when we land, maybe I'll race you to them. If you're a good boy from now on.

Listen to him, will you listen to him? Hey, Anson . . .

Davey, for Chrissakes, shut up for once, will you?

Aah, you guys ain't got no sense of adventure, that's your problem.

Well, we'll see who gets to the rocks first, kid.

Yeah, we'll see. I oughta shoot you with my ray gun right now and put you out of your misery. Bang.

Davey.

Bang. Bang.

Davey . . .

Bang. Bang. Bang.

Bang. Bang. Bang.

"Paul! Paul?"

With a cold shock, Comstock was out of the bed and across the room in an instant. He had the door open before he was fully awake. The chilly morning air hit him and he realized he was still naked. He shivered.

They stared at each other. It had been eight years and so much had changed.

"Hello, Paul."

"Hello, Anson," Comstock said. The doorknob felt cold in his hand. He pulled it back and stepped aside for Anson McQueen to come in. It didn't seem necessary to invite him.

Comstock closed the door and said, "I'll put some clothes on."

McQueen nodded and looked around for a place to sit as Comstock went to a closet and rummaged inside it for a shirt.

Neither spoke as Comstock dressed and made coffee. When the coffee was poured and they were sitting at the table near the window, Comstock finally cleared his throat.

"I'm sorry I hung up on you," he said.

McQueen shook his head, frowned, and waved one

hand in the air over the table. With a shock, Comstock realized that McQueen was uncomfortable.

It didn't suit him. Anson McQueen was a big man and his broad chest and thick neck made him look strong, forceful. Comstock had never seen him look ill at ease. Never. Not even when they had to dig the grave.

"Listen," McQueen said, and cleared his throat. "You know why I'm here, Paul." He hesitated.

Comstock, still surprised at McQueen's discomfort, had a perverse urge to keep quiet and let him squirm. Yes, he thought, the hell with it, I'll be damned if I'm going to make it easy for him. Okay, Anson, he said to himself, if you want me, come and get me. If you can. He remained silent, studying intently the plume of steam rising from his coffee.

"Look," McQueen said, starting over again. "I know how you feel. I know what you're thinking. But, Paul, you have to understand, I didn't have any other choice. We've reached a point now where"—he hesitated, sucked in a deep breath, and went on—"where none of us have any choice. I know that sounds melodramatic, Paul, but it's the truth. I was in Washington last week, spoke to Senator Clarke. They're going to pull the money rug right out from under us. You have to come back in, that's all."

Comstock felt the tautness in his muscles, knotted as if ready to spring. A vein in the back of his right hand was pulsing regularly. Finally, he managed to lift his head and look in the general direction of McQueen's face. He avoided meeting the eyes that were searching for his own.

"Why, Anson? Tell me why you need me. Tell me why you can't leave me alone."

"All right, Paul, I'll tell you. Do you want the easy answer or the honest one?"

Comstock said nothing.

"Okay, plain and simple, then,'" McQueen said. "You are needed because the gods, such gods as there are, have decreed, in their infinite wisdom, that you become the great living symbol of the space program in all its glory and all its tragedy." He sounded tired.

Comstock wondered if he had rehearsed that speech. It had come too easily to the man's lips and yet it sounded as if he were speaking a foreign language that he had memorized phonetically. McQueen was never given to flowery or poetic speech, not even in mockery or irony. He was not a man with a great deal of sensitivity to irony.

To his surprise, Comstock felt that he was perhaps more at ease in this conversation, or whatever it was, than McQueen. He was surprised because McQueen had always been a powerful man, in his dealings with people as well as in his career. Now he was Director of the Space Program, including the Mars Mission, and Comstock knew that he hadn't gotten there by being hesitant or weak. And yet here he was hesitating and stumbling over rehearsed lines.

Comstock wondered if it was an act. He raised his eyes and this time let them meet McQueen's directly.

"And what about the dead symbol?" he said, the words coming soft and slow. That was cruel, he knew, but wasn't it cruel of McQueen to be here in the first place? Wasn't it?

"Paul, Davey's been dead for eight years," McQueen said.

"I know," Comstock said, hearing and surprised by the sudden gentleness in his own voice. "And I think I killed him. I think you killed him too, Anson, but mostly I think I killed him."

There was another long pause and this time it was McQueen's turn to stare into the wisps of steam from his coffee.

"Paul, listen. There are people in this world who would say things like this are incredibly complicated, I know that. But they're not complicated. They're simple. Look. In a sense, well . . . Okay, we need you for the sheer public relations value of your presence. Now maybe it was just chance or luck, *bad* luck if you want to call it that, that made you the . . . symbol you are in the eyes of the public. But you are and that's all there is to it. Now Washington is threatening to cut off the funds, and this time they'll do it. I've been talking to them. And listening. This time they mean it."

"Why this time?" Comstock said. "What's different about this time?" But he already knew the answer. The newspapers and the reports that came in the mail had been telling this story for a long time. All the indications were that the Mars Mission was going to be a spectacular end to the entire space program. Men would go there, walk on another planet again, but perhaps for the last time, then return home, be patted on the back, and the whole thing would be dead. There would be nothing else.

So McQueen wanted to do something spectacular.

"Paul, there are a million things to spend money on," Comstock heard him saying. "Not everybody sees this the way we do. The way *you* do."

"Why don't you go?" Comstock said suddenly.

"I can't," McQueen answered. "It seems I'm not the hero type. Just a good administrator. And I have a heart murmur."

"Convenient."

"Paul . . ."

"Sorry. But, Christ, Anson, after all these years!"

Then, in an instant, he was standing. He was breathing heavily and his ears felt hot. He heard a movement behind him as he turned away and he knew that Anson was standing too.

The words were coming. He could feel them, pushing their way past the lump in his throat, in one of those awful moments when you know you're about to say something that will destroy you but lack the power to stop yourself. They were coming. Anson, for God's sake, please . . .

"Anson, for God's sake, please, you can't tell me . . . I . . . Anson, he wouldn't be there if we hadn't been so goddamn . . . so . . . god . . ." He was sobbing, hard, dry, choking sobs that wrenched his chest and made his throat ache.

He felt his fists clenching and unclenching. There was a knot in his stomach, twisting his intestines. He swung around. McQueen was watching him, wary, eyes narrowed. Comstock could feel the blood rushing to his face, turning it red.

"For Christ's sake!" he screamed. "Anson! I buried him but I didn't sign up for any fucking perpetual care!"

McQueen watched, balanced on the balls of his feet. When he spoke, his voice was soft.

"Yes, you did, Paul. We all did."

"You bastard," Comstock whispered. "You goddamn lousy bastard administrator." But the anger was gone from his voice now, leaving only the pain and the ache in his throat.

McQueen moved then and sat down heavily at the table.

"You better pack," he said. "I'll make more coffee while you get your things together."

"Now? I . . ."

"We've been working on this for two and a half years. You've got four months to catch up."

Comstock started to move away, then turned back. "I've kept up on all the literature," he said quietly, watching McQueen's face.

McQueen nodded. "Good," he said, without looking up. He began gathering the coffee cups and spoons.

He knew they were glad to have him, that they respected him, that he had been a model and an inspiration for many of them, and that they resented him intensely.

Every day something happened to remind him of it, to keep him aware of it. If he entered the cafeteria alone, they were all preoccupied with food and conversations and didn't notice him until he chose a table and sat down. As far as possible, they avoided meeting his eyes. They didn't invite him home to dinner. They didn't include him in the banter natural to men undergoing severe pressure and barely-contained excitement. They were unfailingly polite.

They were waiting for "the bounce," as they had secretly taken to calling it. Comstock occasionally overheard the term. It needed no explanation for him.

It was simple, as McQueen was so fond of saying about so many things. The six-man crew for the mission had been named long ago, along with four back-up crewmen. Now he was going. That meant one man had to be dropped, bounced.

Comstock had no idea which man McQueen had in mind or when he would make the announcement. But he knew it had to be soon. There were only six weeks left. The final crew had to learn to work comfortably together and, besides, it was cruel to let the man to be bounced go right down to the wire without telling him. He made up his mind to ask McQueen about it, hoping at the same time that McQueen would not ask him to make the decision. Comstock already knew which of the six men he would bounce. And he knew for all the wrong reasons. Or rather, he corrected himself, for *the* wrong reason.

But he didn't have to ask McQueen about it after all. Five weeks to the day before the scheduled launch date, McQueen pulled at his arm in a corridor. They were alone, at least for the moment.

"I'm bouncing Vanelli," McQueen said, without preamble or explanation. "I'll tell him tonight and announce it tomorrow."

They stared at each other for a long second, then McQueen turned and went back down the corridor the way he had come. He had been following him, Comstock realized, watching for the right moment, when they would be alone but would not be able to talk about it.

McQueen had disappeared around a corner before Comstock reacted.

So it was Vanelli. Vanelli, the nice-looking young kid who, of all of them, showed the most visible excitement about his great adventure. Vanelli.

David Vanelli. Everybody called him Davey. In two and a half months of training, Comstock had never once addressed him by his first name.

Slowly, eyes almost closed, Comstock continued down the corridor.

He was busy, too busy to think. He had time measured in weeks to master what the others had spent years learning. He didn't doubt his ability to do it. He didn't stop to consider the question, because he knew what would happen if he let his mind wander from the drill or the exercise or the lecture or the practice manual. So he just worked.

And then, two mornings after McQueen told him about Vanelli, he was running by himself on the outdoor, red clay track, counting laps, counting steps, and ahead of him was a running figure in a white warm-up suit that caught the bright morning sunlight.

He faltered, felt, heard the gravel crunch underfoot. His mouth was open, panting for air. He had no time to will the vision away, the vision of the running white fig-

ure on the red ground in front of him. The air burned in
his lungs. He opened his mouth to scream . . .

Davey!
Yeah!
Come on, hurry up.
After you, sir.
Race you to the rocks.
Hey!
Davey!
Oh . . .
Jesus!
JESUS!

. . . but nothing came out. His body pitched forward,
off balance. His legs pumped faster.

Then he was standing, gasping, chest heaving, in
the bright sunlight. He closed his eyes and threw his
head back to suck air into his lungs and the sunlight
shone through his eyelids with a frightening pink glow.

The days passed, and the nights. Somehow.

And he knew McQueen was watching him.

Then McQueen sent for him. They hadn't talked privately since Comstock had arrived. Comstock had the
uneasy feeling, when the idle thought flickered through
his mind, that McQueen had been taking pains to avoid
private meetings. But now McQueen had sent for him.

The big man braced his arms against the edge of his
desk and leaned forward, his heavy shoulders hunched
up around his neck.

"You're doing well," he said.

Comstock said nothing and waited, doggedly using the
time to review the morning's briefing session in his mind.

McQueen looked down at his hands, then up again at
Comstock. "How do you feel?" he said.

Comstock's muscles stiffened, but he forced his body
to remain seated casually in the chair. So, he thought.

"I'm fine, Anson. You know that." And let that be
the end of it, he added to himself. Let that be the end
of it.

McQueen nodded absent-mindedly and Comstock
sensed that it wasn't an act, not this time, that McQueen
was thinking about something else. He relaxed the ten-

sion of his body slightly but kept his eyes on McQueen's tired-looking face.

"They're closing in on us, Paul," McQueen said. And now he sounded tired as well as looked it. His voice was guttural, as if he needed to clear his throat but wasn't aware of it. Or simply didn't care. Comstock wondered which it was, but still said nothing. Best to let him talk, he thought. If he wants to talk personally, let him do all the talking. Not me.

"Senator Clarke is the best friend we have in Washington," McQueen said. "He's done everything he can for the space program, short of signing up for a flight." McQueen snorted. "But right now, with the appropriations debate coming up, it looks like he's fighting a losing battle. You know, Paul, ten years ago I wouldn't have believed it. But it's the truth. They're going to kill our appropriation. They really are. Just like that," and he snapped his fingers. It made a hard ugly sound in the silent room.

Comstock kept his eyes on the man's face, trying to read what the man was not saying out loud. There was something . . .

"At least he's been able to accomplish one thing. And I shouldn't say 'at least,' considering what a grandstand play it is."

He looked at Comstock for a reaction, got none, and went on.

"He used a little leverage with the scheduling committee. They'll be voting on the space bill in the middle of the mission, with all the publicity going full blast and headlines every day and anything else we can wangle out of it to put some pressure on Washington. Anything we can use to keep this whole operation alive."

His voice trailed off softly. Then he hunched forward further on the desk, bringing his head down even lower. Comstock noticed the network of tiny lines around his eyes and wondered if he was aging the same way himself.

"Cheap trick, huh?" McQueen said softly.

"Cheap trick," Comstock said in the same tone. Somewhere inside him, far away, he felt an almost forgotten urge to grin, but it faded away before it reached the surface. He nodded and said again, "Cheap trick."

McQueen sighed gently and sat up in his chair.

"I thought you'd want to know about that," he said, and this time his eyes evaded Comstock's.

Comstock rose and walked silently to the door of the office. He paused with one hand on the doorknob and turned back to face McQueen. The words escaped him, as if he were thinking them for the first time as he heard himself saying them out loud.

"I only work here, Anson," he said. "I'm just a traveling salesman. I don't direct company policy."

He turned and closed the door, but something about McQueen's expression puzzled him as the door blocked it out. As he resumed his schedule for the day, he tried but could not readily name the expression.

Then, at dinner that evening, he realized what it was and why it had puzzled him. He had never seen McQueen look gentle before.

And then there were no days or nights left and the launch was a few hours away.

There was a line of officials, grinning and excited as they shook hands and slapped the shoulders of the six of them in turn. McQueen was last in line, closest to the elevator that would carry them up the side of the rocket. He and Comstock exchanged handshakes and hearty poundings on the back just as all the others did. Then the six of them turned and waved to the crowd and the cameras before following the technicians into the elevator.

The elevator gate clanked shut in front of Comstock, its rattling looseness a sharp contrast to the sleek body of the rocket behind him. The elevator jerked once, then again, and slowly, vibrating beneath his feet, began to rise.

Comstock's eyes met McQueen's, locked, then flicked away. It was no more than a moment, but there was something there, something in Anson's eyes, that he did not want to see, especially not now.

The elevator rose with labored slowness, jerked again, and halted about two feet up. For an instant, the scene was frozen. Then someone—Comstock thought it was McQueen—jumped forward to the button panel. The elevator shuddered, then slowly descended and came to rest level with the platform.

McQueen pulled the gate open. "Hell of a thing," he

said. "Instead of going on a little jaunt, you guys get stuck in an elevator." There were dutiful laughs all around.

"Built by the lowest bidder, huh?" someone said behind Comstock. Another voice said, "That old joke." And another muttered, "I hope we don't have to listen to jokes like that for months."

Comstock barely heard the voices. He was thinking about climbing the scaffolding to the top of the rocket.

A mechanic started to tug at a trapdoor that led to the elevator gears, but McQueen ordered him away. "We're not taking any chances," he said. "You guys are too valuable. So you walk." There was some good-natured grumbling. Comstock heard someone say, "A journey of a thousand miles . . ."

He started up the steps. He was last in line. The thought flashed through his mind that he shouldn't be last. Suppose he slipped. Or something. There should be a tech behind him. But in the shifting around and the moment of confusion, he had ended up last. It wasn't heights that scared him, just . . .

The helmet was in his left hand. He realized it with a jolt when he stretched out both hands to grasp the rails. He could only hold on with one hand. Drops of sweat beaded suddenly on his forehead and prickled his skin.

He reached the first landing, the first turning. How many more? He knew but he forced the idea of counting out of his mind. Just keep climbing.

One more flight of steps. Another landing. He turned and started up again. More steel steps. More. Another flight. Keep climbing. Don't count.

The steps swayed very slightly beneath his feet. They were white-painted steel, molded with a pattern of treads. Solid. But all around him was open space. The structure was meant to be functional, nothing more. Another flight. There were eleven steps in each flight. He focused his eyes on the step directly ahead at eye-level.

He was sweating inside the suit. It was designed to keep him alive on Mars. Here it was just cumbersome. They only wore them for the visual effect, for the cameras and the folks back home. His face was drenched in sweat. He couldn't wipe it away. One hand gripped the helmet. The other was sliding tightly along the thin pipe railing.

He was falling behind the others.

Another flight, another turning. A breeze drifted across his face as he turned, then came around and blew across the sweat on the back of his neck. He shivered. His foot hesitated on the next step. He went up another flight, eyes riveted straight ahead. The scaffolding drifted slowly past. Careful with the steps. Be . . .

Careful with the steps.

The toe of his right boot hit the lip of the next step. His hand clenched the flimsy railing. The sudden movement jerked his eyes free from the steps rising in front of him. He saw the ground below.

The tower. The fire tower. Of course. Keep climbing, keep climbing. Careful with the steps.

Careful with the steps.

Culley. That was it. Culley, waiting for a fire, all his life spent waiting for a fire, and all the while hoping never to see it.

Going home to another man's grave.

The steps of the scaffold swayed more now. Unavoidable at this height. The breeze was stronger. It felt cool on his crew-cut head. A drop of sweat ran into his eye. He shook his head, trying to clear it. He thought he could feel the structure reflect his own movement, the shifting of his own weight.

The face of Culley-McQueen-Davey floated by, whipped away.

Going home to another man's grave.

And something else . . .

The others were now a whole flight ahead of him, around the next turning.

He kept climbing.

You sit and watch and wait. It was all so simple, really. You . . .

He turned and started up another flight. He kept himself from looking up to see how many were left. He was afraid it might be more than he thought.

. . . sit and watch and wait. So simple. The breeze, stronger and more insistent now, whispered the words at him. You go to Mars, you refuse to come back, it's easy if you do it right, plan it right, time it right, watch your supplies, your air. You sit and watch and wait and stick it out and don't go crazy and then they have to send another ship, another flight, to get you. They have to, everybody will be watching, they have to. The ship is built, it could be done, it could be done in time, you'd still be alive, waiting. *I'd* still be alive.

He was at the top. The railing slid out from under his right hand. He was stooping forward. He straightened up quickly.

The cage at the top was small and crowded. Three of the others had already climbed through the doorway. The two ahead of him were waiting till the first ones were settled.

"What took you so long, buddy? You're keeping everybody waiting. Changed your mind?"

Comstock looked up and wrenched his mouth into a grin.

The words would not come but it didn't matter. The others had turned away.

He paused, found himself breathing deeply, drawing the cool air deep into his lungs. He was surrounded by wire mesh and somehow it was enough to make him feel safe.

He stepped forward and grasped the mesh with his right hand. It was warmer than he expected, not cool like the air.

He looked down and saw McQueen. The figure was far below, but Comstock knew it was him, separated from the other figures, back away from the base of the rocket to get a good view, and waving. The arm of the tiny figure far below semaphored back and forth in slow motion.

Comstock freed his fingers from the wire mesh and slowly began to move his arm.

A voice yelled from inside the doorway. "C'mon, Comstock. What the hell you waiting for?"

The single word formed silently on his lips.

Fire.

He moved his arm in a long slow arc once more, then turned, crossed the narrow platform, and stepped carefully through the doorway.

KID PHOTON

≈≈≈≈≈≈≈≈≈≈≈≈≈≈≈≈≈≈≈≈≈≈≈≈≈≈≈≈

by Steven Bryan Bieler

Steven Bryan Bieler (the last name rhymes with Steeler) is a native of Massachusetts currently residing in Seattle and is the proud possessor of a strange-job list which, we think, wins the *New Dimensions 11* award for this issue; among them are numbered cashier, chauffeur, cook, dishwasher, janitor, newspaper reporter, secretary, security guard, schoolbus driver, ticket agent, typist, waiter, and warehouse worker. Impressive, no? In addition, Bieler has published science fiction in *Unearth* and poetry in *Dark Horse*.

He appears here with a deceptively simple story about poetry, and children, and robots, and growing up, and that unnameable thing which marks the difference between those who do and those who can't. From the evidence of "Kid Photon," Bieler possesses that unnameable thing to a pleasing and impressive degree.

AN ICE CREAM SUNDOWN, PEARL WROTE, scribbling industriously. The sky and its assembled topping of clouds are a mixed dish of blueberry mint and shredded strawberry, with a ripple of peach sown in. She stopped and studied her dairy product prose. She squinted speculatively at the sundown in question and shifted uncomfortably on her perch of crumbly shale high above the rocky, crumbly world. Yes, a sundown could resemble a dish of ice cream in point of color, but what about taste? Was that important? Pearl had never eaten ice cream; she was a robot, and not built for digestion. She sighed, or performed the mechanical equivalent of sighing, ripped the sheet of paper from its pad and let it fly on the wind. Another poem shot to hell.

It is not easy being the robot attendant for an observatory on a quiet ringed planet, when you would much rather be Percy Bysshe Shelley.

Her time sense told her she could stay no longer from her official duties. She had learned some useful obscenities from miners in her area, and she utilized one of them now. But she might as well try to eat ice cream as execute the action it described. This did not improve her irritability.

She stood carefully on the precarious shale, a lithe figure the color of copper coins, and picked her way down the spine of the ridge and into the valley under the first stars and the thin racing Rings. Pebbles slid from under her in tiny avalanches and were replaced by more pebbles from higher up. "Stupid rocks," she said. She would have spit if she could. Broken stone was the chief physical characteristic over most of her world. "I wish you all the fates a rock finds unpleasant!"

True night came down and the Milky Way filled the rifts between clouds with wheatfields of light. She paused to orient herself by this aid. Her professional persona gave way to her hidden desire. Starry thumbtacks pin the clouds to a black backing, she composed, but could go no further. Stars were her job; she did not feel romantic or inspired by them. People might be, but robots were blocked by too analytical an outlook. Stellar masses and luminosities, unclear reactions and molecular gasses overpowered her poetic observations. Pearl fired off another choice expression, this time one that nobody could perform.

A night wind blew in puffs and whispers. Rock dust hovered and fell. Pearl climbed cursing over a succession of boulders clogging the ragged valley floor. A weathered rock face gave way under her mass and she dropped a short distance. She jumped to her feet and kicked pebbles in all directions. She shook a steel fist at the eroding boulder. "Damn you rock and the mother who bore you!" She kicked more pebbles at it.

"Don't make a move!" hissed an excited voice, low to the ground.

Pearl froze. Her interior temperature flared and she hastily compensated. She amplified her senses to their limits, especially her hearing and night vision. She tapped her reserve energy reservoir. Her metal muscles tensed. She had heard the wild rumors of dangerous men lurking hereabouts, the criminal detritus of a civilized galaxy. Were the rumors true?

"Turn around, slow," the high-pitched voice commanded.

Pearl turned and faced her adversary. He was about five years old and towered as high as her knees. He was dressed in dirty leather pants, shirt, and embroidered jacket. Two chubby hands gripped the handle of a plastic blaster, undoubtedly built for the child by some harassed uncle or older brother.

The robot's internal systems returned to normal and she experienced feelings similar to relief and vexation.

"Oh, Luis, what did I ever do to you! Can't you leave me alone?"

"The name ain't Luis, ma'am," the little boy said. "It's Kid Photon."

It was hard to be a cranky robot in the company of Luis. "Pleased to meet you, Kid," Pearl said, and extended her hand. Kid Photon holstered his blaster, took her huge hand in both of his tiny ones, pumped it vigorously, released it and trained the weapon on her again.

"Are you going to fry me with that thing, Kid?"

The blaster's open mouth wavered, then pointed away. "Reckon not," its owner said. The blaster went back into its holster, a pliable black plastic arrangement outlined with shooting-star studwork.

"My circuits thank you. You're out kind of late, aren't you, Luis? I mean, Kid Photon?"

"I thought you might need me, Pearl."

"You did?"

"Yup. Reckon you could always use an extra gun, ma'am."

The previous week Kid Photon had been Captain North Star, inspired by the gift of a glittering uniform hat with a visor so heavy it continually fell down over his face, and Pearl had put in several hours as his brave starship. Before the hat a set of miniature hand tools and an apron with pockets had sparked the creation of Doctor Mechano, Robotical Surgeon, and Pearl had narrowly escaped exploratory operations on her feet, arms, and head.

"I'm glad you were thinking about me. This certainly is rough country." She regarded the microscopic gunslinger shrewdly. "Listen, Mr. Photon, you know it is getting very late. What are you really doing out here?"

"Will you tell?" he asked anxiously.

"Of course not."

"I ran away from home."

"Now why did you do that? Your parents must be terribly worried. They'll have searching parties out soon."

Kid Photon kicked at the pebbles beneath him. "They're mad at me. I didn't do my chores 'cause I had to fight off the pirate space guys from the Rings."

"Pirates are always a problem."

"So I ran away 'cause they were gonna punish me."

He looked at her, his black eyes reflecting stars and Rings. "And I think I'm afraid of the dark."

Pearl's time sense nagged her again. The observatory was staffed only by her and required her presence to begin the evening's work. "You know, I've always wanted to start my own gang. But I need someone who's good with a gun." She pretended to consider the boulders around her, the tip of one steel finger meditatively placed where her lips would have been were she organic. "Who should I pick . . ."

"Pick me! Pick me!"

"Oh, Luis! I mean, Mr. Photon! Would you like to join my gang?"

"You bet!"

"All right then, you are now the first member of the Deadly Pearl Gang. I'm the boss. Will you do exactly as I tell you to?"

"Yup!"

"I've always admired your vocabulary. I see I'll have to make you my second-in-command. If anything happens to me you'll take over. Do you think you can handle the responsibility?"

"Sure. I ain't a baby, you know."

"I know." She got down on her knees. "I want you to ride on my shoulders. We'll get to the observatory quicker and you'll be able to watch for pirates and other bad guys."

The walk consumed half an hour. The pirate space guys never put in an appearance, which was fortunate because Kid Photon fell asleep and his dreaded plastic blaster worked only for him. Pearl transferred her passenger to her cradled arms. He was very light for a gunslinger and posed her few problems in transportation.

The observatory rested on the summit of the tallest pile of rocks in the vicinity. By day the view seemed to stretch around the world. Luis implicitly believed this and was convinced he could see himself from the top of Observatory Summit, as it was called, if he only had the use of sufficiently powerful optical aids. One afternoon, after liberating and discarding as deficient several of the observatory's portable ocular devices, he tried to dismantle a telescope two or three times larger than Pearl. His scientific career ended the same afternoon.

The summit was littered with giant wind-sculpted stones,

their attitudes belligerent in the star- and Ring-light. Like soldiers, Pearl decided, trudging by with her passenger: standing guard over the dome in the service of Science. She thought for a moment she was getting somewhere poetically, but just then Kid Photon awoke and jumped to the ground, waving his blaster and squeaking, "Pirates! Pirates!" and she had to chase after him to prevent his disappearance in a sudden rockslide. She carried him inside and put him to work sorting computer printouts by color, but only after he had inspected the dome's interior for lurking menaces and other threatening phenomena.

The dome was quite commodious and even with a population of six telescopes of various mechanical races, their attendant photographic and analytical equipment, one computer, one control surface, one living area for the attendant (a space screened by a folding wall and filled with back issues of the *Galactic Poetry Review*), the attendant herself, and one small boy, there was ample room for getting into trouble, and so Pearl kept careful watch over her visitor. The computer had been waiting impatiently for its instructions for the evening and had some impolite things on its mind, all of which it flashed on its data screen as soon as it perceived Pearl before it. "Don't nag," Pearl complained, and typed the required information into the system. Immediately the data screen cleared and ports opened in the dome, telescopes moved into position on silent tracks, supporting equipment hummed, and astronomical data flooded in. Pearl stole a moment to contact Luis' parents and inform them of his whereabouts, something she did three or four times a week. They thanked her and promised to be by as soon as possible. She returned to her visitor.

Pearl had been worrying about feeding Kid Photon, but she could have spared herself needless use of her anxiety circuits. Her gang had not ventured forth into the wilderness unprepared. Photon's pockets were filled with an assortment of baked goods, fruits, nuts, berries, and candy of all kinds. He had made a neat pile of them atop a stack of blue computer paper detailing stellar positions over several nights. The robot picked out a piece of candy from the pile. It was a flawless geometrical cylinder, pink, with a white starburst glowing inside it.

"Are you going to eat this?" she asked, incredulous.

"Yup," he said, through a mouthful of blue cake with raisins. "For dessert."

Pearl examined the pile. She found candy shaped like rocket ships with little fins ornamenting the sides, candy like raging volcanoes, candy like Valentine wishes, candy of all colors, violet, yellow, lavender, orange, the color of stars on a clear night and clouds on a sunny day. She held one up to light its interior.

"I could open a chem lab with the stuff you've got here," she said.

"Yup." Kid Photon was an experienced outdoorsman. He expertly squeezed his collection of fruit to obtain their juices before turning his contemplation to the candy. Decisions here were difficult. "If we was up here during the daytime we wouldn't have to worry about those pirates, Pearl."

"Why is that, Kid? Are they afraid of heights?"

"Of course not," he said scornfully. "Pirates love being up high. They come from space, don't they?"

"I guess one follows the other. But why are we safe now?"

"We ain't safe now. If it was the daytime we'd be safe now, because they'd all be asleep, that's why." After considerable deliberation he popped a candy with twelve legs and a wiggling tail into his mouth.

"Those pirates are awfully lazy," Pearl commented.

"They sure are. See, look up there!" And he pointed through an open port to the flying Rings, blazing bright as they arced through the night sky.

"What am I looking at?"

"The Rings, silly. You know how invisible they are when the sun is out? That's 'cause the pirates are all sleeping. But at night the Rings are lots brighter. That's 'cause the pirates are awake then."

"You mean they get up at night and they turn on all the lights."

"Yup. 'Cause the sun is gone, and they gotta see."

"Why don't they just sleep at night and be pirates during the day?"

" 'Cause they're lazy."

"You sure know a lot about pirates, Mr. Photon."

"Reckon so, ma'am."

"You get bothered much by pirates, out around your way?"

"Yup. I guess 'cause we run a big mine," he said proudly. "It's an oil-shale mine. We have a whole lotta people working for us and we make so much oil the pirates come after us almost every week."

"How come?"

"I think they need the oil for their spaceships."

"Those pirates are smart."

"Sure are."

Pearl made her rounds of the dome, Kid Photon trailing watchfully behind. If a telescope in its programmed course vacated an open port the Kid was instantly there, blaster atomizing pirate space fleets with every snap of the trigger. "You pirates you!" he cried, adding a series of frightening noises produced with his lips and tongue. Pirate ships being constructed of inferior materials, no doubt a consequence of their owners' slothful habits, the plastic blaster slew them in droves.

During a lull in the hostilities and while Pearl was distracted elsewhere, Kid Photon sat himself at the computer keyboard and began entering a historical account of his part in the great battle. The data screen rapidly filled with a jumble of letters and mathematical symbols. The computer made a brave attempt at translation and surrendered. The screen cleared itself and flashed back: INVALID TRANSACTION IDENTIFICATION PLEASE RESUBMIT, which bothered the busy gunslinger not at all, not being able to read. He continued his activities. The computer flashed another INVALID message, replaced it with PROBLEM AROSE DURING ORDER ENTRY PLEASE CANCEL & RESUBMIT, got tough with THIS UNIT CANNOT OBEY INSTRUCTIONS OF CURRENT OPERATOR, and finally resorted to activating the emergency lighting system to catch Pearl's attention. The flashing red lights brought the robot running. "You old nag, he was just playing," Pearl admonished as she lifted the protesting Photon from his seat. Luis typed one last sentence with his foot before he was totally out of reach. The computer was indignant and did not hesitate to say so. "You are too a nag," Pearl declared and turned her back on it. She put Luis back to work on the colored paper project, where she found him a short time later using a stack of soft white paper for a pillow, blaster forgotten while he slept. The pirates had evidently retired to lick their wounds and hatch new plots.

Luis' mother arrived at midnight in a mining copter.

Pearl met her as the craft put down on the cramped landing area occupying the summit with the observatory. They walked into the dome making polite conversation about the weather and each other's work. They had met many times through Luis but this forced familiarity did little to make them comfortable with each other. The mother could not wholly assure herself that a machine, no matter how intelligent, was the proper playmate for her son; and the robot dealt so exclusively with machines it was unsure how to deal with people. Friendship seemed impossible.

Kid Photon was soon made comfortable in the copter, from which he waved happily to Pearl before falling asleep again. The mother paused for a few words before leaving. "You won't have to worry about my son interfering in your work anymore, Pearl."

"Why is that, Lita?"

"Our company is transferring us to a new world. It's just been opened to exploration and it's a great opportunity for us."

"Well, congratulations! When are you leaving?"

"Tomorrow. They needed people quickly and we were offered the position just this evening. It's so sudden, but it's such an opportunity! We couldn't pass it up."

"I don't blame you," Pearl said, and there followed some aimless chatter about moving and career advancement.

Lita offered her hand and Pearl shook it. "Thank you for taking care of my son," she said.

"It was my pleasure."

"Maybe we'll come back one day to visit."

"That would be nice." Even Pearl could see how polite a promise this was.

"I'm sorry Luis can't come by to see you before we go, but there won't be enough time."

"I understand. He'll forget all about me soon enough, I'm sure."

"Good-bye, it was nice knowing you."

"Good-bye, you too."

The copter lifted into the night. Pearl walked back to the dome and made her rounds. Soon she needed to check something. She referred to the stacks of computer paper. She was using some yellow sheets and a special writing stylus to untangle a mathematical complication when she noticed the plastic blaster. They had forgotten the toy. She picked it up with her free hand. She examined it from every angle. It was scratched and dented from much contact with hard surfaces. She sighted along the barrel and worked the action. She thought of Luis and his delight in the gun. She thought of Luis and she thought of Luis some more and she thought of Luis never coming back, Luis growing up and forgetting all about her, and she disregarded her astronomical problems. She stared out an open port at the racing Rings and listened to the quiet borne on the night winds. She stared a long time.

Pearl put the blaster down and turned a sheet of yellow paper over. The side exposed was blank. She pressed the stylus to it. The computer, having flashed several messages on its screen about matters it considered important, gave up and turned on the warning lights. Pearl did not answer. She was writing her first poem.

THE FEAST OF SAINT JANIS

by Michael Swanwick

Michael Swanwick's first science fiction story was written in junior high school; although he's been writing ever since, "The Feast of Saint Janis" represents only his second sale, his first having been to *Destinies.* Born in Schenectady, New York, he grew up in Vermont and Virginia and received a B.A. in English from the College of William and Mary. In the traditional manner of writers, he has held down a number of strange and interesting jobs: as a yardman for a tourist motel, a short-order cook for McDonald's, a something for the Pennsylvania Department of Health's Bureau of Laboratories. He currently works for the National Solar Heating and Cooling Information Center at the Franklin Institute in Philadelphia. None of these foreshadows in the least the stunning, absorbing tale which follows, of a strange future America and the gods who serve it. On the evidence of this story alone, it is obvious that Swanwick is a writer to watch in the 1980s.

Take a load off, Janis,
And
You put the load right on me ...
          —"The Wait" (trad.)

WOLF STOOD IN THE EARLY MORNING FOG watching the *Yankee Clipper* leave Baltimore harbor. His elbows rested against a cool, clammy wall, its surface eroded smooth by the passage of countless hands, almost certainly dating back to before the Collapse. A metallic gray sparkle atop the foremast drew his eye to the dish antenna that linked the ship with the geosynchronous *Trickster* seasats it relied on to plot winds and currents.

To many the wooden *Clipper,* with its computer-designed hydrofoils and hand-sewn sails, was a symbol of the New Africa. Wolf, however, watching it merge into sea and sky, knew only that it was going home without him.

He turned and walked back into the rick-a-rack of commercial buildings crowded against the waterfront. The clatter of hand-drawn carts mingled with a mélange of exotic cries and shouts, the alien music of a dozen American dialects. Workers, clad in coveralls most of them, swarmed about, grunting and cursing in exasperation when an iron wheel lurched in a muddy pothole. Yet there was something furtive and covert about them, as if they were hiding an ancient secret.

Craning to stare into the dark recesses of a warehouse, Wolf collided with a woman clad head to foot in chador. She flinched at his touch, her eyes glaring above the black veil, then whipped away. Not a word was exchanged.

A citizen of Baltimore in its glory days would not have recognized the city. Where the old buildings had not been torn down and buried, shanties crowded the streets, taking advantage of the space automobiles had needed. Sometimes they were built *over* the streets, so that alleys became tunnelways, and sometimes these collapsed, to the cries and consternation of the natives.

It was another day with nothing to do. He could don a filter mask and tour the Washington ruins, but he had already done that, and besides the day looked like it was going to be hot. It was unlikely he'd hear anything about his mission, not after months of waiting on American officials who didn't want to talk with him. Wolf decided to check back at his hostel for messages, then spend the day in the bazaars.

Children were playing in the street outside the hostel. They scattered at his approach. One, he noted, lagged behind the others, hampered by a malformed leg. He mounted the unpainted wooden steps, edging past an old man who sat at the bottom. The old man was laying down tarot cards with a slow and fatalistic disregard for what they said; he did not look up.

The bell over the door jangled notice of Wolf's entry. He stepped into the dark foyer.

Two men in the black uniforms of the political police appeared, one to either side of him. "Wolfgang Hans Mbikana?" one asked. His voice had the dust of ritual on it; he knew the answer. "You will come with us," the other said.

"There is some mistake," Wolf objected.

"No, sir, there is no mistake," one said mildly. The other opened the door. "After you, Mr. Mbikana."

The old man on the stoop squinted up at them, looked away, and slid off the step.

The police walked Wolf to an ancient administrative building. They went up marble steps sagging from centuries of foot-scuffing, and through an empty lobby. Deep within the building they halted before an undistinguished-looking door. "You are expected," the first of the police said.

"I beg your pardon?"

The police walked away, leaving him there. Apprehensive, he knocked on the door. There was no answer, so he opened it and stepped within.

A woman sat at a desk just inside the room. Though she was modernly dressed, she wore a veil. She might have been young; it was impossible to tell. A flick of her eyes, a motion of one hand, directed him to the open door of an inner room. It was like following an onion to its conclusion, a layer of mystery at a time.

A heavy-set man sat at the final desk. He was dressed in the traditional suit and tie of American businessmen. But there was nothing quaint or old-fashioned about his mobile, expressive face or the piercing eyes he turned on Wolf.

"Sit down," he grunted, gesturing toward an old, overstuffed chair. Then: "Charles DiStephano. Comptroller for Northeast Regional. You're Mbikana, right?"

"Yes, sir." Wolf gingerly took the proffered chair, which did not seem all that clean. It was becoming clear to him now: DiStephano was one of the men on whom he had waited these several months, the biggest of the lot, in fact. "I represent—"

"The Southwest Africa Trade Company." DiStephano lifted some documents from his desk. "Now this says you're prepared to offer—among other things—resource data from your North American *Coyote* landsat in exchange for the right to place students in Johns Hopkins. I find that an odd offer for your organization to make."

"Those are my papers," Wolf objected. "As a citizen of Southwest Africa, I'm not used to this sort of cavalier treatment."

"Look, kid, I'm a busy man, I have no time to discuss your rights. The papers are in my hands, I've read them, the people that sent you knew I would. Okay? So I know what you want and what you're offering. What I want to know is *why* you're making this offer."

Wolf was disconcerted. He was used to a more civilized, a more leisurely manner of doing business. The oldtimers at SWATC had warned him that the pace would be different here, but he hadn't had the experience to decipher their veiled references and hints. He was painfully aware that he had gotten the mission, with its high salary and the promise of a bonus, only because it was not one that appealed to the older hands.

"America was hit hardest," he said, "but the Collapse was worldwide." He wondered whether he should explain the system of corporate social responsibility that African business was based on. Then decided that if DiStephano didn't know, he didn't want to. "There are still problems. Africa has a high incidence of birth defects." *Because America exported its poisons; its chemicals and pesticides and foods containing a witch's brew of preservatives.* "We hope to do away with the problem; if a major thrust is made, we can clean up the gene pool in less than a century. But to do this requires professionals—eugenicists, embryonic surgeons—and while we have these, they are second-rate. The very best still come from your nation's medical schools."

"We can't spare any."

"We don't propose to steal your doctors. We'd provide our own students—fully trained doctors who need only the specialized training."

"There are only so many openings at Hopkins," DiStephano said. "Or at U of P or the UVM Medical College, for that matter."

"We're prepared to—" Wolf pulled himself up short. "It's in the papers. We'll pay enough that you can expand to meet the needs of twice the number of students we require." The room was dim and oppressive. Sweat built up under Wolf's clothing.

"Maybe so. You can't buy teachers with money, though." Wolf said nothing. "I'm also extremely reluctant to let your people *near* our medics. You can offer them money, estates—things our country cannot afford. And we *need* our doctors. As it is, only the very rich can get the corrective surgery they require."

"If you're worried about our pirating your professionals, there are ways around that. For example, a clause could be written—" Wolf went on, feeling more and more in control. He was getting somewhere. If there wasn't a deal to be made, the discussion would never have gotten this far.

The day wore on. DiStephano called in aides and dismissed them. Twice, he had drinks sent in. Once, they broke for lunch. Slowly the heat built, until it was sweltering. Finally, the light began to fail, and the heat grew less oppressive.

DiStephano swept the documents into two piles, returned one to Wolf, and put the other inside a desk drawer. "I'll look these over, have our legal boys run a study. There shouldn't be any difficulties. I'll get back to you with the final word in—say a month. September twenty-first. I'll be in Boston then, but you can find me easily enough, if you ask around."

"A month? But I thought . . ."

"A month. You can't hurry City Hall," DiStephano said firmly. "Ms. Corey!"

The veiled woman was at the door, remote, elusive. "Sir."

"Drag Kaplan out of his office. Tell him we got a kid here he should give the VIP treatment to. Maybe a show. It's a Hopkins thing, he should earn his keep."

"Yes, sir." She was gone.

"Thank you," Wolf said, "but I don't really need . . ."

"Take my advice, kid, take all the perks you can get. God knows there aren't many left. I'll have Kaplan pick you up at your hostel in an hour."

Kaplan turned out to be a slight, balding man with nervous gestures, some sort of administrative functionary for Hopkins. Wolf never did get the connection. But Kaplan was equally puzzled by Wolf's status, and Wolf took petty pleasure in not explaining it. It took some of the sting off of having his papers stolen.

Kaplan led Wolf through the evening streets. A bright sunset circled the world and the crowds were much thinner. "We won't be leaving the area that's zoned for electricity," Kaplan said. "Otherwise I'd advise against going out at night at all. Lot of jennie-deafs out then."

"Jennie-deafs?"

"Mutes. Culls. The really terminal cases. Some of them can't pass themselves off in daylight even wearing coveralls. Or chador—a lot are women." A faintly perverse expression crossed the man's face, leaving not so much as a greasy residue.

"Where are we going?" Wolf asked. He wanted to change the subject. A vague presentiment assured him he did not want to know the source of Kaplan's expression.

"A place called Peabody's. You've heard of Janis Joplin, our famous national singer?"

Wolf nodded, meaning no.

"The show is a recreation of her act. Woman name of Maggie Horowitz does the best impersonation of Janis I've ever seen. Tickets are almost impossible to get, but Hopkins has special influence in this case because—ah, here we are."

Kaplan led him down a set of concrete steps and into the basement of a dull, brick building. Wolf experienced a moment of dislocation. It was a bookstore. Shelves and boxes of books and magazines brooded over him, a packrat's clutter of paper.

Wolf wanted to linger, to scan the ancient tomes, remnants of a time and culture fast sinking into obscurity and myth. But Kaplan brushed past them without a second glance and he had to hurry to keep up.

They passed through a second roomful of books, then into a hallway where a gray man held out a gnarled hand and said, "Tickets, please."

Kaplan gave the man two crisp pasteboard cards, and they entered a third room.

It was a cabaret. Wooden chairs clustered about small tables with flickering candles at their centers. The room was lofted with wood beams, and a large, unused fireplace dominated one wall. Another wall had obviously been torn out at one time to make room for a small stage. Over a century's accumulation of memorabilia covered the walls or hung from the rafters, like barbarian trinkets from toppled empires.

"Peabody's is a local institution," Kaplan said. "In the twentieth century it was a speakeasy. H. L. Mencken himself used to drink here." Wolf nodded, though the name meant nothing to him. "The bookstore was a front and the drinking went on here in back."

The place was charged with a feeling of the past. It invoked America's bygone days as a world power. Wolf half-expected to see Theodore Roosevelt or Henry Kissinger come striding in. He said something to this effect and Kaplan smiled complacently.

"You'll like the show, then," he said.

A waiter took their orders. There was barely time to begin on the drinks when a pair of spotlights came on, and the stage curtain parted.

A woman stood alone in the center of the stage. Bracelets and bangles hung from her wrists, gaudy necklaces from her throat. She wore large tinted glasses and a flowered granny gown. Her nipples pushed against the thin dress. Wolf stared at them in horrified fascination. She had an extra set, immediately below the first pair.

The woman stood perfectly motionless. Wolf couldn't stop staring at her nipples; it wasn't just the number, it was the fact of their being visible at all. So quickly had he taken on this land's taboos.

The woman threw her head back and laughed. She put one hand on her hip, thrust the hip out at an angle, and lifted the microphone to her lips. She spoke, and her voice was harsh and raspy.

"About a year ago I lived in a rowhouse in Newark, right? Lived on the third floor, and I thought I had my act together. But nothing was going right, I wasn't getting any . . . action. Know what I mean? No talent comin' around. And there was this chick down the street, didn't have much and she was doing okay, so I say to myself: *What's wrong, Janis?* How come she's doing so good and you ain't gettin' any? So I decided to check it out, see what she had that I didn't. And one day I get up early, look out the window, and I see this chick out there *hustling!* I mean, she was doing the streets at *noon!* So I said to myself, Janis, honey, you ain't even trying. And when ya want action, ya gotta try. Yeah. Try just a little bit harder."

The music swept up out of nowhere, and she was singing: "Try-iiii, Try-iiii, Just a little bit harder . . ."

And unexpectedly, it was good. It was like nothing he had ever heard, but he understood it, almost on an instinctual level. It was world-culture music. It was universal.

Kaplan dug fingers into Wolf's arm, brought his mouth up to Wolf's ear. "You see? You see?" he demanded. Wolf shook him off impatiently. He wanted to hear the music.

The concert lasted forever, and it was done in no time at all. It left Wolf sweaty and emotionally spent. Onstage, the woman was energy personified. She danced, she strutted, she wailed more power into her songs than seemed humanly possible. Not knowing the original, Wolf was sure it was a perfect recreation. It had that feel.

The audience loved her. They called her back for three encores, and then a fourth. Finally, she came out, gasped into the mike, "I love ya, honeys, I truly do. But please—no more. I just couldn't do it." She blew a kiss, and was gone from the stage.

The entire audience was standing, Wolf among them, applauding furiously. A hand fell on Wolf's shoulder, and he glanced to his side, annoyed. It was Kaplan. His face was flushed and he said, "Come on." He pulled Wolf free of the crowd and backstage to a small dressing room. Its door was ajar and people were crowded into it.

One of them was the singer, hair stringy and out-of-place, laughing and gesturing widely with a Southern Comfort bottle. It was an antique, its label lacquered to the glass, and three-quarters filled with something amber-colored.

"Janis, this is—" Kaplan began.

"The name is Maggie," she sang gleefully. "Maggie Horowitz. I ain't no *dead* blues singer. And don't you forget it."

"This is a fan of yours, Maggie. From Africa." He gave Wolf a small shove. Wolf hesitantly stumbled forward, grimacing apologetically at the people he displaced.

"Whee-howdy!" Maggie whooped. She downed a slug from her bottle. "Pleased ta meetcha, Ace. Kinda light for an African, aintcha?"

"My mother's people were descended from German settlers." And it was felt that a light-skinned representative could handle the touchy Americans better, but he didn't say that.

"Whatcher name, Ace?"

"Wolf."

"Wolf!" Maggie crowed. "Yeah, you look like a real heartbreaker, honey. Guess I'd better be careful around you, huh? Likely to sweep me off my feet and deflower me." She nudged him with an elbow. "That's a joke, Ace."

Wolf was fascinated. Maggie was *alive,* a dozen times more so than her countrymen. She made them look like zombies. Wolf was also a little afraid of her.

"*Hey.* Whatcha think of my singing, hah?"

"It was excellent," Wolf said. "It was—" he groped

for words "—in my land the music is quieter, there is not so much emotion."

"Yeah, well *I* think it was fucking good, Ace. Voice's never been in better shape. Go tell 'em that at Hopkins, Kaplan. Tell 'em I'm giving them their money's worth."

"Of course you are," Kaplan said.

"Well, I *am,* goddammit. Hey, this place is like a morgue! Let's ditch this matchbox dressing room and hit the bars. Hey? Let's party."

She swept them all out of the dressing room, out of the building, and into the street. They formed a small, boisterous group, noisily wandering the city, looking for bars.

"There's one a block thataway," Maggie said. "Let's hit it. Hey, Ace, I'd like ya ta meet Cynthia. Sin, this is Wolf. Sin and I are like one person inside two skins. Many's the time we've shared a piece of talent in the same bed. Hey?" She cackled, and grabbed at Cynthia's ass.

"Cut it out, Maggie." Cynthia smiled when she said it. She was a tall, slim, striking woman.

"Hey, this town is *dead!*" Maggie screamed the last word, then gestured them all to silence so they could listen for the echo. "There it is." She pointed and they swooped down on the first bar.

After the third bar, Wolf lost track. At some point he gave up on the party and somehow made his way back to his hostel. The last he remembered of Maggie she was calling after him, "Hey, Ace, don't be a party poop." Then: "At least be sure to come back tomorrow, goddammit."

Wolf spent most of the next day in his room, drinking water and napping. His hangover was all but gone by the time evening took the edge off the day's heat. He thought of Maggie's half-serious invitation, dismissed it and decided to go to the Club.

The Uhuru Club was ablaze with light by the time he wandered in, a beacon in a dark city. Its frequenters, after all, were all African foreign service, with a few commercial reps such as himself forced in by the insular nature of American society, and the need for polite conversation. It was *de facto* exempt from the power-use laws that governed the natives.

"Mbikana! Over here, lad, let me set you up with a drink." Nnamdi of the consulate waved him over to the bar. Wolf complied, feeling conspicuous as he always did in the Club. His skin stood out here. Even the American servants were dark, though whether this was a gesture of deference or arrogance on the part of the local authorities, he could not guess.

"Word is that you spent the day closeted with the comptroller." Nnamdi had a gin-and-tonic set up. Wolf loathed the drink, but it was universal among the service people. "Share the dirt with us." Other faces gathered around; the service ran on gossip.

Wolf gave an abridged version of the encounter and Nnamdi applauded. "A full day with the Spider King and you escaped with your balls intact. An auspicious beginning for you, lad."

"Spider King?"

"Surely you were briefed on regional autonomy—how the country was broken up when it could no longer be managed by a central directorate? There *is* no higher authority than DiStephano in this part of the world, boy."

"Boston," Ajuji sniffed. Like most of the expatriates, she was a failure; unlike many, she couldn't hide the fact from herself. "That's exactly the sort of treatment one comes to expect from these savages."

"Now, Ajuji," Nnamdi said mildly. "These people are hardly savages. Why, before the Collapse they put men on the moon."

"Technology! Hard-core technology, that's all it was, of a piece with the kind that almost destroyed us all. If you want a measure of a people, you look at how they live. These—*yanks*," she hissed the word to emphasize its filthiness, "live in squalor. Their streets are filthy, their cities are filthy, and even the ones who aren't rotten with genetic disease are filthy. A child can be taught to clean up after itself. What does that make them?"

"Human beings, Ajuji."

"Hogwash, Nnamdi."

Wolf followed the argument with acute embarrassment. He had been brought up to expect well from people with social standing. To hear gutter language and low prejudice from them was almost beyond bearing. Suddenly it *was* beyond bearing. He stood, his stool making a scraping noise as he pushed it back. He turned his back on them all, and left.

"Mbikana! You mustn't—" Nnamdi called after him.

"Oh, let him go," Ajuji cut in, with a satisfied tone, "you mustn't expect better. After all, he's practically one of *them*."

Well, maybe he was.

Wolf wasn't fully aware of where he was going until he found himself at Peabody's. He circled the building, and found a rear door. He tried the knob; it turned loosely in his hand. Then the door swung open and a heavy, bearded man in coveralls leaned out. "Yes?" he said in an unfriendly tone.

"Uh," Wolf said. "Maggie Horowitz told me I could drop by."

"Look, pilgrim, there are a lot of people try to get backstage. My job is to keep them out unless I know them. I don't know you."

Wolf tried to think of some response to this, and failed. He was about to turn away when somebody unseen said, "Oh, let him in, Deke."

It was Cynthia. "Come on," she said in a bored voice. "Don't clog up the doorway." The guard moved aside, and he entered.

"Thank you," he said.

"*Nada,*" she replied. "As Maggie would say. The dressing room is that way, pilgrim."

"Wolf, honey!" Maggie shrieked. "How's it going, Ace? Ya catch the show?"

"No, I—"

"You shoulda. I was good. Really good. Janis herself was never better. Hey, gang! Let's split, hah? Let's go somewhere and get down and boogie."

A group of twenty ended up taking over a methane-lit bar outside the zoned-for-electricity sector. Three of the band had brought along their instruments, and they talked the owner into letting them play. The music was droning and monotonous. Maggie listened appreciatively, grinning and moving her head to the music.

"Whatcha think of that, Ace? Pretty good, hey? That's what we call Dead music."

Wolf shook his head. "I think it's well named."

"Hey, guys, you hear that? Wolf here just made a funny. There's hope for you yet, honey." Then she sighed. "Can't get behind it, huh? That's really sad, man. I mean they played *good* music back then; it was real. We're just echoes, man. Just playing away at them old songs. Got none of our own worth singing."

"Is that why you're doing the show, then?" Wolf asked, curious.

Maggie laughed. "Hell no. I do it because I got the chance. DiStephano got in touch with me—"

"DiStephano? The comptroller?"

"One of his guys, anyway. They had this gig all set up and they needed someone to play Janis. So they ran a computer search and came up with my name. And they offered me money, and I spent a month or two in Hopkins being worked over, and here I am. On the road to fame and glory." Her voice rose and warbled and mocked itself on the last phrase.

"Why did you have to go to Hopkins?"

"You don't think I was *born* looking like this? They had to change my face around. Changed my voice too, for which God bless. They brought it down lower, widened out my range, gave it the strength to hold onto them high notes and push 'em around."

"Not to mention the mental implants," Cynthia said.

"Oh, yeah, and the 'plants so I could talk in a bluesy sorta way without falling out of character," Maggie said. "But that was minor."

Wolf was impressed. He had known that Hopkins was good, but this—! "What I don't understand is why your government did all this. What possible benefit is there for them?"

"Beats the living hell out of me, lover-boy. Don't know, don't care, and don't ask. That's my motto."

A long-haired, pale young man sitting nearby said, "The government is all hacked up on social engineering. They do a lot of weird things, and you never find out why. You learn not to ask questions."

"Hey, listen, Hawk, bringing Janis back to life isn't weird. It's a beautiful thing to do," Maggie objected. "Yeah, I only wish they could *really* bring her back. Sit her down next to me. Love to talk with that lady."

"You two would tear each other's eyes out," Cynthia said.

"What? Why?"

"Neither one of you'd be willing to give up the spot-light to the other."

Maggie cackled. "Ain't it the truth? Still, she's one broad I'd love to have met. A *real* star, see? Not a god-dammed echo like me."

Hawk broke in, said, "You, Wolf. Where does your pilgrimage take you now? The group goes on tour the day after tomorrow; what are your plans?"

"I don't really have any," Wolf said. He explained his situation. "I'll probably stay in Baltimore until it's time to go up north. Maybe I'll take a side trip or two."

"Why don't you join the group, then?" Hawk asked. "We're planning to make the trip one long party. And we'll slam into Boston in just less than a month. The tour ends there."

"That," said Cynthia, "is a real bright idea. All we need is another nonproductive person on board the train."

Maggie bristled. "So what's wrong with that? Not like we're paying for it, is it? What's wrong with it?"

"Nothing's wrong with it. It's just a dumb idea."

"Well, *I* like it. How about it, Ace? You on the train or off?"

"I—" He stopped. Well, why not? "Yes, I would be pleased to go along."

"Good." She turned to Cynthia. "*Your* problem, sweets, is that you're just plain jealous."

"Oh Christ, here we go again."

"Well, don't bother. It won't do you any good. Hey, you see that piece of talent at the far end of the bar?"

"Maggie, that 'piece of talent,' as you call him, is eighteen years old. At most."

"Yeah. Nice though." Maggie stared wistfully down the bar. "He's kinda pretty, ya know?"

Wolf spent the next day clearing up his affairs and arranging for letters of credit. The morning of departure day, he rose early and made his way to Baltimore Station. A brief exchange with the guards let him into the walled trainyard.

The train was an ungainly steam locomotive with a string of rehabilitated cars behind it. The last car had the word PEARL painted on it, in antique psychedelic lettering.

"Hey, Wolf! Come lookit this mother." A lone figure waved at him from the far end of the train. Maggie.

Wolf joined her. "What do you think of it, hah?"

He searched for something polite to say. "It is very impressive," he said finally. The word that leapt to mind was grotesque.

"Yeah. Runs on garbage, you know that? Just like me."

"Garbage?"

"Yeah, there's a methane processing plant nearby. Hey, lookit me! Up and awake at eight in the morning. Can ya take it? Had to get behind a little speed to do it, though."

The idiom was beyond him. "You mean—you were late waking up?"

"What? Oh, hey, man, you can be—look, forget I said a thing. No." She pondered a second. "Look, Wolf. There's this stuff called 'speed,' it can wake you up in the morning, give you a little boost, get you going. Ya know?"

Awareness dawned. "You mean amphetamines."

"Yeah, well this stuff ain't exactly legal, dig? So I'd just as soon you didn't spread the word around. I mean, I trust you, man, but I wanna be sure you know what's happening before you go shooting off your mouth."

"I understand," Wolf said. "I won't say anything. But you know that amphetamines are——"

"Gotcha, Ace. Hey, you gotta meet the piece of talent I picked up last night. Hey, Dave! Get your ass over here, lover."

A young, sleepy-eyed blond shuffled around the edge of the train. He wore white shorts, defiantly it seemed to Wolf, and a loose blouse buttoned up to his neck. Giving Maggie a weak hug around the waist, he nodded to Wolf.

"Davie's got four nipples, just like me. How about that? I mean, it's gotta be a pretty rare mutation, hah?"

Dave hung his head, half blushing. "Aw, Janis," he mumbled. Wolf waited for Maggie to correct the boy, but she didn't. Instead she led them around and around the train, chatting away madly, pointing out this, that, and the other thing.

Finally, Wolf excused himself, and returned to his hostel. He left Maggie prowling about the train, dragging her pretty boy after her. Wolf went out for a long lunch, picked up his bags, and showed up at the train earlier than most of the entourage.

The train lurched, and pulled out of the station. Maggie was in constant motion, talking, laughing, directing the placement of luggage. She darted from car to car, never still. Wolf found a seat and stared out the window. Children dressed in rags ran alongside the tracks, holding out hands and begging for money. One or two of the party threw coins; more laughed and threw bits of garbage.

The the children were gone, and the train was passing through endless miles of weathered ruins. Hawk sat down beside Wolf. "It'll be a slow trip," he said. "The train has to go around large sections of land it's better not to go through." He stared moodily at the broken-windowed shells that were once factories and warehouses. "Look out there, pilgrim, *that's* my country," he said in a disgusted voice. "Or the corpse of it."

"Hawk, you're close to Maggie."

"Now if you go out to the center of the continent . . ." Hawk's voice grew distant. "There's a cavern out there, where they housed radioactive waste. It was formed into slugs and covered with solid gold—anything else deteriorates too fast. The way I figure it, a man with a lead suit could go into that cavern and shave off a fortune. There's tons of the stuff there." He sighed. "Someday I'm going to rummage through a few archives and go."

"Hawk, you've got to *listen* to me."

Hawk held up a hand for silence. "It's about the drugs, right? You just found out and you want me to warn her."

"Warning her isn't good enough. Someone has to stop her."

"Yes, well. Try to understand, Maggie was in Hopkins for *three months* while they performed some very drastic surgery on her. She didn't look a thing like she does now, and she could sing but her voice wasn't anything to rave about. Not to mention the mental implants.

"Imagine the pain she went through. Now ask yourself

what are the two most effective painkillers in existence?"

"Morphine and heroin. But in my country, when drugs are resorted to, the doctors wean the patients off them before their release."

"That's not the point. Consider this—Maggie could have had Hopkins remove the extra nipples. They could have done it. But she wasn't willing to go through the pain."

"She seems proud of them."

"She talks about them a lot, at least."

The train lurched and stumbled. Three of the musicians had uncrated their guitars and were playing more "Dead" music. Wolf chewed his lip in silence for a time, then said, "So what is the point you're making?"

"Simply that Maggie was willing to undergo the greater pain so that she could become Janis. So when I tell you she only uses drugs as painkillers, you have to understand that I'm not necessarily talking about physical pain." Hawk got up and left.

Maggie danced into the car. "Big time!" she whooped. "We made it into the big time, boys and girls. Hey, let's party!"

The next ten days were one extended party, interspersed with concerts. The reception in Wilmington was phenomenal. Thousands came to see the show; many were turned away. Maggie was unsteady before the first concert, achingly afraid of failure. But she played a rousing set, and was called back time and time again. Finally exhausted and limp, her hair sticking to a sweaty forehead, she stood up front and gasped, "That's all there is, boys and girls. I love ya and I wish there was more to give ya, but there ain't. You used it all up." And the applause went on and on . . .

The four shows in Philadelphia began slowly, but built up big. A few seats were unsold at the first concert; people were turned away for the second. The last two were near-riots. The group entrained to Newark for a day's rest and put on a Labor Day concert that made the previous efforts look pale. They stayed in an obscure hostel for an extra day's rest.

Wolf spent his rest day sight-seeing. While in Philadelphia he had hired a native guide and prowled through the rusting refinery buildings at Breeze Point. They rose to the sky forever in tragic magnificence, and it was hard to believe there had ever been enough oil in the world to fill the holding tanks there. In Wilmington, he let the local guide lead him to a small Italian neighborhood to watch a religious festival.

The festival was a parade, led first by a priest trailed by eight altargirls, with incense burners and fans. Then came twelve burly men carrying the flower-draped body of an ancient Cadillac. After them came the faithful, in coveralls and chador, singing.

Wolf followed the procession to the river, where the car was placed in a hole in the ground, sprinkled with holy water, and set afire. He asked the guide what story lay behind the ritual, and the boy shrugged. It was old, he was told, very very old.

It was late when Wolf returned to the hostel. He was expecting a party, but found it dark and empty. Cynthia stood in the foyer, hands behind her back, staring out a barred window at black nothingness.

"Where is everybody?" Wolf asked. It was hot. Insects buzzed about the coal-oil lamp, batting against it frenziedly.

Cynthia turned, studied him oddly. Her forehead was beaded with sweat. "Maggie's gone home—she's attending a mid-school reunion. She's going to show her old friends what a hacking big star she's become. The others?" She shrugged. "Off wherever puppets go when there's no one to bring them to life. Their rooms, probably."

"Oh." Cynthia's dress clung damply to her legs and sides. Dark stains spread out from under her armpits. "Would you like to play a game of chess or—something?"

Cynthia's eyes were strangely intense. She took a step closer to him. "Wolf, I've been wondering. You've been celibate on this trip. Is there a problem? No? Maybe a girlfriend back home?"

"There was, but she won't wait for me." Wolf made a deprecating gesture. "Maybe that was part of the reason I took this trip."

She took one of his hands, placed it on her breast. "But you *are* interested in girls?" Then, before he could shape his answer into clumsy words, she whispered, "Come on," and led him to her room.

Once inside, Wolf seized Cynthia and kissed her, deeply and long. She responded with passion, then drew away and with a little shove toppled him onto the bed. "Off with your clothes," she said. She shucked her blouse in a complex, fluid motion. Pale breasts bobbled, catching vague moonlight from the window.

After an instant's hesitation, Wolf doffed his own clothing. By contrast with Cynthia he felt weak and irresolute, and it irked him to feel that way. Determined to prove he was nothing of the kind, he reached for Cynthia as she dropped onto the bed beside him. She evaded his grasp.

"Just a moment, pilgrim." She rummaged through a bag by the headboard. "Ah. Care for a little treat first? It'll enhance the sensations."

"Drugs?" Wolf asked, feeling an involuntary horror.

"Oh, come down off your high horse. Once won't melt your genes. Give a gander at what you're being so critical of."

"What is it?"

"Vanilla ice cream," she snapped. She unstoppered a small vial and meticulously dribbled a few grains of white powder onto a thumbnail. "This is expensive, so pay attention. You want to breathe it all in with one snort. Got that? So by the numbers: Take a deep breath and breathe out slowly. That's it. Now in. Now out and hold."

Cynthia laid her thumbnail beneath Wolf's nose, pinched one nostril shut with her free hand. "Now in fast. Yeah!"

He inhaled convulsively and was flooded with sensations. A crisp, clean taste filled his mouth, and a spray of fine white powder hit the back of his throat. It tingled pleasantly. His head felt spacious. He moved his jaw, suspiciously searching about with his tongue.

Cynthia quickly snorted some of the powder herself, restoppering the vial.

"Now," she said. "Touch me. Slowly, slowly, we've got all night. That's the way. Ahhhh." She shivered. "I think you've got the idea."

They worked the bed for hours. The drug, whatever it was, made Wolf feel strangely clear-headed and rational, more playful and more prone to linger. There was no urgency to their love-making; they took their time. Three, perhaps four times they halted for more of the powder, which Cynthia doled out with careful ceremony. Each time they returned to their lovemaking with renewed interest and resolution to take it slowly, to postpone each climax to the last possible instant.

The evening grew old. Finally, they lay on the sheets, not touching, weak and exhausted. Wolf's body was covered with a fine sheen of sweat. He did not care to even think of making love yet another time. He refrained from saying this.

"Not bad," Cynthia said softly. "I must remember to recommend you to Maggie."

"Sin, why do you do that?"

"Do what?"

"We've just—been as intimate as two human beings can be. But as soon as it's over, you say something cold. Is it that you're afraid of contact?"

"Christ." It was an empty syllable, devoid of religious content, and flat. Cynthia fumbled in her bag, found a flat metal case, pulled a cigarette out, and lit it. Wolf flinched inwardly. "Look, pilgrim, what are you asking for? You planning to marry me and take me away to your big, clean African cities to meet your momma? Hah?

"Didn't think so. So what do you want from me? Mental souvenirs to take home and tell your friends about? I'll give you one: I spent years saving up enough to go see a doctor, find out if I could have any brats. Went to one last year and what do you think he tells me? I've got red-cell dyscrasia, too far gone for treatment, there's nothing to do but wait. Lovely, hah? So one of these days it'll just stop working and I'll die. Nothing to be done. So long as I eat right, I won't start wasting away, so I can keep my looks up to the end. I could buy a little time if I gave up drugs like this"—she waved the cigarette, and an ash fell on Wolf's chest. He brushed it away quickly—"and the white powder, and anything else that makes life worth living. But it wouldn't buy me enough time to do anything worth doing." She fell silent. "Hey. What time is it?"

Wolf climbed out of bed, rummaged through his

clothing until he found his timepiece. He held it up to the window, squinted. "Um. Twelve . . . fourteen."

"Oh, *nukes*." Cynthia was up and scrabbling for her clothes. "Come on, get dressed. Don't just stand there."

Wolf dressed himself slowly. "What's the problem?"

"I promised Maggie I'd get some people together to walk her back from that damned reunion. It ended *hours* ago, and I lost track of the time." She ignored his grin. "Ready? Come on, we'll check her room first and then the foyer. God, is she going to be mad."

They found Maggie in the foyer. She stood in the center of the room, haggard and bedraggled, her handbag hanging loosely from one hand. Her face was livid with rage. The sputtering lamp made her face look old and evil.

"Well!" she snarled. "Where have you two been?"

"In my room, balling," Cynthia said calmly. Wolf stared at her, appalled.

"Well that's just beautiful. That's really beautiful, isn't it? Do you know where I've been while my two best friends were upstairs humping their brains out? Hey? Do you want to know?" Her voice reached a hysterical peak. "I was being *raped by two jennie-deafs*, that's where!"

She stormed past them, half-cocking her arm as if she were going to assault them with her purse, then thinking better of it. They heard her run down the hall. Her door slammed.

Bewildered, Wolf said, "But I—"

"Don't let her dance on your head," Cynthia said. "She's lying."

"Are you certain?"

"Look, we've lived together, bedded the same men—I know her. She's all hacked off at not having an escort home. And Little Miss Sunshine has to spread the gloom."

"We should have been there," Wolf said dubiously. "She could have been killed, walking home alone."

"Whether Maggie dies a month early or not doesn't make a bit of difference to me, pilgrim. I've got my own problems."

"A month—? Is Maggie suffering from a disease too?"

"We're all suffering, we all— Ah, the hell with you too." Cynthia spat on the floor, spun on her heel and disappeared down the hallway. It had the rhythm and inevitability of a witch's curse.

The half-day trip to New York left the troupe with playtime before the first concert, but Maggie stayed in seclusion, drinking. There was talk about her use of drugs, and this alarmed Wolf, for they were all users of drugs themselves.

There was also gossip about the reunion. Some held that Maggie had dazzled her former friends—who had not treated her well in her younger years—had been glamorous and gracious. The predominant view, however, was that she had been soundly snubbed, that she was still a freak and an oddity in the eyes of her former contemporaries. That she had left the reunion alone.

Rumors flew about the liaison between Wolf and Cynthia too. The fact that she avoided him only fed the speculation.

Despite everything the New York City concerts were a roaring success. All four shows were sold out as soon as tickets went on sale. Scalpers made small fortunes that week, and for the first time the concerts were allowed to run into the evening. Power was diverted from a section of the city to allow for the lighting and amplification. And Maggie sang as she had never sung before. Her voice roused the audiences to a frenzy, and her blues were enough to break a hermit's heart.

They left for Hartford on the tenth, Maggie sequestered in her compartment in the last car. Crew members lounged about idly. Some strummed guitars, never quite breaking into a recognizable tune. Others talked quietly. Hawk flipped tarot cards into a heap, one at a time.

"Hey, this place is fucking *dead!*" Maggie was suddenly in the car, her expression an odd combination of defiance and guilt. "Let's party! Hey? Let's hear some music." She fell into Hawk's lap and nibbled on an ear.

"Welcome back, Maggie," somebody said.

"*Janis!*" she shouted happily. "The lady's name is Janis!"

Like a rusty machine starting up, the party came to life. Music jelled. Voices became animated. Bottles of alcohol appeared and were passed around. And for the remainder of the two days that the train spent making wide, looping detours to avoid the dangerous stretches of Connecticut and New York, the party never died.

There were tense undertones to the party, however, a desperate quality in Maggie's gaiety. For the first time, Wolf began to feel trapped, to count the days that separated him from Boston and the end of the tour.

The dressing room for the first Hartford concert was cramped, small, badly lit—like every other dressing room they'd encountered. "Get your ass over here, Sin," Maggie yelled. "You've gotta make me up so I look strung out, like Janis did."

Cynthia held Maggie's chin, twisted it to the left, to the right. "Maggie, you don't *need* makeup to look strung out."

"Goddammit, yes I *do*. Let's get it on. Come on, come on—I'm a star, I shouldn't have to put up with this shit."

Cynthia hesitated, then began dabbing at Maggie's face, lightly accentuating the lines, the bags under her eyes.

Maggie studied the mirror. "Now *that's* grim," she said. "That's really grotesque."

"That's what you look like, Maggie."

"You cheap bitch! You'd think *I* was the one who nodded out last night before we could get it on." There was an awkward silence. "Hey, Wolf!" She spun to face him. "What do *you* say?"

"Well," Wolf began, embarrassed, "I'm afraid Cynthia's . . ."

"You see? Let's get this show on the road." She grabbed her cherished Southern Comfort bottle and upended it.

"That's not doing you any good either."

Maggie smiled coldly. "Shows what *you* know. Janis always gets smashed before a concert. Helps her voice." She stood, made her way to the curtains. The emcee was winding up his pitch.

"Ladies and gentlemen . . . Janis!"

Screams arose. Maggie sashayed up to the mike, lifted it, laughed into it.

"Heyyy. Good ta see ya." She swayed and squinted at the crowd, and was off and into her rap. "Ya know, I went ta see a doctor the other week. Told him I was worried about how much drinking I was doing. Told him

I'd been drinkin' heavy since I was twelve. Get up in the morning and have a few Bloody Marys with breakfast. Polish off a fifth before lunch. Have a few drinks at dinner, and really get into it when the partying begins. Told him how much I drank for how many years. So I said, 'Look, Doc, none of this ever hurt me any, but I'm kinda worried, ya know? Give it to me straight, have I got a problem?' And he said, 'Man, *I* don't think you've got a problem. *I* think you're doing just *fine!*'" Cheers from the audience. Maggie smiled smugly. "Well, honey, *everybody's* got problems, and I'm no exception." The music came up. "But when I got problems, I got an answer, 'cause I can sing dem ole-time blues. Just sing my problems away." She launched into "Ball and Chain" and the audience went wild.

Backstage, Wolf was sitting on a stepladder. He had bought a cup of water from a vendor and was nursing it, taking small sips. Cynthia came up and stood beside him. They both watched Maggie strutting on stage, stamping and sweating, writhing and howling.

"I can never get over the contrast," Wolf said, not looking at Cynthia. "Out there everybody is excited. Back here, it's calm and peaceful. Sometimes I wonder if we're seeing the same thing the audience does."

"Sometimes it's hard to see what's right in front of your face." Cynthia smiled a sad, cryptic smile and left. Wolf had grown used to such statements, and gave it no more thought.

The second and final Hartford show went well. However, the first two concerts in Providence were bad. Maggie's voice and timing were off, and she had to cover with theatrics. At the second show she had to order the audience to dance—something that had never been necessary before. Her onstage raps became bawdier and more graphic. She moved her body as suggestively as a stripper, employing bumps and grinds. The third show was better, but the earthy elements remained.

The cast wound up in a bar in a bad section of town, where guards with guns covered the doorway from fortified booths. Maggie got drunk and ended up crying. "Man, I was so blitzed when I went onstage—you say I was good?"

"Sure, Maggie," Hawk mumbled. Cynthia snorted.

"You were very good," Wolf assured her.

"I don't remember a goddamned thing," she wailed. "You say I was good? It ain't fair, man. If I was good, I deserve to be able to remember it. I mean, what's the point otherwise? Hey?"

Wolf patted her shoulder clumsily. She grabbed the front of his dashiki and buried her face in his chest. "Wolf, Wolf, what's gonna *happen* to me?" she sobbed.

"Don't cry," he said, patting her hair.

Finally, Wolf and Hawk had to lead her back to the hostel. No one else was willing to quit the bar.

They skirted an area where all the buildings had been torn down but one. It stood alone, with great gaping holes where plate-glass had been, and large nonfunctional arches on one side.

"It was a fast-food building," Hawk explained when Wolf asked. He sounded embarrassed.

"Why is it still standing?"

"Because there are ignorant and superstitious people everywhere," Hawk muttered. Wolf dropped the subject.

The streets were dark and empty. They went back into the denser areas of town, and the sound of their footsteps bounced off the buildings. Maggie was leaning half-conscious on Hawk's shoulder, and he almost had to carry her.

There was a stirring in the shadows. Hawk tensed. "Speed up a bit, if you can," he whispered.

Something shuffled out of the darkness. It was large and only vaguely human. It moved toward them. "What—?" Wolf whispered.

"Jennie-deaf," Hawk whispered back. "If you know any clever tricks, this is the time to use 'em." The thing broke into a shambling run.

Wolf thrust a hand into a pocket and whirled to face Hawk. "Look," he said in a loud, angry voice. "I've taken *enough* from you! I've got a *knife* and I don't care *what* I do!" The jennie-deaf halted. From the corner of his eye, Wolf saw it slide back into the shadows.

Maggie looked up with a sleepy, quizzical expression. "Hey, what . . ."

"Never mind," Hawk muttered. He upped his pace, half-dragging Maggie after him. "That was arrogant," he said approvingly.

Wolf forced his hand from his pocket. He found he

was shivering from aftershock. *"Nada,"* he said. Then: "That is the correct term?"

"Yeah."

"I wasn't certain that jennie-deafs really existed."

"Just some poor mute with gland trouble. Don't think about it."

Autumn was just breaking out when the troupe hit Boston. They arrived to find the final touches being put on the stage on Boston Commons. A mammoth concert was planned; dozens of people swarmed about making preparations.

"This must be how America was all the time before the Collapse," Wolf said, impressed. He was ignored.

The morning of the concert, Wolf was watching canvas being hoisted above the stage, against the chance of rain, when a gripper ran up and said, "You, pilgrim, have you seen Janis?"

"Maggie," he corrected automatically. "No, not recently."

"Thanks," the man gasped, and ran off. Not long after, Hawk hurried by and asked, "Seen Maggie lagging about?"

"No. Wait, Hawk, what's going on? You're the second person to ask me that."

Hawk shrugged. "Maggie's disappeared. Nothing to scream about."

"I hope she'll be back in time for the show."

"The local police are hunting for her. Anyway, she's got the implants; if she can move she'll be on stage. Never doubt it." He hurried away.

The final checks were being run, and the first concertgoers beginning to straggle in when Maggie finally appeared. Uniformed men held each arm; she looked sober and angry. Cynthia took charge, dismissed the police, and took Maggie to the trailer that served as a dressing room.

Wolf watched from a distance, decided he could be of no use. He ambled about the Commons aimlessly, watching the crowd grow. The people coming in found places to sit, took them, and waited. There was little talk among them, and what there was was quiet. They were dressed brightly, but not in their best. Some carried winejugs or blankets.

They were an odd crew. They did not look each other in the eye; their mouths were grim, their faces without expression. Their speech was low, but with an undercurrent of tension. Wolf wandered among them, eavesdropping, listening to fragments of their talk.

"Said that her child was going to . . ."

". . . needed that. Nobody needed that."

"Couldn't have paid it away . . ."

". . . tasted odd, so I didn't . . ."

"Had to tear down three blocks . . ."

". . . blood."

Wolf became increasingly uneasy. There was something about their expressions, their tones of voice. He bumped into Hawk, who tried to hurry past.

"Hawk, there is something very wrong happening."

Hawk's face twisted. He gestured toward the light tower. "No time," he said, "the show's beginning. I've got to be at my station." Wolf hesitated, then followed the man up the ladders of the light tower.

All of the Commons was visible from the tower. The ground was thick with people, hordes of ant-specks against the brown of trampled earth. Not a child among them, and that felt wrong too. A gold and purple sunset smeared itself three-quarters of the way around the horizon.

Hawk flicked lights on and off, one by one, referring to a sheet of paper he held in one hand. Sometimes he cursed and respliced wires. Wolf waited. A light breeze ruffled his hair, though there was no hint of wind below.

"This is a sick country," Hawk said. He slipped a headset on, played a red spot on the stage, let it wink out. "You there, Patrick? The kliegs go on in two." He ran a check on all the locals manning lights, addressing them by name. "Average life span is something like forty-two—*if* you get out of the delivery room alive. The birthrate has to be very high to keep the population from dwindling away to nothing." He brought up all the red and blue spots. The stage was bathed in purple light. The canvas above looked black in contrast. An obscure figure strolled to the center mike.

"Hit it, Patrick," A bright pool of light illuminated the emcee. He coughed, went into his spiel. His voice boomed over the crowd, relayed away from the stage by a series of amps with timed delay along each rank, so that his voice reached the distant listeners in synchronization with the further amplification. The crowd moved sluggishly about the foot of the tower, set in motion by latecomers straggling in. "So the question you should ask yourself is why the government is wasting its resources on a goddamned show."

"All right," Wolf said. "Why?" He was very tense, very still. The breeze swept away his sweat, and he wished he had brought along a jacket. He might need one later.

"Because their wizards said to—the damn social engineers and their machines," Hawk answered. "Watch the crowd."

". . . *Janis!*" the loudspeakers boomed. And Maggie was on stage, rapping away, handling the microphone suggestively, obviously at the peak of her form. The crowd exploded into applause. Offerings of flowers were thrown through the air. Bottles of liquor were passed hand over hand and deposited on the stage.

From above it could not be seen how the previous month had taken its toll on Maggie. The lines on her face, the waxy skin, were hidden by the colored light. The kliegs bounced off her sequined dress dazzlingly.

Halfway through her second song, Maggie came to an instrumental break and squinted out at the audience. "Hey, what the fuck's the matter with you guys? Why ain't you *dancing?*" At her cue, scattered couples rose to their feet. "Ready on the kliegs," Hawk murmured into his headset. "Three, four, and five on the police." Bright lights pinpointed three widely separated parts of the audience, where uniformed men were struggling with dancers. A single klieg stayed on Maggie, who pointed an imperious finger at one struggling group and shrieked, "Why are you trying to stop them from dancing? I want them to dance. I *command* them to dance!"

With a roar, half the audience were on their feet. "Shut down three. Hold four and five to the count of three, then off. One—Two—Three! Good." The police faded away, lost among the dancers.

"That was prearranged," Wolf said. Hawk didn't so much as glance at him.

"It's part of the legend. You, Wolf, over to your right." Wolf looked where Hawk was pointing, saw a few couples at the edge of the crowd slip from the light into the deeper shadows.

"What am I seeing?"

"Just the beginning." Hawk bent over his control board.

By slow degrees the audience became drunk and then rowdy. As the concert wore on, an ugly, excited mood grew. Sitting far above it all, Wolf could still feel the hysteria grow, as well as see it. Women shed chador and danced atop it, not fully dressed. Men ripped free of their coveralls. Here and there, spotted through the crowd, couples made love. Hawk directed lights onto a few, held them briefly; in most cases the couples went on, unheeding.

Small fights broke out, and were quelled by police. Bits of trash were gathered up and set ablaze, so that small fires dotted the landscape. Wisps of smoke floated up. Hawk played colored spots on the crowd. By the time darkness was total, the lights and the bestial noise of the revelers combined to create the feel of a Witch's Sabbath.

"Pretty nasty down there," Hawk observed. "And all most deliberately engineered by government wizards."

"But there is no true feeling involved," Wolf objected. "It is nothing but animal lust. No—no involvement."

"Yeah." Onstage, Maggie was building herself up into a frenzy. And yet her blues were brilliant—she had never been better. "Not so much different from the other concerts. The only difference is that tonight nobody waits until they go home."

"Your government can't believe that enough births will result from this night to make any difference."

"Not tonight, no. But all these people will have memories to keep them warm over the winter." Then he spat over the edge of the platform. "Ahhhh, why should I spout their lies for them? It's just bread and circuses is all, just a goddamned release for the masses."

Maggie howled with delight. "Whee-ew, man! I'm gettin' horny just looking at you. Yeah, baby, get it on, that's right!" She was strutting up and down the stage, a creature of boundless energy, while the band filled the night with music, fast and urgent.

"Love it!" She stuck her tongue out at the audience and received howls of approval. She lifted her Southern Comfort bottle, took a gigantic swig, her hips bouncing to the music. More howls. She caressed the neck of the bottle with her tongue.

"Yeah! Makes me horny as sin, 'deed it does. Ya know," she paused a beat, then continued, "that's something I can really understand, man. 'Cause I'm just a horny little hippie chick myself. Yeah." Wolf suddenly realized that she was competing against the audience itself for its attention, that she was going to try to outdo everybody present.

Maggie stroked her hand down the front of her dress, lingering between her breasts, then between her legs. She shook her hair back from her eyes, the personification of animal lust. "I mean, shit. I mean, hippie chicks don't even wear no underwear." More ribald howls and applause. "Don't believe me, do ya?"

Wolf stared, was unable to look away as Maggie slowly spread her legs wide and squatted, giving the audience a good look up her skirt. Her frog face leered, and it was an ugly, lustful thing. She lowered a hand to the stage behind her for support, and beckoned. "Come to momma," she crooned.

It was like knocking the chocks out from a dam. There was an instant of absolute stillness, and then the crowd roared and surged forward. An ocean of humanity converged on the stage, smashing through the police lines, climbing up on the wooden platform. Wolf had a brief glimpse of Maggie trying to struggle to her feet, before she was overrun. There was a dazed, disbelieving expression on her face.

"Mother of Sin," Wolf whispered. He stared at the mindless, evil mob below. They were in furious motion, straining, forcing each other in great swirling eddies. He waited for the stage to collapse, but it did not. The audience kept climbing atop it, pushing one another off its edge, and it did not collapse. It would have been a mercy if it had.

A hand waved above the crowd, clutching something that sparkled. Wolf could not make it out at first. Then another hand waved a glittering rag, and then another, and he realized that these were shreds of Maggie's dress.

Wolf wrapped his arms around a support to keep from falling into the horror below. The howling of the crowd was a single, chaotic noise; he squeezed his eyes shut, vainly trying to fend it off. "Right on cue," Hawk muttered. "Right on goddammed cue." He cut off all the lights, and placed a hand on Wolf's shoulder.

"Come on. Our job is done here."

Wolf twisted to face Hawk. The act of opening his eyes brought on a wave of vertigo, and he slumped to the platform floor, still clutching the support desperately. He wanted to vomit, and couldn't. "It's—they—Hawk, did you *see* it? Did you see what they did? Why didn't someone—?" He choked on his words.

"Don't ask me," Hawk said bitterly. "I just play the part of Judas Iscariot in this little drama." He tugged at Wolf's shoulders. "Let's go, pilgrim. We've got to go down now." Wolf slowly weaned himself of the support, allowed himself to be coaxed down from the tower.

There were men in black uniforms at the foot of the tower. One of them addressed Hawk. "Is this the African national?" Then, to Wolf: "Please come with us, sir. We have orders to see you safely to your hostel."

Tears flooded Wolf's eyes and he could not see the crowd, the Commons, the men before him. He allowed himself to be led away, as helpless and as trusting as a small child.

In the morning, Wolf lay in bed staring at the ceiling. A fly buzzed somewhere in the room, and he did not look for it. In the streets iron-wheeled carts rumbled by, and children chanted a counting-out game.

After a time he rose, dressed, and washed his face. He went to the hostel's dining room for breakfast.

There, finishing off a piece of toast, was DiStephano.

"Good morning, Mr. Mbikana. I was beginning to think I'd have to send for you." He gestured to a chair. Wolf looked about, took it. There were at least three of the political police seated nearby.

DiStephano removed some documents from his jacket pocket, handed them to Wolf. "Signed, sealed, and delivered. We made some minor changes in the terms, but nothing your superiors will object to." He placed the last corner of toast in the side of his mouth. "I'd say this was a rather bright beginning to your professional career."

"Thank you," Wolf said automatically. He glanced at the documents, could make no sense of them, dropped them in his lap.

"If you're interested, the *African Genesis* leaves port tomorrow morning. I've made arrangements that a berth be ready for you, should you care to take it. Of course, there will be another passenger ship in three weeks if you wish to see more of our country."

"No," Wolf said hastily. Then, because that seemed rude, "I'm most anxious to see my home again. I've been away far too long."

Di Stephano dabbed at the corners of his mouth with a napkin, let it fall to the tablecloth. "Then that's that." He started to rise.

"Wait," Wolf said. "Mr. DiStephano, I . . . I would very much like an explanation."

Di Stephano sat back down. He did not pretend not to understand the request. "The first thing you must know," he said, "is that Ms. Horowitz was not our first Janis Joplin."

"No," Wolf said.

"Nor the second."

Wolf looked up.

"She was the twenty-third, not counting the original. The show is sponsored every year, always ending in Boston on the Equinox. So far, it has always ended in the same fashion."

Wolf wondered if he should try to stab the man with a fork, if he should rise up and attempt to strangle him. There should be rage, he knew. He felt nothing. "Because of the brain implants."

"No. You must believe me when I say that I wish she had lived. The implants helped her keep in character, nothing more. It's true that she did not recall the previous women who played the part of Janis. But her death was not planned. It's simply something that—happens."

"Every year."

"Yes. Every year Janis offers herself to the crowd. And every year they tear her apart. A sane woman would not make the offer; a sane people would not respond in that fashion. I'll know that my country is on the road to recovery come the day that Janis lives to make a second tour." He paused. "Or the day we can't find a woman willing to play the role, knowing how it ends."

Wolf tried to think. His head felt dull and heavy. He

heard the words, and he could not guess whether they made sense or not. "One last question," he said. "Why me?"

DiStephano rose. "One day you may return to our nation," he said. "Or perhaps not. But you will certainly rise to a responsible position within the Southwest Africa Trade Company. Your decisions will affect our economy." Four men in uniform also rose from their chairs. "When that happens, I want you to understand one thing about our land: *We have nothing to lose.* Good day, and a long life to you, sir."

DiStephano's guards followed him out.

It was evening. Wolf's ship rode in Boston harbor, waiting to carry him home. Away from this magic nightmare land, with its ghosts and walking dead. He stared at it and he could not make it real; he had lost all capacity for belief.

The ship's dinghy was approaching. Wolf picked up his bags.